CAPTURED

A RED HORSEMEN MC SERIES NOVEL

RAVEN AMOR

Captured

First Edition published in 2021.

Text Copyright ©Raven Amor

All rights reserved.

The moral right of the author has been asserted.

Editing by Imogen Wells

Cover Design by TRC designs.

CAPTURED

A RED HORSEMEN MC SERIES NOVEL

RAVEN AMOR

To my Tribe-love you, ladies.

ICE

I walk over to the guy in the bar, not saying a word, but people move out the way as if I'm Moses parting the fucking Red Sea. I'm not biblical. Fuck, I would catch on fire if I ever stepped into a church. There isn't enough holy water to save my soul. No, I'm the darkest myth brought to reality. The devil himself.

Wayne turns just as I approach. "Ice, man?" I don't speak to him but feel my lips curl back, baring my teeth. I feel the weight of my brothers beside me. I yank him off his stool before chucking him to the floor, lifting my boot, I kick him in the face. Blood covers the onlookers, who all start backing away. I bend down.

"You think you can sell on Horsemen turf? Where's Cane?" A garbled groan comes from his lips as blood spills over. When I see movement to my right, I drop Wayne's head back down and smirk as Lance's steps falter. I swing my fist, hearing the bone of his jaw crack. Fuck, is it made of glass? Before landing one in his gut, that has him bent over heaving. I lift my boot, kicking him to the ground.

in the same bloody mess as his friend.

Two of their sidekicks try jumping over the bar, but Rev grabs one as I grab the other.

"Where the fuck do you think you're going," I spit in his face, slamming my head into his, causing him to fall like a loose noodle. I watch Rev grab the other one, slamming his knee into his face before tossing him to the floor like a rag.

When the sound of smashing glass has my head whipping to the side, I see Cane scrambling over the crates towards the back door. Jumping the table, I hear cursing behind me knowing my brothers hate their VP going ahead. It's too late now; the blood is pumping too hard, and anger taints my vision like a bloodthirsty animal. I had a taste, but it wasn't enough. I need to quench the hunger.

Pushing the door open into the back alley, I know Cane is still here because I can sense him. Like the vermin he is and hiding amongst the trash.

"Die like a fucking man," I growl, my fingers hovering over my piece.

When I sense the movement behind me, I turn to see Cane. His gun trained on me. "I'm not going to fucking die here in the same place as my old man."

"Should have thought of that before selling on our turf."

I watch as dark figures step up behind him, and before Cane has a chance to react, Rev and Cas have him on his knees, the gun on the floor.

I walk up to him, picking it up, smirking at the irony as I squeeze his jaw until his mouth opens. I shove the barrel in, hearing the crack of his front teeth. My grin grows as he moans painfully around the metal as I force it down his throat until he is heaving.

"You were going to shoot me? Kill me?" Snot and tears cover his face as he shakes his head. His eyes begging me for his life. Begging for a mercy I will never give.

I turned my humanity off a long time ago.

Pulling the gun out, a thread of snot follows. Relief shines momentarily in his eyes before I raise the gun, and he opens his mouth to plead. A shot vibrates through the alley as he falls back, eyes still open. I stand there watching the dark pool gather around him. The color drains from his eyes as his soul escapes, and I feel jealous. He is free. No longer held in this hell. A prisoner to his addictions and own mind.

RAE

I look up at the old wooden sign, flicking my eyes to the wrinkled paper in my hand and making sure I have the right address. The shop is rustic, and a sheen of dust covers the window as though it's stuck in a time capsule. I almost expect a group of cowboys to step out, tilting their hats in greeting. The only thing giving away it's more modern is the black, gothic looking sign.

Fuck it's hot. The air burns like the fires of Hell as it licks over my skin and dryness from the dust coats the back of my throat. I take a breath, remembering why I am here.

Pushing open the door, a brass bell goes off overhead. I almost laugh out loud at its delicate, tinkling sound. It is so out of place to the rest of the deco. The four walls are deep cherry in color with ebony frames of artwork. The floor is checked black and white and a black leather couch, that you can tell is used often from the permanent indents, sits against the right wall. A glass table sits in front with a few magazines that are covered with tattoo models and some black portfolios.

I'm immediately drawn towards the artwork. It's amazing, true artistry. Most of the work is dark, devils, grim reapers, and skulls. You cannot deny the workmanship in each of the designs. Whoever has drawn them has some incredible kick-ass talent. I can't stop from reaching out and tracing the lines of a magnificent black and grey dragon with the tip of my finger.

It wasn't like most dragons other artist like to ink; it lacked the oriental style. It didn't hold the bold lines, they were finer. Instead, it crossed over to a realistic style. The tattooist had used white to highlight the scales, smoothing out the transitions between the shades, giving it a 3D effect that made the dragon look like it was just about to take flight. Breathtaking.

I turn, hearing a loud exhale, to see a girl, I'm guessing is around twenty. Her hair is dyed burgundy, tumbling around her shoulders and down her back. Blue eyes, the same color as forget-me-nots, and full lashes fan them making them pop.

Her face is flawless, free of makeup and the color of porcelain. I am shocked to see she has virginal skin. Well, no ink that I could see. After only two days in the first shop I worked, I was under the gun having my skin branded. Now, I have a grey shaded skull covering my shoulder, with a red rose coming from its mouth and dripping with pearls and a butterfly. A grey clock with hands stopped at nine, and three blood-red roses. The date 18.10.17 is written in Roman numerals. A new piece that starts on my hip and curves around my leg is of a dreamcatcher and feathers. Down one side of my torso are the words *'color in the dark world'* with watercolors splashed down my ribs.

Some people try to hide their scars using ink to cover them. I use it to show mine. Every piece is a part of the story that I have lived and fought to survive. You can't tell by looking at them, but I know.

Her brow raises, an expression somewhere between pissed off and bored. Resting bitch face. I'm the queen of that look. Placing a hip against the desk, she pins me with a glare.

"Look, it's been a long day, so I'll get straight to the point. Sketch is busy. He doesn't want to fuck you." She must see something cross my face, so she carries on, "Look, sweetheart, it isn't personal." She nods, waving her hand up and down my body. "Those tits and that ass. Still, it doesn't matter." She shrugs. "Don't bother giving me your number. As soon as you leave, I will chuck it. He already has as much free pussy as he can get from the club. He doesn't need or want some ink bunny," she finishes.

Ink bunny! I tilt my head to the side and take a deep breath. Trying to control my anger. I shouldn't let her get under my skin, but I'm tired and edgy.

I'm used to people judging me by how I look, the clothes I wear, and the ink branded on my skin. But an ink bunny? I've worked in enough shops to know the women she's talking about. They hang around the shop and the artist like flies. Love the taste of ink and would fall into any of their beds.

I bite my tongue, until I can taste the metallic undertones, to stop my mouth running away with me. I know she is only doing her job. I don't want to argue with her. It isn't her fault I had to pack up my life once again. That I just arrived, after driving almost nonstop for the last week across the country to get here. Finally, after years of running, I followed my mom's last words to come to Harrison. In what? Desperation? Curiosity?

"If you ever find the sun missing from your sky, go there. Promise me."

Mom had grown up in the small, quaint town of Harrison, on the edges of southern Arizona. Surrounded by red sands and heat that made you feel like the devil himself lives here, and tall mountains that looked as if their peaks touched the sky. It wasn't her favorite memory. Mom could never hide the pain that crossed her beautiful face every time she mentioned it. Her brown eyes would glass over and seem to be unfocused lost in a memory. That was when she would tell me to come here if ever the sun disappeared.

My sun had fallen from its sky a long time ago.

Maybe that was it? I missed its warmth and its light.

I've become too familiar with the dark, and it has become my friend, my solace and protector.

I bite my cheek from saying what I really want to, but she needs to understand something. "I'm not looking for any ink, and I am certainly not looking to hook-up with some guy called Sketch, or any other guy in fact...I am here for the job."

I wasn't lying on both counts. I have all the ink I want, and I'm not looking to date anyone.

My heart is still unscathed, but the rest of me is like a cracked mirror, with sharp, ragged pieces, covered in blood and soul. I've felt the type of pain that alters you in a way that you'll never be the same. It leaves you no choice but to change, to guard yourself against ever feeling hurt again.

Now, I live by two rules: Never trust anyone and move on within a couple of months.

I stay away from anything connecting me to a place, and that includes relationships and friends.

Here isn't going to be any different. I'm going to follow my mother's last words, then leave.

The girl's brows drop as she peers at me as if searching for the truth. Apparently, she doesn't find it, as she crosses her arms over her chest.

"What's your name?" Her voice holds a bite, ready to call me out on my bullshit.

I put my hand out, smiling. It is one a pageant queen would be proud of. It's the same fake one I use to cover my face every day.

"Rae."

Her brows go into her hairline, eyes travel up as if she's missing something. "You're Rae?" It comes out slowly.

I nod as slowly as her words. Then a wicked smirk, one that spells trouble, lights her face and mischief fills those blues.

"Be right back."

Before she disappears through a backdoor, she glances over her shoulder one more time and grins at me.

I focus on the buzz of the tattoo machine, which I can hear, and it makes my fingers twitch. It has only been a week, but it feels as if I'm going cold turkey, withdrawing, and now, this close, my body recognizes that sound. It hums with the buzz, and I want to get my hands on it. I needed it, craved it, even.

As a kid, I loved to draw. It didn't matter if it were crayons, chalk or pencils, anything I could get my hands on that made a mark, I was pulled to. I loved the sharp lines, and how they became something beautiful. My mother used to say I saw the world differently, that I saw beauty in everything. I used to agree with her. Only, life has shown me how wrong I was. Now, all I see is darkness and pain. Beauty is just a hallucination. A facade covering depravity, and the truth of what happens in this world, the true evil that doesn't just exist on movie screens but walks past you on the street.

It wasn't until a few years ago, when I stopped in Vegas, that the girl who let me crash with her happened to be going out with an artist called Rex. He saw some of my drawings I had left out by mistake after another nightmare. Said he saw raw talent in my designs and invited me to come by to have a look and see how it all worked.

I hadn't even considered tattooing as art, but curiosity had me turning up at his shop, Marked. I will never forget my first time walking in there, the smell of antiseptic, the buzz of the machine.

It sent a thrill through my body, something I hadn't felt

since I was young and had opened a whole case of watercolors for the first time. I still remember my mom's words as she handed them to me. 'This world needs more beauty and color, my darling, and you are the one to do it'.

As soon as I held the gun in my hand it was like something clicked inside of me. How it felt, vibrated through me, sinking into my bones. It felt like a part of me. It wasn't long before I found out that my flare was old school and old English.

Rex said he hadn't seen work like mine since 'Jerry the Sailor', which is the biggest compliment you could have in the ink world. Famous for his tattooing of sailors, his work was amazing and is still recognized today.

The buzzing from the machine stops, followed by the low, husky sound of a guy's voice. I'm too far away to make any sense of it, but he doesn't sound happy.

After a beat, heavy booted footsteps make their way closer. Sketch, I assume, stops in front of the door, his arms crossing over his broad chest, his stance intimidating. I rake my eyes over him. I might have been off men, so far out of the dating game, I wasn't even in it, but that didn't mean I couldn't spot a good-looking guy when I saw one. I had no doubt Sketch had women falling into his bed whenever he snapped his fingers. I could almost see why the ink bunnies had such a hard time staying away.

His dark hair was styled in a faux Mohawk, with the sides shaved. Fire flames were inked on each side in black and grey with hints of oranges and yellows. More tattoos covered his arms, including a skull on his right hand and the words 'Ride Free' across his knuckles.

Towering over me and the other woman, his height matched by a hard as stone body that looked like he worked out. My eyes gravitated to the trimmed beard covering his strong jawline as his teeth scraped across the lip ring, with a matching ring through his eyebrow. Intense, deep, chocolate eyes appraise me and dismiss me as something dark ripples through them, lurking just beneath the surface.

This man has demons. There is an air of danger that drapes around him like a blanket. A part of me understands it and wants to run as fast as possible, not wanting him to see my own. But I keep my feet rooted to the floor, even as I feel my heartbeat race. My nails biting into my skin, causing pain to keep me here and stopping me from sinking into the past.

Sketch takes me in. He undresses me with a single look as he scans me from my blood-red heels to my dark raven hair.

Like he is amused by me, his lips curve as if I'm the punch line of a joke that nobody's told me about.

It has my spine snapping straight as I tip my chin out. I am not a weak girl. Not anymore.

How would he act if he knew he was facing a murderer? The invisible crimson that unquestionably covers his hands, drenches mine too.

"Sorry, sweetheart, but the job is gone."

Trust no one.

"I drove all week to get here! You said it was solid," I hiss through my teeth. I'm far from the girl I grew up as, no pearls and poised smiles, or polished words cover me. His tongue would have been cut out and shoved back in until he choked on it back home for lying.

What the hell am I going to do now? I only know how to ink. I could wait tables for a while, but that wouldn't keep me over. I need to feel the machine in my hand, the buzz flowing through my body. It's what grounded me, kept me from falling down the rabbit hole I always walked the edge of.

I only planned to stay a month or two. It was coming up to my parent's anniversary. Maybe that's what made me come here.

Following lost whispers of my dead mother. God, I'm going fucking crazy.

The thought digs in its claws at my insides, holding me in its grip, as memories flood around me. Still able to hear the drip of their blood, the copper smell so strong. The tear that ran down her face, the way her pearls turned red. I will never erase it from my memory. Remembering the promise I made to their lifeless eyes.

Sketch tilts his head, looking at me the same way the redhead had earlier, like I am a puzzle to solve. What's the matter with this town?

"What's your name?" I tilt my chin higher and force my feet to hold me steady as those dark eyes drill into me, searching, questioning the secrets he no doubt sees in mine, but ones he will never find the answers to.

"Rae. I sent you my portfolio. You said that the job was mine. Rex recommended me."

Rex is the only one who has even come close to seeing beneath the veil I hide behind. He had barely peeked over the walls, but as soon as I realized what was happening, I left. We've kept in contact every few months, but that's it. I never made plans to call, to see him again. It's safer that way. Sketch's eyes widen, brow rising, as the girl tries to hide a laugh behind a cough, making my eyes dart between them both.

"You're a bitch!" It falls from his mouth with a gruff snort.

"How would you know what I am? You've just met me!" I speak through my teeth, making my jaw hurt, acting like the bitch he just called me. I shake my head, trying to reign it all in because I need this job.

"Bitch means woman," the red head explains. "He means you've got a pussy, not a dick. I'm Layla, by the way."

I give her a tight smile before looking back at Sketch, who lifts his chin in agreement.

"Yeah, I thought that was pretty obvious…Wait! Am I missing something?"

"Yeah, a whole shit load," she replies, leaning over the counter, her mouth quirking into a smirk. "Sketch was expecting Rae to be a guy."

I blink, and my mouth pulls into a frown. "My name is Rae, short for Arya." The words spill out fast. Hearing my real name sounds strange. I haven't used it in so long. I can't remember the last time someone even said it. Rae is the only name I ever give. No last name, no middle name, just Rae. I haven't been Arya in four years, she died that night.

RAE

Layla grins, elbowing Sketch in the ribs, who is staring at my eyes. It's not unusual. Many people have commented on them over the years. They are navy blue, but they can look more violet at times. If I'm happy, they turn a shade lighter, to a bluish-purple, and when I'm sad, they turn darker. Since that day, the day that destroyed me. They still have a slight tinge of lilac, but are darker than usual, leaning more towards the navy.

My mother's eyes were like warm chocolate. She said I had the eyes of the greatest man she ever knew. I assume mom was talking about my grandfather, her dad, who died before I was born.

He rubs his jaw, tugging the lip ring between his teeth like he is trying to decide. "Sorry, sweetheart, but I can't have you working here."

I hate the doubt that creeps in. After mom died, it's like she took all the color from my world, and I hid my art, it was my secret, something no one could take away from me. Since Rex had taught me to ink, my confidence had grown. Nothing beats the feeling of watching someone walk out the door with my designs on them, knowing it was there for life. My art is something that I would never be; free.

It is the one thing I have left in this world.

"You said you liked my work. So, what's the problem?" I'm proud of the strength in my voice. I will never show weakness, not again.

"Some of the best I've seen, that's the problem. Got a lot of fucking brothers coming in here." He shakes his head, like he can't believe he's letting me go. "I know they will all want you inking' them." I can't help the grin. The ink world is still mainly men. Yes, there are some kick-ass women artists, but it was still hard to get that recognition. My smile slips as he raises a brow, motioning up and down my body. "You look in the mirror? Because, sweetheart, you look exactly like them pin-ups up there." He points to some photos, artwork of the 1950s pin-ups. Sketch's lip curls up. "They'll take one fucking look at you and lose their nuts, and that shit is messy."

I roll my eyes as a grin slides over my lips. This is something I know how to deal with. Sketch isn't the first to say that about the way I dress, and that I look like a pin-up.

I used to hate my hourglass figure because my boobs are heavy, my waist tight, and the way my hips flare. I always looked at the willowy type of girls in school with envy, like the girl in front of me, slight and feminine with subtle curves.

It was what he had noticed about me. The body of a woman, yet I wasn't one yet.

When he caught me crying, hiding from the world, and told me it was my fault my body was too tempting for men—a temptress. I had been raised my whole life to dress and act a certain way. I was screaming behind the pearls and poised smiles. Itching in my own skin to be set free. The wildness in me roared to be let out, it was in my blood not to roll over, to not be controlled. Yet, I chained it up, starved it like an unruly beast. Believed every one of his sweet lies, thinking he was protecting me. I played the part perfectly. Becoming everything, he wanted; meek, and timid. His plaything.

When I ran, I knew I had to be different, and as far from that girl as I could be. An appointment hadn't shown up, and I was looking at a magazine in Rex's shop when I came across pictures of pin-up models. It took me a while to get up the courage to try something so bold. His voice sometimes still found me, gave me nightmares. Still made my body shiver. Made me want to run and never stop, to hide in the darkest part of the world.

When I finally found the courage to try the style and bury Arya. I liked how the tight pencil skirts hugged my hips making them look smaller. The way the tops would frame my boobs in a sultry way before clutching my tight stomach. On my feet were heels meant for the bedroom, and my hair was dyed dark raven. I liked the blood-red lipstick I always wore—it had become my trademark, my armor.

It was something Arya would never have worn. Arya was gone, and I became Rae.

Rae is stronger. Rae would survive. She could deal with the terror and darkness and make it her friend. She would not break the same way Arya would have. She wouldn't be weak.

Rae is a mask I wear to keep the world out. I hide behind her, bury all my nightmares and fears behind the walls she built up. Rae is my redeemer.

"I've worked in plenty of studios." I've got heaps of attitude to give back. "You think just because I haven't got a dick that swings in the wind, I haven't got the balls to say no?" Now it's my turn to snort. "Trust me, it's because of that reason I can say no! I promise you; I will not go all fangirl over the guys who come in here."

Layla turns her head to look at Sketch, a smile pulls at her lips. "I like her, and we really need someone."

I have a feeling getting her approval is a big thing.

Sketch rubs his neck, looking at me. Excitement dances through me. I'm getting through to him.

"Fuck!" he curses under his breath before looking me dead in the eyes. I've had a lifetime of experience with that intense look. Most of my family has the same stone-cold glare that makes grown men piss themselves. Where theirs makes my skin crawl, Sketch's doesn't. His is a different darkness.

"A fucking month's trial," he growls.

It's only then I realize how much getting this job meant to me. "Thank you!" I say, unable to hide the smirk covering my face. Sketch shakes his head, laughing. It doesn't reach all the way to his eyes, but it's a good sound, sort of gritty and rough, like he doesn't do it often.

Walking over to the counter, he chucks me a bunch of keys which I catch. "Have your ass here by nine tomorrow. The apartment above is free. It's yours to do what you want with it. Don't forget, I fucking warned you." His laughter follows him as he walks through the door before I hear the gun start up again.

I turn to Layla, who is smirking at me. "Are they really that bad?" Her grin grows.

"Oh, you have no idea. Come on, I'll show you the apartment."

We walk up the steps on the side of the shop, our footsteps echoing. Metal: good. I can hear someone coming.

"It's not much," Layla says as she pushes open the door, letting me walk in first.

It is a small space, with an open floor plan living room and kitchen and a narrow hallway with two doors. The living area has a two-seater brown couch, with a patchwork throw. A cream rug sits in front. Mismatched wooden furniture surrounds it, acting as a tv unit and side tables. Posters of motorbikes with girls sitting in a myriad of different erotic positions covers some of the walls.

"They were Ink's, but he's…umm away." Layla curses as she rips some down, making me laugh. I couldn't care less about the decoration.

The kitchen units are white and look newer than the rest of the place. I walk straight over to the window in the kitchen, which looks over the main street. I do the same in the living room. This side looks over a high wall and a parking lot. Walking down the hall, I open the first door. A medium-sized double bed sits on one wall with the same mix of wooden furniture. More posters of bikes and some sketches also cover one wall. The window is facing the street the same as the kitchen.

I cross the hall, opening the second door, which is a small shower room. Arya would never stay in a place like this. It is beneath her, nothing like the luxury she was used to. For Rae, it's perfect.

I feel my muscles relax for the first time in a week, and I can't help the smile.

"I'll take it."

RAE

After Layla leaves, I bring up all my bags. My whole life in three bags makes for a sad scene, but it's easier when I have to leave in a hurry.

I don't bother to put stuff away because I won't be here that long. I take another look around, and this place is luxury compared to some of the vermin infested places I have stayed. It's a roof over my head and bed to sleep in which is more than I've had in a while.

My stomach reminds me that I haven't eaten anything other than a few granola bars for the last two days. I knew I couldn't stop for long, and that taking the back roads would make my journey longer. But it was a necessity to survive. Then I remember the little diner when I drove in earlier.

Heat knocks into me as soon as I open the door. The place smells like a stove burning, with dust from the desert getting stuck in my throat, but the town is charming. I see two young girls laughing and joking. The sight makes me stop. Mom walked down these streets when she was the same age. Did she have a best friend? Did she giggle, link arms like those two? Was she happy here?

I walk through the diner's door, and it looks like it has been here for years. Making my way through the red plastic chairs and silver round tables, a lump forms in my throat as I can't help feeling my mother around me. Raising more questions; did she have a favorite milkshake, or order the same thing every time?

Taking a seat in the back booth, to keep an eye on the front door and the only exit. I glance around. No one would imagine my mother sitting at one of these tables, drinking through a straw, fingers covered in grease from her meal. Can you imagine what they would have said? I hear her voice like a whisper carried on the wind, almost as if she is laughing, and I can't help but smile as an image of her face flickers through my mind.

"Can I help you?"

I am jolted out of the daydream to see a young girl with blonde hair, tied in a ponytail and a bubble gum smile, wearing a white t-shirt with Maggi embroidered on it in red and a name tag saying, Polly-Anne. A pen hovering over a notebook.

"Sorry." I quickly pick up the menu, scanning over everything, and the picture of a big burger makes my mouth water.

"Number eleven with a side of fries and a strawberry milkshake, please."

Taking my order, she smiles before bouncing off with the innocence of youth still surrounding her.

I remember being like that, and the worst thing to happen at that age was the boy you liked didn't like you back. An innocent outlook on the world, and then the illusion crumbles around you, like sand, knocking off those rose-tinted glasses. There is no longer a place to hide and you are left seeing the truth of this world. The pain, the soul ripping pain, that does not ease with time. But you learn to live with it, like a noose around your neck that someday will leave you unable to breathe.

Everything he did was, supposedly, preparing me for my place in the family that was carved out for me, which I would never accept. The place that cost me everything.

The smell hits me first, making my stomach growl just as the waitress places down the burger, fries, and milkshake.

"Thanks," I say around a fry, starving now that the food is this close. As much as I want to scoff all the food down, I can't help old habits kicking in as I pick up the knife and fork, cutting the burger. I can practically feel his eyes burning into me, even though he is not here. He is still haunting me from the grave.

The food turns sour in my mouth.

"Everything okay, dear?" I look up to see a woman with grey hair tied on top of her head, dark brown eyes full of wisdom, and the lines on her face show a road map of adventures, laughter, and sorrow.

"Yes, sorry, I had a large lunch." It's a lie that falls artfully from my lips, like a well-rehearsed line from a play. Because that is all my life has been, acting, playing the part, it may have taken on different roles, but it's all the same. I hate how I fall back into the role so easily, how it doesn't matter the miles between us, or the persona I put on, it still creeps over me like ivy tangling around a tower. Those invisible chains still hold me in the past.

"You look really familiar. Have we met?" she asks, her eyes taking in my features with a glimmer of recognition, then it's gone.

"No, but my –" Our conversation is cut short as noise fills the small diner. I watch as some men walk in, all of them loud and gruff. Dressed the same in jeans, white shirts, and black leather vests. Even from across the room, you can feel the danger that emanates from these guys. The control they hold as the rest of the diner falls silent, closing in on themselves as they try to make themselves invisible. The men don't even blink an eye at the tension that now covers the diner as they push two tables together. Some lounging in seats, others sitting on them backward.

"I better go," the woman babbles before dashing off to meet them. I nod as the last three walk in together, fluidly, like a pack.

When I feel all the small hairs on my body stand up, I take a quick look, my eyes landing on piercing icy blues. The color sends a shiver through me as they hold me there in their cool pools.

Someone calls him, breaking the connection. Allowing me to blink, I take in the rest of him. Tall, with midnight-black hair that falls on his forehead. Cheekbones as chiseled as his jaw, which holds a dark trimmed goatee and frames sensual lips. He is handsome, savagely so. Broad shoulders, with ink that covers his arms, making them into a piece of living art. Muscles I didn't even know existed make the t-shirt pull and show the strength he holds, and the power within him. A trimmed waist leads to thick thighs, covered in dark denim. Pure male, raw, and red-blooded.

His eyes slide back to me, locking with mine. The air in the diner vanishes, and my breath catches in the back of my throat as everyone else falls into muted greys while he stands out in full color.

My heart starts to pound as his eyes change from cold and calculating to a blue that reminds me of a methane flame. I can feel its searing heat from here as he takes in every inch of me. When his brows slam down, a cruel smirk twists his lips as another guy slaps his back holding their order. He shoots me one more angry glare before walking out.

Like everyone else in the diner, my eyes follow them out, watching as they all get on bikes, but not the ones you see weaving through traffic. These are a mixture of leather and chrome. Looking as deadly and dangerous as the men that ride them. The bikes start-up, filling the air with a loud roar as the man with the icy blues lifts a hand, his fingers moving in a circular motion. As they prepare to ride, I quickly pull out some money to cover the bill, and a tip, before racing for the door. Standing in the parking lot watching them ride away, the vibrations still shaking the ground. It is a powerful feeling that I feel throughout my whole body. I frown; it was as if my body remembered it.

They soon disappear, and I start to walk back to the apartment. The air has a bite to it now, making me wrap my arms around myself. I look over my shoulder, my eyes scanning the streets, trying to see any movement in the shadows.

It is not until I close the door behind me, that I let out a breath. Will there ever be a day I can stop?

I shake my head, already knowing the answer. You don't draw royal blood and not get punished. I know what awaits me, how my life ends. It won't be growing old with the love of my life surrounded by family. It will be tortured and painful and have me begging for death. But they will have to catch me first.

I walk into the shop early the next morning, nightmares mixed with fear that constantly leaves me on edge and with little sleep. I can't remember the last time I slept a whole night, felt safe enough to just close my eyes. This morning, I styled my hair into loose curls, picked out skinny black jeans and a black crop top with the slogan 'I'm smiling, this should scare you' in red. Blood-red, five-inch heels match my lipstick. I had time to call into the diner and get some coffee.

"Hey." Layla smiles as soon as she sees me. Coming around the counter, she gives an appreciative glance. Her eyes go wide when she sees what's in my hands. "Please tell me one of them is for me?"

"Yeah." She grabs it, taking a mouthful and moaning as she does.

"Come on, I'll show you where you will be working." Following her towards the back of the shop, I spot Sketch bent over a drawing pad, shading in a skull surrounded by fire. I walk in and place a coffee down beside him. He looks at the cup before smelling it.

"It's just coffee." I raise my brow as he leans back in the chair.

"Nah, this is Maggi's, best damn coffee around." He smirks as his eyes flick behind me. "Anythin' you need, ask Red."

Red? I don't question it, instead, smile. Layla shows me the storage room first, and it's a complete mess. Nothing has a place, just shoved on the shelves. "Is it always like this? How do you do stock checks?"

"Sketch is booked up most of the time and has no time. I've just been helping out with the desk while trying to fill out college applications, so…" Layla waves her hand to the mess before closing the door.

"You're going to college?" A small frown appears as she shrugs.

"I was meant to go two years ago. I just couldn't leave this place. Now…" I don't miss the way she cuts herself off as she leads me to the room I will work in. It is a nice size with a black chair that lays into a bed. All the equipment is brand new. Walls, white and bare, with black gloss cupboards that run along the back wall.

"You can do anything you want."

"Thanks. I heard Sketch call you Red?" Instantly, her muscles tense.

"Yeah, it's a nickname." Every word is covered with attitude. I pull my tattoo gun out, fingers gliding over its decorated steel.

"Is that what you prefer?" Her eyes narrow as she waits a beat before nodding, and I produce one of my pageant smiles.

"You did all this?" Sketch looks between the store cupboard and me. With no clients, I had to keep busy. Stop my mind from wandering, taking me to places I do not want to visit. So, I started to arrange the cupboard, now everything has a place and is easy to find. I hand over a piece of paper.

"This too. This column is everything we have and how much." I point to what I mean. "This is what we are running low on, and the last column is things we should order every time, gloves, needles, that sort of thing. I'll add it to the computer and do a stock check every Saturday?" When he doesn't say anything, I grab the paper out of his hand. "Don't worry."

Before I can walk off his big hand wraps around my arm, making me freeze. Looking over my shoulder, he lets go of my arm as if he can feel the tension in my body.

"You did fucking good," he says with a rough voice. He opens his mouth to say more when the sound of a ringtone breaks the air between us. I've heard Sketch's mobile go off a few times, but this is more of a high-pitched tone. He reaches in his pocket and pulls out a small one. I know it's a burner phone, something that can be lost easily. I keep my face neutral, but when his eyes flick to mine, his face grows darker with each second.

"On my way," is all he utters before pushing past me, heading straight out the door. I meet Red at the desk.

"Is everything okay?" I ask, watching as Sketch mounts a bike, peeling into the road leaving dust in his wake as he speeds off.

"Club," is all she says, not lifting her eyes as she flicks the page in the book in front of her before writing something down.

The bell goes off, making me turn to see a guy walk through the door.

"Princess." He grins, Red shoots him a look that would have most men's balls shrivel up. Which strangely makes his smile widen.

"Sketch isn't here, but Rae can do your ink if you want?" His eyes slide over me, taking me in slowly. He grins, showing off a missing tooth.

"Yeah, go get him. I'll have sweets here, keep me company."

His voice is huskier as he answers Red, but his eyes stay on mine.

I can't help the smile as I lean against the desk. "I am Rae."

His eyes widen in disbelief and bounce between Red and me.

"She's a fucking bitch." Not this again, I nod.

"Yeah, no dick. Is that going to be a problem?" I add a little sass to my voice, arching a brow.

After a beat, he shakes his head, walking past me to the room and taking a suspicious look at Red, as if he's not sure to believe her.

As I follow him back, I can't help thinking this is more than just a tattoo shop.

ICE

We all drop our mobiles and guns in the box before entering church. It isn't a place where we pray for our fucking sins or ask for God's mercy and forgiveness. Too much darkness and blood have been spilled to save our souls. There's only one place we will be going, and I'll welcome it with open arms.

Church is the heart of the club. Where every decision is made. Where our secrets are confessed, and where the horrors of yesterday are etched into the walls. I take the seat to my dad's right as his VP. Revenant, or Rev as he's known, takes his seat opposite me as Sergeant in Arms. His weird gold and brown eyes stare off as he plays with the blade of his favorite knife. Our secretary and money man, Jellybean, sits next to him, with that fucking goofy grin. The darkness of this world hasn't touched him like it has the rest of us. He seems immune to it. Cas, or Cas-a-fucking–Nova, our Road Captain, drops down next, doing his buttons up, his hair a mess, no doubt where some cum bucket has just had her fingers in it. Shooting me a fucking smirk, you never see the fucker without a grin, or joke. His eyes reveal the truth, everything he's hiding. Like a pressure cooker, one day he will explode, blowing away the facade he hides behind.

I wait for the rest of the brothers to come in. My leg bounces from the fucking restless tension, when my thoughts turn to the bitch at the diner.

All that dark hair that is long enough to tie around my wrist as I drive into her from behind and pale skin that would pink up beautifully from my handprint. Red fuck-me lips that I already know would look good wrapped around my cock. Only, she had fucking innocent bitch written all over her. Feeling my dick growing, I reach down to adjust it in my jeans, realizing my leg had slowed down. Nothing normally stops the twitches, the restlessness that beats through me as if it is my master, controlling me. Holding me in its dark manic touches, leaving me a prisoner in my own mind.

"Sorry, boss, I was at the shop." I look up to see Sketch walking in.

Luther, our president, and my father, nods. "You get anyone to fucking help out yet?"

"Yeah, hired someone today," he replies, falling into the seat next to me.

My father's eyes take in the whole table before he slams down the gavel.

"Word coming in is we have fucking foot soldiers sniffing about where they shouldn't fucking be. Coming into our fucking town has crossed a fucking line."

The air in the room turns deadly as each brother sits straighter. Foot soldiers are fucking Mafia men. The lowest on the totem pole, dispensable, they mean nothing to the men on top; the fuckers that had sent them to my town.

"Who?" I snarl. There are all different cartels and mafias

around. Some we learned to play nicely with, and others, not so fucking much. I know it's fucking bad when every one of his muscle's tenses, his eyes turning lethal.

"Mendez."

Mendez are the fucking worst; A mafia family from New York, our rivals that have drawn blood and lost lives on both sides.

The head, Marco, is as bearable as a fucking toothache, and his youngest son, Carlo, is a bastard if all the talk is real. He has his fingers in the darkest of pies, including sex trafficking and slavery. There was an older son, Gino, who was murdered with his family a few years back. The word on the street is the hit came from inside, but not even we believe the Mendez are that fucked up. We all turn to Cas, that smirk that lands bitches in his bed is gone, replaced by a snarl, teeth bared. Buck, his pop, was one of the men they had taken from us, body parts dismembered and left outside the club lot. Piece by piece, like macabre gifts. It was a fucking dark time for the club. Declaring an outright war to an already blood feud.

"Cas?" I call his name, knowing how fucking close to the edge he is. Triggered by just the name. His jaw locks, muscles moving under his skin before his eyes turn to me, and it's like looking at a reflection. My own. He stands, as if he can't fucking stay still. Walking to the wall, he punches it, letting deep grunting sounds out as red streaks the plasterboard. Rev goes to stand, but I shake my head. I know this feeling, the rage so close to the surface it feels like it will rip your fucking skin off. It will completely take over, destroy everything, and everyone around you. My eyes glance back to Cas to see he's breathing like a fucking bull. His eyes turn to us, looking around the table before letting out a deep breath and collapsing in his seat. The inferno, ready to explode, coming off him in dark waves has me readying for anything. I might not be able to save myself, but I'll fucking save Cas from himself. A few beats pass before he nods. His eyes catch mine, and I lift my chin. They will pay. We will make them fucking suffer.

"We know why these fuckers think it's okay to come to our town?" Jellybean growls, the grin no longer on his face. He's fully focused like us all.

Luther shakes his head. "No, just fucking been lurking. Those motherfuckers cause shit, we are fucking waiting. We all fucking clear?" A round of aye's fill the room. I light up a smoke as my fucking leg starts bouncing again. We had faced shit, no fucking doubt, but a lot more is always coming. It comes with this life. Usually ending in a rain of fucking bullets. We will die as we lived; in violence covered and in blood.

"We've got a run in the morning." Prez looks straight at me. Giving me a warning glare, I know that fucking look, but I'm too wound up. Anger simmering in my veins, my lips curl into a smirk as I blow out smoke.

"I'll play fucking nice." I inhale another drag before grinning.

"Ice, you will be fucking leading. Cas, I want a new route and no fucking surprises. Rev, you go and take Storm. Can't lose this fucking deal with the Irish."

He's right. The club couldn't afford to fucking lose it. We got a sweet thing going with them. Arms were our biggest trade. It also meant we controlled whose hands they fucking ended up in, and they were all fucking sold as soon as we received them, bringing in big money.

"Going to let Rags and the fucking other chapters know to keep eyes on the ground. Call in on your way back, see if he's heard anythin'." That's his paranoia talking, it came hand in hand in this life. Rags is his best friend, but I know he needs me to see his reaction face to face.

My father's and Rags' pops started the club when they got back from the war in the early 70s; then a few of their war brothers soon joined in. My father didn't sign up for the military, he was immersed in the fucking club early, but Rags did. On his second tour, he was captured. Reported M.I.A. Every fucker thought he was dead, including his Ol' Lady and his son, Bolt. Bolt wasn't his Ol' Lady's kid. His mother had been a fucking junkie, an ex-club girl. With Rags dead, his bitch of a mother took him; he was only seven at the time, and she made a run for it. Talk is, Rags' Ol' Lady was devastated, not only losing Rags to the war, but his son, who she loved like her own, and ended up marrying some rich fucking suit and moved away. Then Rags rose from the dead. He was held captive for three years. He was tortured in a way that even made chills go down our spines, broken, and by the time he got his shit together, Rags realized he'd fucking lost everything.

Then the club got a call from child services that a boy had been found in a motel room, starving and fucking dirty. It was Bolt, and Rags and my father rode straight away to get him and brought back a shell of a boy from the one I fucking remembered. It took a few years, but Bolt and I repaired that bond we had when we were kids. We were both teenagers when Rags pulled the fucking rug from underneath us again with no real explanation. He couldn't stay in town but didn't want to leave the Horsemen, so he opened another chapter in Ohio. We already had chapters covering most states, but we were the Mother Chapter. My father was the national president and the backbone of the Horsemen. This place was formed by his blood.

Bolt and I had kept in touch. He was the only person outside this club I considered a brother.

"Yeah, ain't checked in with the motherfucker in a while." Too long. Every time I thought about calling or going up, I ended up fighting, drinking, or fucking. Most of the time, all three. It was bullshit, I knew he saw the change in me. How restless I'd become.

"What about the families? We need to bring them in?" Champ asks. He's an old-timer, and Prez's close friend and human fucking lie detector. Ain't lying, that man could fucking see into your soul. He called it a curse. It was fucking freaky. Should have been wearing the VP patch, but an accident had fucked up his back a few years ago stopping him from taking long rides, and a VP needed to make the long runs.

My father shakes his head. "Nah, Sketch will take and bring Layla to and from the shop. We've got enough brothers here if anything should happen."

Sketch nods. "I got it."

Fuck! How had I forgotten? "Alec, his brother-in-law, is in with Mendez, just a runner, but he could have information. He still fucking owes us. Looks like we should call it in."

Alec had got himself into a mess with gambling a few years back, and the good Samaritans we fucking are, we helped him out of a big deep hole, with just a few missing fingers. In exchange for a marker. Now it's time to call it in.

Prez nods. "Yeah, okay. I'll take Johnny, Tracker, and Axel to meet the Irish. When we're on our way back, you can leave with the boys and speak to Alec. That way, we will have enough firepower to hold them motherfuckers off if anything happens." We all nod in agreement.

"Just got the word in that Cage will be out in the next few weeks." Everyone yells and starts banging the table. Cage is serving time after being picked up with an unlicensed gun and some weed. He's a lucky bastard and only got a year.

"Any other order of fucking business." A chorus of no's go around before the gavel goes down and calls the meeting to an end.

We all walk out, and I fall beside Sketch. "So, how's the new kid?"

The fucker's lips twitch as if I just told a joke. "If their work is as good as their portfolio and Rex's word, Rae will be fucking solid."

Rae so that's his name. "And you warned him about my sister?

To keep his fucking hands off." Or he will be looking for a new job because you can't ink without them.

Sketch smirks as he heads for the door, walking backward. Has he been smoking the good stuff? "Now that is something I'd pay to see," he cracks up, laughing. The motherfucker. Then leaves to close the shop, and I flip him the bird making him laugh louder.

"Ice." I turn at my father's voice and follow him to his office, knowing what he wants with the look in his eyes.

He takes a seat behind his desk, motioning to the chair for me. Grabbing a bottle of whiskey from his drawer, unscrewing the cap, he takes a long swig before passing it over to me. I take it, bringing it to my lips. The first taste of it makes me hiss, and then I relish the burn.

"I ain't got to tell you to fucking rein that shit in tomorrow. Dead can't talk."

I grit my teeth, I'm known for my fucking hot temper, to be erratic. The wildfire of rage that erratically burns through me makes me see white-hot fucking fury. No one knows what I would do, including myself.

I wasn't only his son. I'm also the club fucking Vice President. Being Luther's son didn't give me the right to the fucking cut on my back. Every inch of the motherfucking leather I wore, I earned through blood and sweat.

I wasn't a part of this life. I am this life. It flows through my veins; it's a part of my DNA and not because of my father, but because this is me. You cut me open, and I bleed oil.

It didn't matter that this was my legacy. I still had to earn everything. Show I deserved my place. Prove I was worthy of being my father's son—the Red Horsemen's VP.

The patch on my chest claiming me as VP was another fucking story. It stole my humanity. I got the patch, my reward, because I pulled the trigger and ended a life. I've ended more fucking lives since and will again in the future. I died that day too, the part that made me human.

But restless energy drove me insane, ate me a-fucking-live and invaded my brain like a motherfucking parasite. It was all laid at the feet of that first one.

At nineteen, I killed someone on my first ride. Every time I close my fucking eyes, all I see is his motherfucking blood spilling from his body. Dark liquid that pooled around him as the dirt drank it. The copper smell that invaded my nostrils, embedded into my fucking soul. The only way I managed to block that shit out and keep my demons on leashes was to shut down. To keep people away. To become cold, cold as fucking ice. That's how I got my road name.

The club was on a ride, to visit another MC, we weren't friendly, but we weren't at war either. Some shit was going down, and Prez had arranged a meet. My father told Sketch and me that we could come. It was our first ride. Cas, Rev, and Cage had got their cut and scar that welcomed them into the Horsemen as a full brother a year before us. Prospecting was a motherfucking bitch, and we both wanted in on the real stuff, wanted to be where it fucking mattered, beside our brothers, with our club.

As we rolled up, their prospect stood up, the asshole straightened. I knew what he was doing as soon as his fucking hand went to his back, pulling out the piece. His whole body fucking shook with fear, and the gun rattled as he raised it. The prospect searched through us, looking for something through those fucking haunted eyes. As soon as they landed on my father, he closed his eyes and fucking pulled the trigger, only the bullet went wide, missing by miles. He couldn't shoot for fuck. I doubt he'd held a gun before.

The fucker tried to shoot the President of the club-the national fucking President-so I shot him right between the eyes. I watched as his body hit the ground, a cold look on my face as I still held the nine in my hand. Everyone thought I was impulsive, that I protected my father - our President. A stone-cold killer.

It wasn't the whole fucking truth. Fuck, if the brothers had reached him, they would have tortured him for days, let him think he was dying, only to wake him up to face a new type of hell.

Marshal, our old enforcer, loved pain and blood; hearing his victims beg for mercy he would never give. He would slowly torture them, one fingernail at a time. Slice pieces of skin from their bodies. Knowing how much they could take to keep them held in the hurricane of pain.

The club would have gutted him, put his head on a stake. Especially, as none of us even had our guns raised. Something made me raise my arm to shoot him first. The fear in those almost black eyes, made me end him quicker than he deserved.

The gates opened and a woman came running out. Her scream filled the night sky, a cry like a wounded animal, that I will never fucking forget. It lives in me, as if it's a part of me. Holding his limp body in her arms as she cried. Whispering to him, stroking his hair with her blood-soaked hands, and begging him to fucking come back to her. That's when we all saw - a fucking kid. A motherfucking kid that was only seventeen! Who should never have been watching the club gate. He wasn't old enough even to prospect. They had used him to do their dirty work. His mother looked up, tears streaked her face, red-rimmed eyes landed straight on mine knowing it was me who took his life.

A mix of hate and shame clung to my fucking skin. I felt it with every breath. It changed something inside me. My mood went from fucking high as a kite, to the deepest pits of fucking hell. My fuse became fucking non-existent. I tried to hold on to it. To the club, my brothers, to the rational side, but it all fell through my hands like fucking sand. It wasn't enough, and when my hot temper came into play, the anger took over. I couldn't see past the white fucking haze, hear past the racing thoughts.

Some part of me had hoped that my baby sister, Layla, would move on from the club. She was so fucking smart; could do anything she wanted. Become the teacher she always dreamt of. Layla deserved to see the world, to experience it. To loosen the chains that the club, my father and I, held her by.

This was it; this is my fate, not hers

"I know what fucking needs to be done," I sneer, getting up and walking to the door.

"Son." I freeze as the name comes from him, turning to look over my shoulder. He opens his mouth, thinks better of it before his shoulders sag, and nods toward the door. "Fuck! Go find yourself some pussy, maybe two, have a fucking drink, let loose tonight." My father knows what's happening, how fucked up my head was. He didn't get it, no one fucking did, not even me.

His son didn't exist anymore, even if he looked at me as if he'd suddenly be reincarnated. That the boy he once knew, had been replaced by the man he now saw looking back at him. The man his club had created. He knew one day I would take it too far. How dangerous I had become. I would end up killing someone or locked up behind bars as an animal like me should be or end up in an early grave. I scared him. Truth? I fucking scared myself.

ICE

"**G**et the fuck up. We're out in five." Cas lifts his head from the pillow, untangling himself from the two fucking snatches in his bed.

"Be there in four." He smirks, scratching his stomach and heading for the shower. The snatches stop in front of me, giving me a look that tells me they'd love to go another round. It's not like Cas and I haven't shared before. We've never crossed swords, but sharing we are good at. They stink of sex and desperation. Even that didn't get my dick to twitch. Fuck, we need some new girls. Walking straight past them, I jog down the stairs to see Rev and Storm already waiting.

My head fucking aches from the whiskey I had drunk, making my stomach roll. I light a cigarette, taking a deep drag as my mobile rings. Grabbing it from my pocket, I see my father's number and swipe to answer. "You all set?" His voice comes through.

"Yeah, Cas is on his way." As if hearing me, he walks down the stairs pulling on his cut. Crystal, one of the snatches, walks out of the kitchen with a flask full of warm coffee. Cas takes it, looking too fucking alert for someone I just had to get up and smirking when he sees the brothers watching him.

"Magic dick." He grins, grabbing his junk, making us all shake our heads at the bastard.

"We are only a few hours out, so leave now, the boys are there until we get back."

"Yeah, I'll message when we stop." I hang up. In this life, tomorrow isn't promised, but we never say goodbye.

Grabbing our shit, we all head outside. It's already warm, letting us know it's going to be a bitch riding all day. All mounting our bikes, I grab the handles, my knuckles whitening as I try to let the calm settle over me. Turning her on, she roars like a beast, and soon the others follow as if answering her call. I lift my fingers in the air, and we all pull out as one. We keep to the speed limit through town, and when Maggi's diner comes into view, there she fucking is. The fucking dark-headed beauty. Dressed in leather pants that hug all her curves and filling out her red shirt, leaving no fucking question that her tits are full and heavy. Looking like pure fucking sin. Raven hair, blowing in a face that looks as if the angels themselves drew her.

My dick grows at the sight of her, and my stomach ripples, thighs tightening as something possessive flies through my fucking veins. The brothers start to slow down as they all spot her, all wolf whistling.

"Keep your eyes on the fucking road," I growl, over the roar, making a few of them turn. I lift my chin, pointing out we need to move. Flexing my wrist on the accelerator and making my girl roar to life. Soon they all join in, picking up speed as we enter the limits of the town, but I can't help looking over my shoulder, taking one last look at the female that's caused all the fucking blood to go to my dick, turning it hard as a fucking diamond. Aching for the dark headed female, I pull the throttle, letting my girl rip up the way. With the wind blowing around me, everything else disappears, no longer a man and his bike, we become fucking one. It is the only time I find peace; my mind slows down as my muscles unwind.

I call for the boys to pull over after four hours, and we all pull up to rest, take a piss, and refuel. As soon as the bikes stop, the chatter begins, everyone is grinning. This is what we all love about the club, the free life and open road. Yeah, the snatches are a good place to chuck your muck, but nothing beats this.

"Fuck, did you see that bitch," Storm says, as he unclips his lid. Knowing who he's talking about makes my lip curl, and all the tension lost on the road rolls back through my muscles.

"Ain't seen her around, wanna take a trip to town when we get back?" Cas smirks, thrusting his hips.

"Stay the fuck away." The words rush out before I can stop them. I don't turn around when it all falls quiet. There was something about that bitch as soon as I set eyes on her. I felt my fucking blood heat, short circuiting my already fucked up brain. As if I'm fucking ravenous, I want to fucking devour her.

"Are you laying claim?" I hear the amusement and surprise in Cas voice.

I snort. "Ain't claiming no fucking bitch." It's God's truth. Yeah, a few of the old-timers had Ol' Ladies, but most of which had turned nomad now. For me, that shit will never fucking happen. No bitch will ever be strong enough to deal with what goes on in my head. To deal with my fucked-up mind. As if on fucking cue, I see Storm's eyes go to my leg, and that's when I notice how fast my finger is tapping against my chain. My silver ring's hitting it, click, click, click, click from the restlessness I feel, and everything in me climbing, knowing I'm going fucking high.

The chatter starts up as everyone grabs their shit, and we take up the picnic benches. I grab my pack of cigarettes, lighting one up, inhaling the smoke like an old friend. My leg bounces as if I can't stay still. Fuck, it's getting fucking worse. My whole-body trembling from its force. By tonight I'll need to find a fucking pussy to take some of the edge off before I turn full fucking manic.

Storm shoots a concerned look at me. I know he's worried about Cas and the shit this is bringing back up for him. We were all tight.

Some of us had grown up together; Cage, Rev, Cas, and me. Cage is currently doing time in the pen for a drop off that fucking went wrong. He had disappeared for a few years, going off to college. After his father was sent up the river, he was mad at the bastard who had used his fists to teach him lessons and drink until he passed out.

Angry at the club for not fucking protecting him, and as soon as the club found out, Relic had what he dealt to Cage returned by a man that owed us a favor on the inside. Cage came back one day, just fucking turned up and wanted in as a prospect, but I didn't miss the secrets in his eyes.

Sketch came from the same town and joined as a prospect. Storm joined straight from the military two years ago. He was Sketch's friend, they went back years, and grew up in the same shitty trailer park. He was still prospecting, but he will get voted in soon. Rev is like my fucking adoptive brother. My father brought him back from a rival club. At thirteen, he was a mess, his body covered in scars, and he didn't speak for months. His demons are different from my own. Rev's demon is born from evil and cruelty.

Brothers amongst brothers. Not by blood or DNA but something more. My ride or die, no matter what.

I lift my chin in return to Storm, letting him know we will keep an eye on him. Rev is sitting off from everyone, playing with that damn knife, running his thumb over the blade. I know it is sharp enough to slice to the bone, and just like the bike is a part of me, the knife is an extension of him. It is fucking crazy watching the way he spins it. Making it dance in the air, the way he's constantly sharpening it, running his fingers over the blade like a caress you would show a lover. What really freaks the brothers out is when he starts whispering bible verses. He's a lone wolf but comes out snarling when a brother needs him. He can see a threat from fucking miles away; he's like Robocop on acid. I'm glad he's on our side because he's someone you want covering your back.

Cas sits there digging into twinkies. If he isn't fucking them, he's eating them. He has a smirk on his face, but his whole body is locked solid, this shit is getting to him. You can taste his hunger, the need for revenge, to spill the blood of those who destroyed his family. And we fucking would; we'd drain them like fucking pigs. They wouldn't be dissolved in acid; we'd cut them up and send their pieces back in pretty little boxes with fucking bows. Mendez cunts weren't the only ones who could send a message.

"Let's move." A round of grunts goes around as we make our way back to the bikes. The midday sun beaming down on us as we get on. "Should get to the motel at six with a clear road," Cas says, not looking at us as he uses the GPS on his phone before nodding.

Arriving at the motel, it looks like something from an old 70's movie, fucking even has flashing neon lights. It's in the next town over from where Alec lives. Didn't want him knowing we were in town, yet. Needing to assess the situation.

Storm comes back with two keys, and taking mine, I walk over to door number nine. The sound of a bitch moaning catches all our attention.

"Do you think I could ask to join in?" Cas asks, looking at the wooden door that separates him, no doubt his dick twitching as the woman behind it moans again.

"Fuck, ain't you scared it's going to fall off?" Storm grunts, as Cas jogs to catch up with us.

"You've hurt its feelings, apologize."

They're still bitching as they enter the room next to mine. Letting out a deep breath, I push open the door, and the musty old smell hits me straight away. There are two twin beds, covered with sheets I'm sure were white and not yellow at some point.

"Where the fuck did he find this place?" I growl, knowing Rev won't answer as he checks over the room as if a fucker is going to jump out from under the bed. I chuck the keys on the small table next to the television. Shrugging out of my cut as I walk to the bathroom, I push open the door, surprised by how clean it looks, even the towels are fresh. Stripping, I crank the water on, ready to get the road dust off. Not even checking the temperature, I stand under the lukewarm stream. As the water washes the road away, the dark-headed beauty's image pops in front of me, sending all the blood straight to my cock. I grab the base, giving it a squeeze as it pounds in time with my heartbeat, heavy in my hand. I move my fist from root to tip, twisting as I get to the head, making me hiss between my teeth as pleasure licks its way up my spine, and my balls become full and heavy. Moving my fist faster, harder, with a twist that has me leaking pre-cum. Using it for extra lubricant, I rest my hand against the wall as red-painted lips flicker behind my eyelids. My back arches as my thighs tense, and my stomach clenches, letting out an animalistic growl as white ropes spray the tiles.

Coming down, my legs feel weak, still shaking from the aftermath. "Fuck!" What the fuck has this bitch done to me? I just rubbed one out in the shower like a fucking horny teenager.

Tying a towel around my waist, I knew I wouldn't fucking sleep, even though I rode for hours, my body was buzzed as if alive. I knew I had to get out, do something. I get dressed quickly.

"You okay, brother?" Rev's rough voice sounded like nails on a chalkboard, his fingers typing on his phone echoing round the room, making me grit my teeth. Intense irritability runs through my veins wiping away any relief I felt. Ripping open the door to see Cas and Storm already there. I growl over my shoulders at Rev.

"Don't need some fucking babysitter." None of them back away from the danger in my tone, instead they mount their bikes.

"Seen a fucking dive bar about an hour away," Cas says, knowing what I fucking need.

We pull up at a bar, old music blares from the open doors as people laugh in the dark corners. I'm off my bike and heading in, walking through the crowd, hearing a few grunts as I push past. Cas and Storm walk to the bar, Rev stays on my fucking heels like a guard dog knowing how impulsive I can be from fucking to fighting, anything to get rid of this fucking restlessness and the racing motherfucking thoughts.

We take a seat in the corner as I grab a smoke to stop my fucking fingers from fidgeting. Cas places a bottle of beer down.

"See anything you like?" he asks, his own eyes scanning the crowds for a place to put his fucking dick for the night.

I grab my beer, downing it in one as my own eyes go to the crowd, and I notice a girl dancing. In a thin top that shows off her plump tits, nipples poking through and jeans that hang off her narrow waist. It's the dark hair that makes my fucking dick twitch. I'm up on my feet, crossing the distance between us, and when her dark eyes find mine as she bites her lips.

"Hey, sweetheart," my voice comes out as cocky as the smirk on my lips.

"Hey," she whispers.

I grab her bony hips, pulling her against me, squashing those tits to my chest. She moves her fucking hips in a way to tell me she's offering more than a fucking dance. I slip my hands down her fucking pants, giving her what she is begging for, and what I want. What I fucking need.

Her lips part as she looks around, lifting her head to kiss me, I turn my head so her lips land on my cheek.

"Don't fucking kiss, but I'll make you feel fucking good." I push my fingers between her wetness, thrusting in and out, making her eyes roll as a low moan comes from her covered by the heavy beats.

I grab her hand, taking her outside, pushing her against a wall. "On your fucking knees," I growl, getting my fucking belt undone and jeans down. The first lick of her tongue, I feel my muscles start to fucking relax. "That's it lick it darlin', best fucking cock you'll ever get." I growl as she takes me in, hot and wet, and my hips thrust hitting the back of her throat. "Yeah, take it all like a good fucking bitch." I grab her hair, feeling the back of her fucking throat. Hearing her gag around me, the wetness from her tears she can't keep at bay hit my balls. "Bet you ain't ever had a dick this fucking big," I hiss, moving my hips back and forth, feeling on top of the fucking world. Nothing could fucking stop me. I stumble forward, getting bumped from behind making the bitch nearly choke on my dick.

"Watch where you're fucking going," a slurred voice comes from behind me.

I turn around, setting my fucking sights on the man that just knocked me. He stares at me laughing. No fucker laughs at me. Cas, yeah, that bastard is a funny fucker, but me no.

Putting my dick away, I cross the distance between us. Before he can open his fucking mouth, I throw my fist, landing it in his jaw, smirking as he yelps in pain.

"What the fuck!" the stupid asshole spits out. Doesn't he know who he's fucking facing? I land another punch to his nose; a sick satisfaction runs through my veins at the tears running down his face and the blood dripping off his chin.

"What's happening here?" I hear Cas' voice breaking through the group of people that have gathered around.

"Fucker disrespecting me," I growl as my blood pumps to the heavy beat of the music. I turn to punch his stomach, sending him to knees.

"Fuck, man. I'm sorry," he gurgles as I bounce from one foot to the other.

"He hears you." Cas slaps my shoulder, and I smirk.

"Yeah, he fucking knows I'm the best."

Storm's lips twitch. "Yeah, you're the fucking best."

"He's high," I hear Rev's low voice, and I smirk, walking back in, the thrill alive in my veins as the adrenalin's pumping like a base to a fucking heavy metal song... Yeah, I'm fucking high. I'm unstoppable, invincible. I feel fucking alive.

ICE

I hate riding in a car, truck, or van. All of it makes me feel caged in, claustrophobic. I spark up another cigarette, already been through two packs as my leg bounces. The restlessness is still racing through my veins, only now I'm fucking exhausted because I've barely fucking slept this last week. I feel the manic phase leaving me fucking weak in its wake. Something you can't afford in this life is a weakness. I can feel the guys eyes on me, watching me like a fucking bomb about to go off. They know there's not a thing they can do, there's no help, not for a fucker like me. I roll my shoulders, getting my head together as Storm glances at me. My face shows nothing. Cold, calculating, and emotionless.

He had rented a van a week ago to do recon before we paid our little friend a visit. Didn't want any fucking surprises knowing the gang MH28 is heavy around here. We hadn't let the leader know we were coming through or staying. It's a fucking dangerous risk we are willing to gamble.

To respect their turf, our cuts were in the back, but it felt wrong. That piece of leather and the patches made us the fucking men we are, showing who we belonged to, that we were The Red Horsemen. Demanded the respect it was owed. The name we have carved from those who had fucking betrayed us. Over the last week, we've watched Alec from down the street as people came and left quickly, their eyes searching around before they scampered away.

Fucking junkies. And if Alec is selling this close to MH28, that means he's on their payroll, or bigger. My fucking thoughts are racing, making them nothing but fucking white noise, taking me to places that has my teeth gritting. I clench my fists, and Storm flicks his eyes to mine.

"We're five minutes out." I lift my chin in response, turning away so he can't see what I'm trying to hide.

The tension in the van grows like a hungry wolf as if it can taste the blood of its prey. The blood thirst makes your mouth water. I look over my shoulder to see Cas staring at the side of the van, body fucking rigid, not even blinking. Lost in the memories of his past. The vengeance he usually hides, spilling to the surface. Rev is doing the same, only spinning his knife and catching it by the blade, and I know if he turned around, his eyes would no longer be gold, but dark. Rev is no longer there; now, his fucking demon has taken over.

We all get out, pulling the hoods up over our faces as we race across the road, slipping into the shadows, staying close to the houses. The street is quiet, apart from a few cats and the sound of a party somewhere in the next neighborhood. I hold two fingers up and flick them, telling Rev and Storm to take the back. Cas and I wait until they are around the side, then I walk up to the door and knock. There is movement and cursing before a shadowy figure comes towards us behind the screen, opening the door, Alec's eyes widen as soon as he sees me.

"Shit."

He frantically tries slamming the fucking door, but I've got my boot ready, and the door hits back, knocking him in the shoulder as he runs down the hall. A smirk crawls across my face as we follow him and hearing him yelp like a fucking pussy, knowing Rev and Storm are waiting for him. As soon as I walk in the living room, the smell of dope hangs heavy in the air, white powder covers the table ready to be bagged.

"No hello, Alec? And I thought we were friends." I slap his cheek, and the sound vibrates through the room, the crack of skin meeting skin.

"Yeah, we're cool, you know that, Ice," he splutters, and nods like a fucking bobblehead. I intimidate the fuck out of him. I do most people. I'm a big guy, but I know what really puts Alec on edge is the coldness in my eyes. Dead, soulless. No remorse.

"So, why did you fucking run? Your pussy ass got something to hide?" He shakes his head so hard I'm surprised he doesn't give himself whiplash.

"No, no. Nothing." I walk around the coffee table, kicking it with my boot and knocking over a few g's worth of drugs. It explodes in a plume of white dust like a snowstorm. His eyes widen before he drops to the floor, trying to gather it up.

"I've got buyers coming in a few hours," he squeaks as he frantically tries to sweep up the powder using his hands. Cas stands on his hand, making him wail in pain. I watch as Cas' lips curl, the excitement in his eyes as he watches the pain cover Alec's. Fuck, he's enjoying this. He's further gone than even I realized.

"We need to ask you a few fucking questions." Alec met Cas a few years back with me, and I know he's searching for the man he saw then. The one with the cocky smirk. Alec's eyes flick to mine, realizing this isn't a drop in call.

Making a dick move, he tries to run, again. Storm grabs him around the neck, digging his two fingers into a pressure point that makes Alec's eyes roll before his fucking body crumples to the floor. Rev grabs a chair, the legs scraping like nails down a chalkboard as Storm grabs the body. Not being careful, he spreads him across it before they both get to work tying his arms and legs down. Cas grabs the dope off the table, putting it in a bag that was on the side, and then he looks up and shrugs. We don't do fucking drugs like a lot of the clubs. My father got out of it years ago, wanting the brothers at a moment's notice, not face first in fucking snow. We all did random drug tests, even the snatches, and anyone that was found having it in their systems paid the price. The brother took a beating, and that was his warning, but a snatch was out on her ass. Although, Prez didn't mind a bit of dope.

We all turn as Alec starts groaning, coming back around and blinking a few times before everything registers. His eyes Ping-Pong between us before landing on mine.

"Ice?" There's fear in his tone, a deep dread that makes my body tingle with excitement as my rage reaches closer to the surface, fueling that need.

I bend down, so we are eye level. "What the fuck are the Mendez motherfuckers doing coming into my town?" The color drains from his face, eyes dart and beads of sweat start to gather on his top lip. I smirk, relishing in his fear. Smelling it seeping from his pores. It draws me in like a drug. Having it so close, I can fucking taste it.

"That's Lonzo, not me. You know this." I draw back my fist and punch him straight in the jaw, watching as blood explodes from his mouth like fireworks on the fourth before sending another straight after. Enjoying the whimpers and pleas that fall from his swollen, bloody lips and watching as he spits out a tooth, knowing the pain that must cause. For a tooth to be ripped out wasn't fucking child's play, it hurt like a bitch and filled every one of your nerves with a pounding pain.

"You know what the fuck I'm talkin' 'bout." I throw another punch, snarling. "We both know that motherfucker can't stop talkin' like a fucking bitch," I sneer. Lonzo, Alec's sister's husband, and a cocky shit, likes to tell everyone who will listen that he's a runner in with the Mendez cunts. Likes to think he's high up when he's the shit on their shoes, dispensable, nothing to them. Licking the blood from his lips, Alec nods.

"Yes, but he hasn't mentioned the Horsemen. I would have told you." Bullshit. I send a fist to his ribs, feeling the connection with the curved bone before they crack under the force, making him wheeze. The air whistles between the gap where his tooth was and his swollen lips before I step aside as Cas steps forward.

"Do you know they killed Buck, one of our men? My father." Alec freezes at the venom in Cas' voice.

"No," he whispers, his whole body starts to shake, and the fear passing through his eyes makes me enjoy this more. Feeding my fucked-up brain as if my body doesn't know what to do. It's trying to shut down, running on fumes from last week, yet adrenaline is pumping around hard causing a sensation of feeling on the edge, yet unable to fly. It's the most dangerous.

"Yeah, cut his fucking limbs off one by one, motherfucking alive before dropping them outside the clubhouse." I watch as a dark patch grows on his jeans and the smell of ammonia fills the air.

"He's fucking pissed himself," Storm states the obvious, making us all turn to see his nose curled up. "That's fucking disgusting."

Turning back to the mess in the chair, Cas takes a step forward. "See my brother." Shoving his thumb in Rev's direction. "He's got an obsession." Alec's lip starts to tremble, his eyes flicking to Rev and the knife he's flipping as Cas' smirk grows. "That knife can cut flesh like fucking butter, but the bone is always a little harder. Ain't that fucking right?" Rev grunts making Cas' smirk turn into something

61

sadistic. "When the knife hits the bones, it crunches, splitting the motherfucking bone. It can take a while."

Alec starts pulling on the ropes, trying to get away as he starts screaming. Cas punches him in the face, and the sound of bone-crunching under the force echoes around the room. Blood pours from his mouth and under his nose as the punches keep coming. I wish it were me causing the pain. The blood covering his face makes my skin itch, knowing I haven't released enough of the anger raging in me.

"Hold back, motherfucker," my voice is like a whip against his skin, his body taut, blood covering his knuckles. He looks over his shoulder straight at me. I can't believe it's me saying this shit. Normally I'm the one being reined in. "Need him fucking breathin'."

He takes a step back, fist-clenching, and I see a look in his eyes. He's not finished, and I watch as his lips peel back as if someone is controlling him before he shuts it down and makes the final step back. I take over his place.

"You ready to fucking talk?" A muffled groan comes from him. With what's left of his mangled lips and shattered face. "I'll call Lonzo." Alec's shoulders slump.

I lift my chin to Storm, and he walks across, picking up the phone and messing about with it. When a ringtone fills the room, Alec's eyes widen.

"What do you think I couldn't fucking break a little code?" Storm mocks as he holds the phone in front of Alec.

"Let on we are here, and Rev will cut your fucking tongue out," I sneer. He nods just as Lonzo's deep voice comes through.

"Hey, man. You'll never guess where I am? Sin nightclub. Man, there's so many fucking women and drinks, none of the cheap shit." Alec's brow comes down when the women are mentioned. If anyone treated Layla like that, I would chop off their fucking dick and feed it to them.

"Cool, man. Thought you might have been in Arizona. Seen a bunch of Mendez men heading that way and didn't know if I should get Maria out if war is brewing with the Horsemen." He deserves an Oscar for an award-winning performance.

"The dirty fucking bikers," a snarl comes through the phone as if our name leaves a bitter taste, making us all grin. "Fuck no, we don't bother with dogs like them, leave them to kill themselves." Each of us turn, what the hell is going on?

Cage ends the call. "What the fuck is going on?"

I don't know, but I don't like it. My gut is telling me we are all missing something. I turn to Alec, gun pointed at his head.

"I won't say anything, please. Maria and Anita, I'm all they've got." At the mention of his sister and niece, my stomach turns as the self–hate and fury clash together. Lifting my gun, I feel that familiar feeling run through my body, turning from fiery rage to cold, as ice fills my veins. I pull my finger back, watching as Alec's body jerks once. His head falls forward with a hole between his eyes. Another mark against my fucking soul. I wait for a stir of emotions, something, anything, but I feel nothing.

We pull up outside Rags' chapter in Ohio. The last fucking three weeks have been a massive waste of fucking time. We've stopped at our chapters, meeting with the presidents to determine if they know or heard anything, and it had to be face to face, we couldn't risk our lines being tapped. Plus, I wanted to see their faces as I asked them. We were only keeping the main officers in the loop. Nothing. Not a fucking peep. Soon as we roll our bikes to the gates, the prospect spots us, and before even asking, he's typing in the code ready for us to pass through, and we all lift our chin in greeting. Pulling up outside the clubhouse, Rags is waiting. Parking up, I stand, stretching my back.

"Good to see you, boy. Luther said you'd be fucking coming by. Are you all staying?" Rags is still fit for his age, towering over most people at 6ft 3 and shoulders just as wide. He keeps the brothers in place and rules them with an iron fist.

"Yeah. Bolt about?" I don't miss the small twitch of his eye as he looks at me before shaking his head.

"Nah. Had a run, left yesterday, early morning." There was something in his voice, a strange undercurrent, and he held my eyes for a second longer before heading inside. A few of the brothers hanging in the main room come over greeting us, some we haven't seen for a year. Bottles of beer are passed around. Hastings, one of the prospects, shows us to the extra bedrooms. We all leave in silence, the last week heavy on our muscles and back.

Hitting thirty next month, I'm beginning to fucking feel it. Everything about this life is hard. Fuck hard, party hard and ride hard. Skipping the room, heading straight for the shower, stripping, and not even waiting for the water to warm, I get in. The cold water catches my breath like shards of fucking glass against my skin. I stay under until it warms up, loosens all the muscles in my shoulders and back. A flash of the dark-haired beauty dances behind my eyelids, the same fucking bitch that's haunted my dreams and stolen more thoughts than I can count. My dick rock solid, I grind my jaw, holding back and refusing to give in.

Getting out, still wet, I pull my jeans up and put my shirt on, grabbing my smokes and piece. Opening the door I see Rev standing against the wall.

"How long have you been there?" He doesn't answer, I bet my fucking bike he's been there all the time I was in the room, protecting me. "Chill man, they are fucking Horsemen." He glances at me out of the corner of his eye as we jog down the stairs. Rev doesn't trust many people; no one that is outside our tight circle.

Since we have been upstairs, the place has filled, music vibrates the floor, everyone is drinking, the snatch is already on the prowl. We grab a beer and walk over to Rags' table, where he's sitting with Swan, his Sergeant at Arms. They both lift their beers in welcome as we take the seats.

"Luther told you we got cunts sticking their nose in places it shouldn't be?" I swear he growls as he shakes his head.

"Yeah, called me three weeks ago. You find anything?"

"Nothing, not a motherfucking word. No one seems to know a fucking thing." He nods, rubbing his jaw, but I swear some tension leaves his shoulders. "You got an idea, old man?"

Rags watches me. His eyes flicking to my features as if trying to read if there's anything I'm not telling him.

"Nah, told Luther I'll keep our ear to the fucking ground, told the boys the same."

Taking a deep pull of beer, I feel the tension coil in my muscles as my finger taps on the beer bottle and my leg bounces underneath the table. Something feels off, a fire licks at my gut as I grab my smokes, putting one between my lips, grabbing my lighter, I take a few drags before leaning forward.

"If they are looking for fucking trouble, we will fucking bury them." I leave my words to hang in the air, the threat surrounding us. Rags and Swan both grunt in agreement. Rev slams his knife into the table. Swan's eyes widen as he leans back in his chair, putting more space between them.

"Agree, never fucking liked the Mendez." The whole room vibrates from the force of his words, threat dripping off each letter. I lift my beer to that; I couldn't agree more. The fucking Mendez time is running out. We are going to take them apart, destroy the motherfuckers till there is nothing left.

Cas and Storm walk past us with three snatches, grinning.

"How's he dealing?" Rags asks, lifting his chin in Cas' direction.

"He's fucking dealin'." I won't betray his trust by spilling his fucking business and gossiping like I've lost my dick. When the music stops, turning to see what's up, I see all the brothers pushing the furniture to the side. "What's going on?" Rags smirks.

"Looks like they want a friendly, club against club." For the first time in days, I grin. Standing up, I rip off my shirt, and walk into the center as the men form a circle around us, and then Tank walks in, smiling at me. He a big fucking bastard, muscles as wide as he is tall. Bald head covered in ink. Tank grew up on the streets and knows how to fucking fight.

We are both grinning, circling each other as adrenaline pumps through me, making the blood race through my veins. Tank swings his leg out, but seeing it coming, I dodge it. The brothers start to shout around us. Running at me, he grabs me around the waist, allowing me to throw two kidney punches that make his body arch as he hisses. Swinging with his left, he catches my jaw and lip. I lift my hand, rubbing my blood away, grinning. Dancing around each other.

"You punch like a fucking pussy," I taunt him, through a bloody grin. He races at me. We both go for it, a mixture of blurred images, arms, legs, blood covering both of us. I throw a hard left, knocking his shoulder. He comes back at me, throwing a right to my ribs, a kick to my shin, sending me to my knee, and he grins, holding his hands in the air. This is what I want. Pain.

Pain that I deserved for breathing another fucking day. Pain so I never fucking forgot. Pain for punishment.

Pain to know I'm still fucking alive.

Because I was a fucking piece of shit that shouldn't be breathing.

I'm a motherfucker that destroys everything and everyone around me. My boys have stuck around, knowing the destruction I cause. They all still hold fucking hope for me when there is none. My head is too fucked, and the crazy thoughts too strong. I will fucking never return from the darkness.

My instinct kicks in, animalistic, built into us all—a feeling to fight for survival. I turn, taking a punch to the back before jumping while twisting and laying a kick to his fucking jaw. Surprise covers his features before his eyes roll, and his body falls to the floor with a loud thud. The brothers go mad, pounding their feet. It matches my hard breathing. Sweat from my hair glistens on my body, highlighting the blood running down my skin, painting my body crimson. When a snatch walks into the ring, my prize, she grins, licking her lips as she walks towards me, pushing her tits into my side. The blood is still pumping, knowing it won't last and the relief my body feels as the restlessness escapes through the cuts is only temporary, I chuck my arm over her shoulder, seeing Cas and Storm smirking as Rev hands me a beer.

"Let's get this fucking party started." The whole room goes crazy as I point my beer neck towards my boys. "Tomorrow, we go home."

RAE

"What do you think?" I ask, biting back my grin at Davis' gasp when he sees it.

"Rae, it's fucking amazing."

"Fuck, girl." I recognize Sketch's voice, surprising me, I spin in my chair to see him standing just inside the door. Coming closer for a better look, he doesn't say anything else, but takes a photo then squeezes my shoulder, nodding. Unable to hide my smile as I wipe the blood from Davis' leg before rubbing the ointment and covering. Bright colors take up half his calf; a pin-up dressed in a white shirt with the buttons open revealing her cleavage and tiny denim overalls with a spanner in her hand, an oilcloth hanging from one of the pockets. Long blond hair falling over her shoulder and down her back with a red headband. Her one leg kicked back, wearing blood-red heels as she leans on a Harley.

"So, about that date?" Davis asks, sitting up on the chair. He works in the town as a mechanic and came in a couple of weeks ago to drop some parts in for Sketch's bike, and ever since he has been coming in asking me out for a drink. Last week he scheduled an appointment. A last-ditch effort, one that would never happen.

"Sorry, Boss' orders. No making customers lose their nuts. That shit gets messy." I repeat Sketch's words from my first day. The man himself grunts behind me as Davis frowns. I smile, handing him his aftercare before he goes to pay Red.

I wasn't sure what the big fuss was. Why was Sketch worried about me working here? Yeah, the men could be a little boisterous and intense at times, but nothing I couldn't handle. They have treated me with more respect than I expected.

Layla prefers to be called Red. She is sassy and can banter with the best of them and doesn't take shit off Sketch, and he seems to be amused by it. I walk out, seeing them both by the register.

"I think you broke Davis' heart." Red smirks at me. I roll my eyes and shake my head at her dramatics. She had warmed up to me over the last few weeks.

"He'll live." I smirk. Sketch keeps quiet, but I feel his eyes on me, making me turn.

"Davis' ink is fucking good. Sort out some designs and put them in folders if you wanna." I glance at Red, who's grinning back at me.

"I'll help you."

I didn't know how to feel. I have never put my drawings in a portfolio before. I had been asked a few times but always refused. It was like leaving breadcrumbs, a paper trail that anyone could find. But something about leaving a little of myself here felt right. Like it belonged here, and I knew in months to come, I would smile knowing there's a part of me still here.

"Yeah, I'm free now, I'll look through my sketches and put some in later, if you're sure?" He studies me before lifting his chin, his eyes staying with me a beat longer before he goes back to his room. I still often catch him looking at me. It wasn't in the 'I want you' way or one that made me feel uneasy.

It was as if he were trying to see something, like he knew me but couldn't place it. That we had maybe met before. A puzzle to solve, and that can't happen. I can't let anyone see behind the curtains to the truth Rae hides.

Luckily, I travelled around a lot, so I didn't have a defined accent that could pin me to one place, and I could easily dodge his questions from years of practice. I had learnt to give information, yet no real detail. Nothing that could be traced back.

The bell goes off, and a few customers walk in, and I leave Red to deal with them as I walk back to my room, which Sketch and Red had decorated for me. I came in Monday morning and Red had surprised me with it. One whole wall was black, and across it, in blood-red graffiti was the word Bitch. A joke from that first day. The bottom looked like it was dripping down the wall. White highlights made it stand out, and above the T was a golden crown with red gems. It made my eyes misty when I saw it. Sketch didn't acknowledge he had done it, but he is warming up to me, impressed that I can banter with male clients but keep it professional. They had no idea I was playing a part, that none of them saw the real me.

They also bought me a new vintage black chair that went down to do bigger pieces and two chairs as Red seemed to be in here more than she was at the desk.

I grab my drawing pad, flicking through the pages. A few rough sketches, harsh lines that are still transforming, pin-ups, and Harleys like the bikes I saw at the diner. I stop, looking towards the door as I hear Sketch's deep voice and Red's laughter. It makes me smile, but also brings a frown to my face.

I was finding it hard being here because of how relaxed I felt. That never happened. How close I've become to Red, even though I never really made friends, it's something that never came easy. It had always suited me as making friends meant opening up and made leaving harder. But I would go. I always did. It is what I did. I had been doing it for so long now, didn't even know if I could stop.

This place settled something inside of me; the anxiety to run isn't as close to the surface as it always was. My skin didn't itch to leave. Fear did not crawl over my skin and hold me prisoner. I didn't look over my shoulder all the time, jump at moving shadows. I didn't have to hold my breath, waiting for something to happen so much.

I walk through the door to the main room spotting Red and Sketch. They had an odd relationship that I still couldn't work out. She swore that nothing was going on, but no one could miss how she looked at him sometimes. Yes, she could deny, deny, deny all she wants, but that look she gives him, the way her eyes would heat and soften at the same time, couldn't lie. There is something between them, but I can't work out what?

Sketch holds his cards close to his chest, and I couldn't work him out. I saw the way his eyes softened when she laughed or smiled. I didn't know if he cared about her or something more.

RAE

I walk out to the front with the sketches, absently handing some over to Red. I hadn't stopped drawing. Like it's alive inside of me, using me as its vessel to escape. I spend every night with a pencil in my hair, or between my teeth as I sit in shorts and oversized shirts drawing until my hand cramps.

"Oh, I love this one." I glance at her, holding one of my favorites. A full bloom rose, bold cherry with black outlines and highlights, with a few white lines to emphasize certain parts. Green stalk with three thorns that had a small teardrop of blood hanging off one of its points.

"It would look amazing on your hip."

Her eyes widen full of excitement as she bites her lip, nodding. "Can you do it for me?"

I go to answer when the floor starts to vibrate. "What the fuck!" I whisper, scared to speak any louder as a loud roar fills the air. Red gets up, jogging to the window. I catch up with her just as twelve motorcycles go past.

All of them were Harleys of different shapes and sizes. Some had big handles, and others were wide. Like the ones the men rode as they drove past me when I was getting coffee my first day. The sun glistens off the metalwork, casting rays of light around. I admit I never thought of a bike as sexy, but these were wild, and sex all wrapped into one dangerous package. The sound vibrated through me, and that feeling washed over me again. A similar feeling that the gun gave me. It filled me with excitement. All the riders were wearing leather waistcoats with the same large patches on the back of them. Across the top were the words Red Horsemen, and underneath a picture of a red horse, that looked terrifying. The war horse of the apocalypse, with the town name written at the bottom. Most of them wore a scarf covering their face that made the bottom half look like a skeleton—an army of the dead. The sight made a shiver run down my spine.

"Looks like playtime is over," Red huffs, crossing her arms over her chest as we watch the remaining bikes pass.

I blink as her words register. "You know them?" She snorts, her eyes still on the road where the bikes have just passed.

"I belong to them." I'm sure I look like a goldfish with the way my mouth is opening and closing, which must look comical because her lips curve upwards. "It's not as bad as it sounds. My brother, Ice, is the VP, and my father is the president."

I am sure she didn't mean the president of the U.S and what the hell is a VP? Her lips twitch even more as she studies me, seeing the confusion on my face.

"Sorry, I forget you're a civilian, you fit so easily with us." Her brows pull down into a frown as she studies me before walking back over to the drawings I'd brought out, picking them up and putting them all in tidy piles. "VP means vice president. Ice is second in command. He's an intense asshole most of the time. Fuck that, all the time." She rolls her eyes, shaking her head as we place my sketches on the table. "They are all assholes and man whores." She scrunches up her nose, her lip curling up as if tasting something sour. "They all have the same motto they live by; pump it and dump it! They don't stay and cuddle, fuck, half of them don't even kiss. They fuck as they live. Hard!"

I'm not sure what I make of her description. It sounded cold and cruel. I didn't understand the whoring. It made my body freeze up, and a cold sweat cover my skin. Did the men treat Red this way?

Is this why she didn't sound happy they were home? I felt sick to my stomach that someone could treat her like that. I knew intense men, and what it was like to live under their sort of power. To have all your choices taken away. To have someone have so much control over you. To suffer in their hands. The anxiety that had kept away was back in full force. Clawing at my throat. Sitting on my chest. Trying to steal my breath, while my thoughts fall over each other as I think back over the past few weeks for any clues Red could have given me, coming up blank. Red never showed any signs she is mistreated, held against her will, but I knew smiles could mask the truth. I know because I had done it to survive.

What I didn't understand was how she wasn't more tainted by their lifestyle? I saw the way she sassed at the men, but their eyes always turned soft, not cold, no anger lingering in their eyes. She wasn't punished. Her eyes were not haunted; no demons hid behind her blues.

It was confusing. I didn't understand how Red had stayed so pure in the darkness I suspected and felt surrounded her.

A frown appears between her brows, and when she sees something cross my face, she smiles as if to reassure me. It holds tension, but it is still a real smile, not like the fake one I hide behind.

"Fuck! I'm explaining it all wrong. They might be intense assholes, but you will never meet more loyal men." She looks out

the window, her eyes lost. "I swear to you I can't even explain that
fucking shit. All of the men you just saw ride past and the rest that
belong to the Horsemen." She points outside. "Would jump in front
of a bullet for each other. For me, without any hesitation. They
protect what is theirs, as in the Club, the brothers, and their family,
with their last breath. Even death couldn't stop them revenging those
that had dared cross us," she snarls. "Never once have I not felt safe."
Red lets out a shuddering breath. "Or loved. I don't mean the type
you see on a hallmark card. It is wild, untamable, raw."

I take in all her words and try to process it all. Trying to
understand it, believe it. An ache appears in my chest.

I never doubted my mother's love. It wasn't what my mother
said. It is what I felt when I was around her, the look in her eyes.

Even in her death, I still felt it wrap around me.

The love Red just explained. Did it exist?

It didn't sound like a weakness. It was not cruel or cold. Red
believes their love makes them stronger. Could she be right? Was I
wrong?

Is love a weakness or strength?

Whenever I remembered my mother, I saw love and beauty,
but when I remember the after? All I can feel is pain buried deep, so
much that it marks your very bone marrow. Has the pain masked the
beauty? Twisted my perception? Hidden it? Was my mother's love
so different because it was the love of a parent?

The love he claimed to have for me wasn't freeing. It was
destroying, cold, and cruel. Haunting. It ripped you apart piece by
piece, killed the person you were, destroyed your soul. Even dead,
he still held me in his grip, my mind now his torture chamber. I still
wasn't free of him.

Is Red's love the beautiful lie, where mine was the cold hard
truth?

Whatever the truth is, her words touch me.

I feel my walls lower slightly, and I am not sure I know what to think about that? I am about to ask more, when Sketch comes racing out in a leather waistcoat, saluting us before running out the door. He chucks his leg over his bike before peeling out in the same direction the other bikes went. I watch as he disappears, only dust left behind in his wake.

"Sketch is one too? I mean, he's wearing the same leather waistcoat."

She barks out a laugh. "That's fucking priceless. They are called cuts, leathers, colors. Don't let them hear you say waistcoat ever." Her face darkens to let me know she is serious, so I nod in understanding – Cuts, not waistcoats. "Their cuts show they belong to the Club, the MC, the Horsemen."

I've heard of MC before and watched documentaries, who hasn't? But I have never actually seen them.

"So, they are a gang?" Her lip curls, baring her teeth as she stares me down.

"Fuck! Never, the Red Horsemen is a motorcycle club. That's what MC stands for. They ain't no fucking gangbangers, never have been."

"I'm sorry. I didn't mean any offense. I've just watched things on TV. They always called them gangs."

Red sighs as she gets up, starting to clean up the magazines on the table. "Sorry, that was bitchy; they are not the only protective ones. Half the shit these programs talk is complete bullshit." Poking out her lips as she studies me intently. "You've got the weekend warriors that bring their bikes out when it's sunny, the biker clubs that only ride in the summer, and then you've got the one percenters, that's what we are."

We both stand, and I know she is giving me the watered-down version. Red, like everyone else, doesn't know where I came from. That I knew to keep my mouth shut when my uncles turned up with bullet wounds and heard the dark whispers of what had happened when they all left the house. Seen the blood stains that no bleach could get rid of. I came from the darkness, much thicker than the one surrounding her. Mine came from pure evil. I wasn't protected or had men watching over me. I stood in the middle seeing the blood that covered them. It was my life, my inheritance, my fucking destiny. One that I hated with every fiber of my body. One that destroyed the girl I was, changed the woman I was becoming.

"Look, they don't go around causing shit, but if someone starts it, then you can fucking bet they will finish it. Horsemen believe in something different, free-living, but most of all, the brothers believe in the club. The club is everything." She speaks with complete passion.

I wasn't foolish even if Red played naive. Maybe she was still draped in the illusion I had been for so many years. But I knew what happened behind closed doors, when their perfect mask slipped to reveal the true man and the evil behind the show.

"Red, I will never judge you on where you come from." I turn off some of the lights before turning to face her. "Trust me, that world out there isn't rosy with sunflowers and fucking rainbows. Plenty of men dressed in designer suits, who speak the right way, that act perfectly, hide evil. I'm curious, that's all, like what's a brother?" She studies me before her whole body relaxes as she finishes locking the safe.

"Patched brothers are full members. They wear the full cuts like the one Sketch is wearing. Yes, Sketch is a brother. Before you become a brother, you've got to prospect."

I tilt my head, not sure she is even talking English anymore. "Prospect?"

"It basically means you're the bitch for the club, and you've got to do what the brothers tell you. No questions, it's a sort of hazing." Her words amaze me, and you can't deny how she speaks about the brothers and the club and what they all mean to her. We turn off all the remaining lights and turn the sign to closed. It's still early evening, so the light comes in from the window. I follow her to the couch.

"Ice was the quickest to prospect at just under a year, it usually takes eighteen months maybe more…All the brothers knew him. As I said, my dad is Luther, the club president, and a founding member along with Rags. My father isn't just the president of this club, he's the national president." She watches me through her lashes, I don't know what she sees, but she carries on. "Ice and I grew up in the club, so did Cas, Cage, and Bolt. He is Rags' son. We are called biker brats, meaning club life is all we've ever known." The more she spoke, the more it seemed to run parallel with my life growing up. Maybe that is why she spilled everything because she saw it in me. Knew I came from a similar experience and that I would have an understanding that most women wouldn't.

Standing up as if she can't sit down, her lips pull down as she frowns. "Something went bad on the run. A week later, Ice was patched." She walks to the window, her whole body tense, anger fills her sapphires, causing them to look more electric. "I've been a part of the fucking club all my life. The clubhouse, it's my home. Those brothers are my family. Dysfunctional as shit, we will never be the Walton's. But still, they are my family, I love them." She grits her teeth, and you can feel the anger flowing from her. "Fuck! I know how shit works even if they try hard to keep that shit away from me. I know he needed to do something massive to get patched in early." She shakes her head. "Even biker brats have got to earn that fucking cut, the brothers' respect and loyalty. No one gets a free pass. Ever."

I watch as she transforms from the girl I've come to know, into the girl that fits in the place she's been describing as all her features harden. "Ice is different to me because women can't patch. They can't belong to the club as a member. Some clubs let women ride, but ours doesn't." She carries on quickly, "After that run, Ice became hot-tempered, fighting all the time. He is so fucking angry. Uses the club girls like he is trying to fuck whatever it is out of his system. Sketch and the rest of the brothers are no saints. Fucking Cas got his name because it stands for Casanova, but Ice... Whatever happened that night changed my brother. That night he became cold. He became Ice."

Red frowns, and her eyes hold a darkness that is never usually there. The conversation is upsetting her. The hitch in her voice tells me how much it hurts, that she bottled it up, waiting to release it all into the world. I feel like she doesn't get upset quickly, so whatever is bothering her is bad. It hurts her, so she doesn't show many people. Red is giving me her trust, and from everything she just told me, trusting an outsider doesn't happen often.

"Hey, want to grab some food," I ask, trying to lighten the situation.

"Yeah!" As Red locks up the shop, she looks over her shoulder at me. "What I told you in there, stays in there. I don't talk about the club to anyone. No one talks about the club. Trust, that means shit here." I know she is serious. I also know what it is like to be betrayed. To feel that knife as it sinks in, cutting you open, and the scars it leaves behind never fade.

"I would never betray your trust." She inspects me carefully before she smiles gently.

"I know, because if you ever did, I would slit your fucking throat myself. You wouldn't know until you woke up choking on your own blood." My eyes widen as she continues to smile sweetly before linking her arm with mine. I want to think that she is joking, but something is telling me she's not.

RAE

"Two beers and chasers," Red shouts over to the barman. After food, she decided we needed to make a night out of it. My heart skipped a beat as the bouncer checked out my ID. I had paid through the teeth for it, but it didn't stop the nerves that crept up my spine as he held the little plastic between his fingers. We have been at Ace's a couple of hours. It was a hole in the wall. The sort of place where you wiped your feet on the way out. Beer on tap, with five-day-old peanuts on the bar and old rock music playing in the background. The best sort of bar for when you wanted to get drunk and forget life. Where no one asked your name, and that was our plan.

Red has lost all the tension in her body. She's now relaxed, and I also find myself relaxing for the first time in years. Letting the music take over my body, dancing to the hard, heavy beats as sweat gathers at my hairline and trickles down my back.

"Thanks! I needed this." She grins, waving her hands in the

air as she sways her hips. The girl's got some serious moves. Men check us out, with that look in their eyes as they watch from the dark corners of the dancefloor. But something is stopping them from coming over to us, which I'm happy about. Like we have our own protective barrier. I didn't need some drunk fool coming on to me. When movement catches my attention, I see a figure standing in the shadows at the edge of the room. Fear crawls up my throat, making every breath painful and fingers dig into my heart. No. Please, God no.

I don't feel the bottle of beer slip from my hand and crash to the floor. The music dies as my heart pounds in my ears. Pins and needles tingle through my fingers as I turn, looking for an escape. Only to be met by another figure hiding in the darkness. How did I forget to check for an escape?

"Rae, Rae." I try to cling to her voice, turning to see Red looking at me with her eyes wide. I try to speak, but it's as if all my words have been captured. I couldn't let her be hurt in the crossfire. This is why I stayed away and didn't let people in. They would slit Red's throat just for talking to me. My eyes scan the bar quickly. "Stay here."

I walk away before she has a chance to question me. Watching as the shadowy figure gets distracted lighting a cigarette. My movements are slow as I come up behind him. My hand disappears into my bag when my fingers brush over familiar, smooth metal. I grab it pulling it out in one fluid motion, pointing it at his skull.

"I've seen you watching us," I growl as his body goes ramrod straight.

"Fuck!" Red growls before taking a step in our direction.

"Stay away, he's been watching us." I push the metal harder against his skull. Her eyes widen, flicking between us.

"Rae, it's okay. He's a prospect," her voice is steady as if she is talking to a cornered animal.

"Prospect?" I lick my lips, and she nods.

"Yeah, my father sent them for protection." She rolls her eyes, crossing her arms.

A shuddering breath leaves me as I lower my gun. The guy turns around staring me down, anger alive in his eyes, coming off him in waves, and I know he is itching to fight back. You didn't hold a fucking gun to guys like him and walk away.

"Sorry, but you're creepy just watching us," I try to explain. I made a foolish mistake not checking my surroundings, looking for an escape. If it had been them, Red would be dead, and I wouldn't have escaped this time. That would be on me. I was not a fool, but I made a stupid mistake that could have cost us our lives.

"Shots! We need a shot!" I shout. I've never had them before. I've only ever drunk a glass of wine served at dinner, never more than one glass and it was meant to be sipped slowly, but I need to deflect. It seems like something a girl is meant to say. I don't wait for her answer, cold climbing up my spine as I shoulder my way through the crowd. The barman spots me and places the towel he is cleaning the glass with over his shoulder. Without asking, he slams a small glass down and fills it with an amber liquid. I grab the drink, downing it in one, coughing and hissing as it burns my throat, but soon a warm sensation follows. I place the glass down, nodding as I try to fix the mask and push all the emotions that were too close to the surface back down. I can't afford to let my guard down like that again. I can't afford to let Red see beneath my carefully crafted veneer. He fills my glass again, and this time I only hiss, enjoying the way it burns through the fear.

"Two beers, please." He gives me a small smile before uncapping them and placing them on the bar. I grab a few bills out. "Thanks." I turn just as Red reaches me. "Here." I pass her a bottle. Her eyes stay on me a beat longer before she takes it, and I see the question dancing in her eyes.

We make it back to the small booth and Red is smiling a goofy smile, swaying to the music, her bottle already empty, and within minutes some guy brings over two more.

"This is Smithy." She chucks her thumb in the direction of the guy. I smile before he disappears back into the crowd. "What happened back there?"

I slide into the booth knowing I've got to give her something. Red is too smart for some bullshit excuse. I shrug, playing with the paper bottle label.

"I used to have panic attacks. I haven't had one in years." Liar, liar, a small voice whisper. Panic attacks held me as their prisoner, locked me in the torture of my own mind. Haunted by dreams and in my waking hours, there was no escape. Fear is my master.

"And holding a gun to a prospect's head?" She smirks, I down the beer.

"I've lived in some rough places."

Red goes to speak, when she frowns and picks up her bag, pulling out her phone. She looks at the number as if she is deciding whether to take the call, and then her shoulder drops as she slips her thumb across the screen, lifting the phone to her ear.

"Yeah. What the fuck... We've had a drink…Fuck…Okay … I'll grab us some coffee…Yeah, okay." Her eyes swing to mine, and as I am only getting the one side, I gather it was about us. Why? I haven't got a clue. Instantly my back straightens, and my chin comes out in a defensive stance. "Yeah, me too." She whispers, hanging up.

The tension I lost is back full force. Red downs her drink, and I follow her lead when she starts to grab our purses, heading towards the door as I follow blindly. Soon as we hit the air, I shiver. The cold sobering us instantly. I'll never get used to that. The boiling hot days and quick temperature drop at night.

She sighs, turning her eyes to me, lips tight together in a thin line, blue eyes looking furious. Whoever was on the phone has pissed her off.

In the short weeks since I moved here, Red's somehow slipped under my radar, worked her way in without my knowledge. I should be packing my bags and hightailing it out of here. Especially after my freak out, but something stronger is keeping me rooted here, something that I am not ready to look into. I am happy to hide behind the lie, telling myself that this place doesn't feel like home. That Red doesn't mean anything to me, that Sketch doesn't, and that it will still be easy to leave this place behind in a few weeks.

"Looks like Storm got patched tonight." I frown, not understanding through my slight buzz. I remember patched means that he has become a brother, a full member, if I've remembered that right. Still, no idea what that has got to do with us?

"Okay?" I leave the question hanging in the air between us. Red's eyes blaze with fury, at who, I am not sure.

"When you get patched, you get the club's ink branded on your skin. Another way to show you belong. Sketch is either passed out or too busy having his dick blown. Storm needs a full back piece. I'll grab us some coffee because it's going to be a hell of a long night. We've got to meet them at the ink shop." I am not sure what she is more pissed about: that our night got interrupted, or that Sketch is having his dick sucked?

But it looks like I have had my crash course into bikers. Red and Sketch were just a glimpse of who I was working for. Who Red belongs to. Now, I'm coming face to face with the Red Horsemen.

ICE

I hear my sister greet my brothers before I see her. Her voice carries through Sketch's ink shop, sounding pissed, then when she comes into my sight, I lift my chin.

"Hey, Red." I try to keep the bite out of my tone. I haven't seen her for over three weeks, and I'm pissed that she wasn't at the club when I got back. Red is always at the clubhouse waiting for us to return.

Instead, Sketch told me she was out having a drink with this fucker Rae. He had smirked when I said the guy better be good people, or he would pay if she got hurt.

She wraps her arms around my waist and squeezes me tight before looking up at me with those big sapphire blues. I know she's trying to see her old fucking brother, how she always does, as if he will fucking reappear. What she doesn't understand is he died ten years ago. I run a hand through my hair and turn away from that motherfucking look. Red needs to stop looking at me like her damn hero. I need that look to die with the memory she has of me dancing around in that fucking head of hers, once and for all.

I hear someone whisper, "Holy Fuck!" Soon there are grunts of agreement, followed by some more curse words, mixed with low whistles. The whole fucking atmosphere changes.

I raise my head to see what's got all my brothers' fucking attention because they usually have the brain span of a fucking goldfish when they're not on club business. Especially after the last ride. I'm fucking surprised they can put a sentence together. What the fuck is happening?

When the crowd parts, I'm stuck looking at a beautiful bitch.

The dark-haired female from the diner. The woman that's haunted my fucking dreams for the last three weeks. The woman who makes me hard and has me with my dick in my hand, just fucking remembering her.

She looks just like the pin-ups from one of Sketch's designs as if she magically came to life. If I hadn't been drinking tonight, I'd swear I was fucking hallucinating.

Bitches like her only exist in men's dirty imaginations. Brought to life in drawings from a man's most carnal thoughts.

But no, here she is, fucking standing and breathing in front of me. Making those fucking big tits rise and fall as if they are playing fucking peek a boo. I didn't have a type of woman. I fucked them all, brunettes, blondes, redheads. Skinny, thick. Beautiful bitches, but this one in front of me gained my attention in a way no one else ever had.

Black hair falls down her back, with curls framing her face, and the poutiest blood-red lips. Fuck, those lips. Lips that were designed to bring a man to his knees. Lips to torment you, dare you to come and take a bite. They are the forbidden fruit. Without even tasting them, you know how fucking sweet they will taste. I learned young where most bitches had their mouths, so I didn't kiss, ever. But if I didn't lick my fucking own as if I could already taste this female. Her body was curvy and tight in all the right places. It was as if the devil himself had carved her. The perfect temptress.

Her face, though, was as beautiful as a fucking angel. It almost hurt to look at all that sin and perfection wrapped into a sexy wild package.

My cock hardens in my jeans at the sight of her. Like I'm a fucking hormonal teenager that doesn't know what to do with his fucking dick.

"Eyes up here," she growls, and I slowly lift my eyes at the sound of the husky voice. Focusing on her face, I get lost in her eyes. Navy in color but, I fucking swear, the more I look at her, they turn brighter, almost looking violet-like as if I was making them change.

With that thought, I leaned in, wanting to watch closer as those purple shades appear. Her eyes were the most unusual color I had ever seen as fucking violet flecks appear. It brought something alive in me, a primordial spark of life. Like something deep within me had awakened and was prowling, raising his head and noticing this female. A shot of fucking adrenaline tore through my veins.

She crosses her arms over her chest, pushing those tits higher, making me bite my cheek to stop the groan from escaping. Kitten didn't seem impressed.

Yeah, I fucking nicknamed her already. Not that I would say that shit out loud, but she was a kitten. I wasn't stupid; I know kittens are all soft until their claws came out.

I wasn't in any doubt this one sat at home sharpening hers. It's something in her eyes that told me underneath all the classy girl, lay a fucking hellcat.

"Where the fuck is Rae? Sketch is...busy," I yell at the room, keeping my eyes on the female. The last time I saw Sketch he was having his dick sucked dry by a club pussy and was already looking for more. Somewhere I wouldn't mind being now. Only it wasn't a club snatch I could see on their knees. My cock turns hard as fucking stone at the thought. I reach down to adjust myself, to squeeze the fucker. It was hurting. It wanted her that much.

I hope she wasn't this Rae's bitch, not that it makes a fucking difference. The only people who had my loyalty were my brothers. Kitten's eyes widen slowly as she watches me squeeze my dick. Oh yeah Kitten, this is all for you.

The bitch sucks in a small breath before shaking her head, like she's trying to fucking shake me loose. Couldn't she see the male in front of her?

Her eyes glance around, widening as if she just noticed everyone else in the room. A flare of panic flashes in her eyes. I watch as her walls come up, her spine straightens before turning and glancing at Storm who is barely fucking conscious. He tries to smile from the chair that he's hanging off and hugs the bottle of rum like it was his motherfucking newborn son.

"He's not having the ink done tonight...his body will just reject it," her voice firm. I crack my neck, gritting my teeth, trying to hold on, and so angry I want to spew all over her. No one ever said no to me, especially bitches. Bitches listened, every motherfucker did. This fucking bitch had a mouth on her and if she weren't careful, I'd shove my cock in between those lips to shut her up.

I'm a trigger-happy motherfucker, everybody knows it. My mood swings got my knuckles split open and bloody most of the time. I'm an intimidating bastard.

Kitten's defiant stance is pissing me off further. The adrenaline rising in me, fucking drains away, replaced by fucking anger flicking in my gut, which somehow made my fucking dick as hard as a fucking diamond. Figure that shit out!

"Look, sugar... Just ask this fucker Rae, okay?" I draw out the sugar, but it sounded anything but sweet. She doesn't back down but just smiles a wicked smile.

"You just did, sugar." She copies my drawl, and I frown,

glancing at the brothers who all wear the same confused- what the fuck- look.

Like a fucking gun butt to the head, it hits me. "You're a fucking bitch!" I hiss, crossing my arms against my chest, making my stance wider as I glare at her. This bitch has a fucking mouth, and if it had been anyone else, she'd already be missing teeth. She had one over on me, she obviously knew who the fuck I was, and I didn't have a fucking clue that Rae was, in fact, a motherfucking bitch!

It was my fucking job to know this shit. It also explains the smirk Sketch was wearing. He knew, the bastard. Her lips turn into a devilish smirk.

"You're quick …A habit of yours, Ice?" she purrs, sweet enough to give you a toothache.

"What the fuck you say?" I hiss. I don't know if I want to strangle her or fuck her, or both.

I take a step closer to her, eyes never leaving hers. A flicker of fear emerges before they turn cold, making my lips twitch at the fear, knowing I'm it's master, and I fucking own it. How intense those feelings are. How they feed me. She stays put, clenching her hands so fucking tight that her knuckles are white. I draw my fingers down her cheekbone.

"You thinking of me fucking you? My cock sliding into your fucking tight pussy, sweets?" My voice comes out husky, slow and with grit, making sure she heard every fucking word.

I'm not sure if it's because this bitch is affecting me more than I liked, or I enjoyed playing with her. No, toying with her. She is different from the club girls. Something new and shiny, something I wanted to dirty as my dick slipped inside her and she screamed my name.

I watch as her breath hitches and her pupils dilate. The pulse at the bottom of her neck flutters, like a trapped butterfly.

Yeah, looks like she is affected like every other bitch. Only this female has innocent stamped all over her. Fuck! I should back the fuck away, walk out the fucking door. Before I break her, destroy her like everything else I touch.

"Sweets? Really? That line usually works for you?" The brothers all whistle, some laugh. I would never admit it, even if I were being tortured in Rev's meat shed, but I like that she gives me sass. Rae wasn't going all mushy and starry-eyed by what it meant to be in front of me. She doesn't see the VP, a Horseman. She sees the man.

"Daddy fuck you up, sweets, didn't get the doll you fucking wanted?"

She chucks her head back laughing, it's a soft, carefree laugh that doesn't hold any darkness, and her eyes glow with amusement. The color changes in them making them shine brighter, that purple almost glows. "Well, considering he only stayed around long enough to get my momma pregnant before moving on and I never played with dolls, I'd say I am all good on that front, but thanks for the concern." She winks. Motherfucking winks.

I search her eyes to see she's fucking telling the truth. Rae didn't give a shit for the man who helped make her.

"Burn, brother." Cas laughs, the prick, as his eyes rake over her, licking his motherfucking lips. I never thought of a female being a smartass as cute, but fuck, it looks good on her.

I'm lucky that it's just these fuckers and not the rest of the club hearing her smart off because they would have my fucking dick for letting a woman get one over on me and think my balls had shriveled up and I had grown a fucking pussy. We both stare each other down. Fuck, all this bitch did was piss me off and make me want her more.

I dig my hands into her hair, finding the back of her neck. Her whole-body shivers in response, causing my hold to tighten as I pull her tight body against mine. I lean close, until I can almost taste her lips, smell all that fucking sweetness. Rubbing my cheek against her, my lips grazing her jaw line, I suck in her earlobe making her shiver and whisper, "Ah, so you're pissed. Your mom was a cum bucket, nothing more than a fucking nameless snatch … A fucking whore. You like it dirty like your mamma, Kitten." My fingers tighten as she tries to pull away. "'Cause I've got a whole club full of fucking boys that are dying to chuck their muck up you and forget by morning." I feel my anger seep out with every word I spit at her.

I feel her body turn as hard as fucking steel, her eyes narrow, but not before I see them become misty, which she quickly tries to blink away. The purple fades into the darkness leaving a dark navy color.

Rae pulls back like I've burnt her, letting my hand fall away. She takes another step back, the only thing you can hear is her heavy breathing. She blinks as if lost somewhere else, shaking her head slightly. I recognize that look, like she's trying to escape the memory. Her eyes glance around as she walks quickly through the crowd, her spine ramrod straight as she picks up her bag. After a beat, she turns, biting that plump bottom lip to stop it trembling as her little chin sticks out.

Her features harden as a darkness appears as she takes a step forward. "I will never be someone's whore, you'll have to kill me first," she snarls, her voice shaking, but it has a strong undercurrent. She's a fucking strong bitch, which makes me crave her more, find out how strong she really is.

I meant to shut her down, not hurt her. Fuck that was a lie. I saw the vulnerability in her. I saw the weakness and brought it straight to the surface, opened her up wide while I took a shot at the fucking bullseye.

I don't apologize, no matter how much my dick wanted in her. This feeling of guilt wasn't something I had felt before because if people didn't like what I said, fuck them. Fuck her.

"Tell Sketch I will be in on Monday for my cheque."

Red walks over to Kitten, her blue eyes pleading. She knows to beg is a weakness that we don't show. This pisses me off for two reasons: One my sister knows better, and I didn't fucking practically raise her to be a fool and show any weakness. Two, it means they are fucking close, and for some unknown reason, that rubs against my skin like a cheese grater.

"Don't go, stay. Ice is a fucking asshole. Everyone knows it, ask anyone." She motions around the room, her voice smaller than I've ever heard it. Kitten smiles a genuine smile.

"Yeah, I kind of like you too, Red … I was always going to leave. I leave, Red, it's what I do." My sister goes to say something but shuts her mouth and nods in acceptance. Like they already get each other.

Kitten walks out the door, back straight, head high in those sexy as fuck heels, without another look back, but her saying she was always going to leave makes me growl. What I can't work out is the fuck why?

ICE

Red looks at me before nodding her head to fucking follow her to the back room. She shuts the door glaring at me, eyes turning electric blue.

"What the fuck, Ice?" I shrug, lighting a smoke. Kitten had fucking unsettled me where no one else had ever been able to, and it made me fucking want her. I didn't even know how to process what the fuck had just happened out there, let alone explain that shit.

"Don't fucking dare shrug. I'm not one of your fucking brothers! I am your sister." She starts pacing the room. "Yeah, you can be an intense asshole, a right bastard at times …But what you did to Rae out there was fucking cruel." She stops pacing and turns to me. "Fuck, Ice, we know that pain. We live in it…That was cold even for you," she growls as she pokes my chest. "I've seen you work your way up in the club. Seen you do things I wish I never had. Heard the stories of what you're capable of, VP." Her words hit my chest like they were fired at fucking point-blank range. I know how much she fucking loves me, and for some fucked up reason, she looks up to me like I'm her motherfucking hero.

I wasn't telling her that Kitten tied me in fucking knots, and she made me feel. For the first time in ten years, I wasn't fucking numb. The racing thoughts cooled fucking down, that intense irritability lying just beneath my skin, I didn't notice it. The restlessness didn't fucking claim me, it was contained. And she quelled my demons with just a fucking look.

"No fucking bitch disrespects me," I snarl, shoving my fingers through my hair as I spark up another smoke. "You are a part of this fucking life. No fucker disrespects the VP, especially not in front of the brothers and especially not fucking little bitches," I sneer, watching as her mouth drops open and closes, shaking her head as she studies me. The look in her eyes when she looks back nearly fucking slays me, which only powers all the emotions back to the surface.

"He's gone... He's really fucking gone." What? Who the hell is she on about? Red is known for going from calm to spitfire in seconds. Honestly, she gives us all a fucking headache trying to keep up with whatever she is talking about.

I feel my muscles tense, grinding my jaw so hard that I'm surprised I haven't broken a fucking tooth. I know one thing, when Red tells me who she is talking about, I'm going to fucking kill him for hurting her. Each of her tears he would pay for. I'd carve his fucking heart out.

"Who?" The venom in my voice makes people run, but she knows I'd never hurt her. I fucking hope it's true because I would never forgive myself if I did.

"My brother."

"What the fuck are you talkin' about? I am sure as fucking shit, that I am here, standing in front of you?"

"Yeah, but you're not here really! I have watched you fucking destroy yourself for years, become cold, calculating, and closed off. I have seen you burn through the fucking club ass …drink yourself fucking stupid …Your eyes are dead, your laugh is fake, …I thought if I left you the fuck alone that you'd pull yourself out of it. Seeing what you just did to Rae. …It was fucking cruel … I love you. I fucking do. But I don't like you very much. In fact, I don't like you at fucking all!" She turns and walks out the door without another word.

I never want Red to see the truth. To know the things I've fucking done, the things I've fucking seen. Maybe this is a good fucking thing that she now sees me, not the brother she wishes for, the one Red remembers. It's better this way. It will keep her safer. She finally sees the man everyone hates. I fucking hate. I fall against the chair, pulling my hair.

"Motherfucker." I turn and punch the wall until my knuckles ache, blood drips from them, and crimson streaks run down the plaster.

I storm out the shop before anyone can say anything. Heading straight to my bike. Starting her up, the roar only makes my blood pump harder. I break every fucking road law, getting to the club within half the time, and hear the low rumble of my brothers' in the distance. Opening the door, the familiar smell of leather, sex, and beer surrounds me. It takes a second for my eyes to adjust before homing in on one fucking person. I break the distance between us, pushing through the crowd of brothers hearing their fucking grunts and just as he turns around, I punch his jaw, sending him to the floor. I land another fucking one to his face, and instantly blood gushes from his nose.

"What the fuck!" Sketch growls, wiping the blood away. We didn't fight. He's one of the brothers I'm closest to.

I stand over him, sneering one word, "Rae."

He stands, rubbing his jaw as his lips twist. Bastard. I punch him in the fucking stomach. He groans, bending over and holding his legs.

"Next fucking one, I hit back," he growls, as Cas and Storm walk over, both laughing with Rev, who's holding a bottle of whiskey. I take my seat, lighting up a smoke as Sketch straightens, looking directly at me, his whole body vibrating with anger. "So, you've met Rae?"

Cas smirks. "Oh, he fucking met her, alright." Then adds, "Never thought I'd see VP lose his fucking dick over a damn bitch."

I shoot a look at him, grabbing the whiskey. Taking a big pull as Sketch sits down, his eyes ping pong between us.

"Fuck! What the fuck happened? Did you fuck her?" There's doubt in his voice. If it had been any other bitch, he wouldn't question me, but he seems so motherfucking sure. That's when it clicks that while we were on our ride, he's been working with her.

"You're sticking your fucking dick in her?" I hiss. His eyes widen for a split second before all his features harden.

"No," he grits out through his teeth.

I lift my chin. "You want to?"

"Fuck sake, no! You know how hard it's fucking been, and the talent Rae's got, it's fucking rare." He clicks on his phone, pulling up ink of a pin-up leaning on a Harley.

"She did that?" It was good, really fucking good.

"Yeah, for Davis earlier. I don't want to fucking lose her because you want to stick your dick in her."

Cas snorts. "Too late for that."

Sketch stands, and I match him, coming toe to toe, my fist clench ready to throw another punch.

"What the fuck did you do?"

I don't say anything, instead blow out a cloud of smoke, so Cas answers. "One minute it was some messed up foreplay, fuck even my dick got hard watchin' them, the next he went for her fucking jugular." Sketch curses, starting to walk away.

"Where the fuck do you think you're fucking going?" The sound that leaves me makes the brothers around us lookup.

Sketch turns, looking over his shoulder. "To ring fucking Rae and try and clean up your fucking mess, again". He shakes his head snarling. "Red is fucking tight with her, and we all know she doesn't get on with bitches. Brothers have been coming in for the last three weeks asking' Rae out, and she told them no every motherfucking time. They respect her. I'm not going to lose her because you wanted to get your fucking dick wet and she said no." He storms off.

I sit back down instead of following and punching him like I want to because the fucker is right, sort of. I've known Sketch needed someone for a long fucking time. He was missing runs because of it and the shop brings in too much money to shut. Red didn't have fucking friends because she always found it hard to mix the lines between club and civilians. I want to cut out the brothers' fucking tongues that asked Rae out. A wave of different emotions builds with an intensity and leave behind an unfamiliar one that means I should care about what Sketch said.

It was the motherfucking truth. But I don't. I'm a bastard going straight to hell.

"Fuck! Your fucking going after her?" Cas asks, looking at me over the rim of his bottle.

I've never lied to a brother, so I don't say anything but take a deep pull of the whiskey instead.

RAE

I don't know why I had such a meltdown at the shop. Yeah, I could see that Ice is dangerous. But he is not the monster I was used to. He didn't hide it behind a sweet smile, or smart suits. He showed it to the world, wore it like a lethal aftershave. God, I forgot to breathe when he came into sight. The men just parted like the Red Sea, and there he was. Icy blues from the diner.

He is beautiful, not in the traditional Hollywood way, but in a sinful way. Rough around the edges, that takes away the polished look. Nose a little crooked like he has been in too many fights. The flaws are almost there to remind you he is real, that he is human. Ink covering both his arms, all grays and dark, which stands out against his sun-kissed skin, letting you know he's spent a lot of time in the sun. I drank him in as my stomach clenched.

My breathing became heavy as my nipples tightened. I had the overwhelming sensation to clench my thighs together, and that is when I realized what I was feeling was pure, raw, desire. I hated that just looking at Ice made me feel what no one else had. I thought they had broken me. Shattered my pieces, and here he is holding them all. Putting them back together again, ready for me to feel every inch of its wild emotion. Even though my mind screams he is nothing but heartbreak.

The way his eyes took in my body. Yeah, men have looked at me. I had hidden from those looks. I learned to hate the way those men stared at me like property. Usually, it would send a cold shiver over my skin and send that urge to run flying to the surface. But it is different with Ice.

Everywhere those eyes touched left a blaze along my body. I could feel Ice's touch from the other side of the room, and God, did my body crave that touch. Instead of needing to run away, I wanted to lean in, rub my cheek against his leather and purr like the kitten he called me.

I ignored how my traitorous body reacted; instead, I crossed my arms over my chest and reminded him where my eyes were. Big fucking mistake, a huge mistake because as his head lifted, I got caught in the gaze of those icy blues. Sending a shiver through me as they held me captive in their cool crystal pools. Just like that day in the diner.

I was surprised to see the cold, calculating look disappear and the heat emerge in them. They burnt bright like the bottom of a flame. Warmth touched me in a place that I thought had died a long time ago, his eyes didn't match the ease of his body or the cocky smirk he was carrying. Swirls of emotions going on inside, all warring together to make the perfect storm. I knew it could easily destroy me.

When he baited me, I knew I should have shut up, kept my mouth firmly closed. Rae should have taken a step back. I didn't know these men, only from what Red had told me, and even though Red belonged to them, I didn't.

I was not stupid; I hadn't kept myself alive by making mistakes. I was the gazelle amongst the lions and poking at the goddamn fucking king. Which meant certain death.

That is when I saw it happen. The way his eyes shut down, so much like the way I did. The color changed from crystal blue to ice shades, and you could see the way they froze over, and hardness appear in them.

I could see the exact time it happened. I had gotten close and caused a reaction in Ice he didn't want. The flame behind his eyes extinguished by a coolness that caused goosebumps to appear across my skin. I missed the burn. I hated the cold, but the cold is what I needed.

Those cold eyes told me more than he ever could. I was no longer standing in front of the man who wanted me. I was now standing in front of Ice, and he wasn't taking any prisoners. He wanted to hurt, cause destruction, leave nothing alive in his wake, and it was all aimed at me. A joker smile covered his face, a sinister look crawled over him before he spat every word and watching with sick satiation as they hit their mark. Mentioning my mother, calling me a whore, telling me I could be one for the club. I couldn't speak past the fucking goddamn lump in my throat. I had no sassy comeback, it was like he right hooked me, and I was knocked out, gone was Rae--she ran, and fucking hid somewhere leaving me open, and I took every one of those hits one by one.

I don't know if it was this place or the fact it was the anniversary of my mother's death in a few days, but I had opened myself up and that meant one thing.

It was time to leave.

Instead of going home, I walk past the apartment. I needed to walk and clear my head.

"Rae ...Rae." I turn and see an out of breath Red running at me like her demons are after her. As I look behind, my spine straightens—my hand inches towards my bag, where the 22 lies.

"What's the matter? Everything okay?" I ask, looking behind her, not seeing anything.

Red nods as she bends over, waving her hand around in some gesture that I'm not even aware is human and making me grin.

"Fuck girl, you can walk fast and in them," she says pointing to my shoes. I smirk, realizing there is no impending danger.

"What are you doing here, Red?"

She frowns, for once she looks young, her age. Red told me she was twenty-one, and when she asked me, I told her what was on my fake I.D., which made me twenty- two.

"Don't go. I wasn't lying earlier, you're my friend. And I don't make friends."

Well shit! I link my arm with hers. "Come on, is there a liquor store?" For one night, I'm going to give in, have a drink, a good time. I am just going to be normal, hiding in a bubble of denial.

Red's whole body relaxes as she smirks. "I know just the place,"

It is only a few more minutes, and we are back outside Aces' bar. Red walks in, within minutes she is back holding up a bottle of Jack. Well shit.

We walk down the street when I look over my shoulder to see a dark car following us.

"Just keep walking, it's been following us since Gables." Gables is the Garage that Davis works at. I slow my pace reaching into my bag, feeling for the cold metal, and my fingers clench around the grip just as the car pulls up beside us.

"What are two lovely ladies doing walking around town? Want a ride?" The driver's slimy voice makes my skin crawl. There's laughter, letting me know there is more than one. More voices rise from the car encouraging him. Red tilts her head before smirking, but it wasn't friendly; it was damn well scary, and you could see the resemblance to her brother shine through. She pulls her arm out of mine before turning towards the car. Shit! Red places her hand on the roof of the car, banging the top, the sound breaking into the night sky before bending to look through the window.

"Jameson, you offering to take me for a ride?" What is she fucking crazy?

"Shit, Layla...we didn't know it was you! Say hi to your brother," he squeaks as the car peels away so fast I cough at the smoke.

Red's not even affected, and she is fucking grinning. That is when I see Red, the Princess of the Horsemen. She might be sweet and act innocent, but there is no denying she has their blood running through her, and a lot stronger than anyone believes.

"Stop looking at me like that. My father is Luther, my brother's Ice. You really didn't think I couldn't fucking hold my own?"

I frown at her words. "I guess. You just don't seem tainted."

She snorts. "You don't live in my world and not get tainted. I could easily walk around town as if I owned it, laying bitches out, and even some fucking men. I could act like everyone expects me to be." She shrugs. "Being a hard bitch, it gets old fast, and I like my nails pretty. Plus, blood is a fucker to get out of your clothes." Our lips twitch before we both burst out laughing.

We climb the stairs to my apartment with the bottle of Jack under my arm.

"So, are you going to stay?"

I look over my shoulder at Red. "I like it here, but I'm going to leave. I guess a few extra weeks won't hurt." I watch as she bites her lip, knowing she wants to say something, but thinks better of it.

I chuck my keys on the table by the door, taking my shoes off, and I moan as I rub my feet, making Red smirk.

"Go make yourself comfy. I'm going to change." She skips over to the sofa before falling on it as if she has been here hundreds of times before. I put the Jack down before walking into my bedroom, grabbing some shorts and a t-shirt. Quickly taking a shower, I get dressed, tying my hair in a messy bun on top of my head—Sans makeup.

I walk back into the living room, and Red lifts her head, then her eyes widen as she takes me in.

"Wow, you really are stunning, and you look younger, much younger."

I smile tightly as I walk to the connected kitchen, grabbing two shot glasses and the Jack Daniels off the side. Red grabs the bottle from my hands, pouring the amber liquid into the two shot glasses.

I flop down next to her on the sofa. "You know, you really are sweet."

She stops pouring the Jack, tilting her head. "Tell anyone, and I'll tell Sketch who really always eats the last donut."

My eyes widen. "How do you… You wouldn't?" She smiles. Fuck that bitch, she so would!

She hands me a glass. "On the count of three. One…Two …Three."

My head is banging like little men are using a jack hammer to knock against my skull. A small hand pushes my shoulder.

"The door!" Red groans, her voice hoarse as she snuggles further underneath the duvet.

That's when I realize the banging is, in fact, my front door. My fingers instantly go for my gun, but they wouldn't knock if they had found me. I would awaken to a gun to my head. I groan, getting out of bed, blinking from the bright light trying to burn my retinas as I pull the blankets back. Then the banging turns into a pounding, making me wince as I rub my forehead and try to make my way to the front door. Jack was such a bad idea.

"Okay...Okay," I half shout, while walking towards the door. I swing it open ready to castrate whoever thinks it is okay to come over at this damn time in the morning. I rub my eyes. Blink. No, he's still there. "Ice?" My voice sounds huskier than usual, I am sure from all the singing we did last night. God, we were really drunk.

Ice's eyes catch alight as they take me in, his nostrils flare, and he licks his lips. That's when I realize I am in a pair of small shorts and a thin tank top, and it's just my luck that my nipples also wanted to join the show and say fucking hello!

I quickly cross my arms over my chest as my nipples tighten. "What do you want, Ice?"

His body jerks before he lets out a grunt, and that's when I notice Sketch next to him. He smirks, making me smile.

"Hey, sweetheart," Sketch says. A low growl sounds from Ice, who is looking at his friend like he wants to kill him, much to Sketch's amusement. Yes, he fucking growled. His icy blue pools turn to me.

"I'm an asshole." His voice is still gruff like he hasn't long woken up.

"Okay?" I am completely confused as to why he is over here. He shakes his head as his eyes narrow, and his lips tighten as he takes a step towards me.

"Okay? That's it! I fucking come here to fucking apologize, and all I get is an O-fucking-K."

Sketch coughs back a laugh. Shaking his head as he covers his mouth. I tilt my head to the side, trying to hide my own smirk. He really has no fucking idea on how to apologize, but I guess it's something he hardly ever does. I'm not letting him off that easy. I kind of like the way he is squirming.

"An apology normally starts with 'I am sorry', but I didn't hear any sort of apology. You just stated something I already knew."

I lean against the door, but it's the wrong move because it brings me closer to Ice. His smell starts to consume me, and it is the perfect mix of man, oil, leather. The heated look in Ice's eyes appears again as he looks between my eyes and lips. Trying to decide something. I know I should slam the door in his face and lock the deadbolt. In slow motion, I watch as he leans closer. I feel his big hand slide through my hair before he grabs the nape of my neck, bringing me closer, causing me to shudder. A shudder, I know he feels, when his grip tightens on my neck. The same pleasure as last night fills my body. Do I want to kiss him? No.

No matter how loud my mind screams to pull away, to join Red under the duvet, and hide from the world, I can't move. My body reacts, tilting automatically and lifting my head upwards towards his.

Ice's lips gently brush mine as if he doesn't know what he's doing, like he's unsure. Something I don't think he ever is. It makes me lean closer as if we are both giving something that none of us has before.

RAE

Just as our lips touch, I hear a distant groan from Red, but before I can move, Ice jumps back like I've burnt him. His lips curl up, baring his teeth, feral.

"You got some fucker in there?" He's gone back to growling. Gone is the man that was here seconds ago, now in his place is the Red Horsemen VP. The man that men fear. The one I only had a glimpse of last night. This man in front of me is pure sin and darkness. Danger rolls off him in waves, and he is as cold as the name he's been given.

I open my mouth to speak, instead a squeak comes out as Ice picks me up and places me to the side. He strolls into my apartment like he's been here before and has every right. It takes a few seconds for my mind to get over the almost kiss and the fact he's just barged in uninvited.

"What the fuck! You can't just walk in here!" He doesn't listen to a word. Pig-headed bastard. "You can't go in there."

He stops, turning as he flashes me a grin that would scare the devil himself and prowls the few steps back towards me. It takes everything in me not to cower back at the glare he is giving me.

He grabs my jaw, tight enough to hold me in position. "Who's going to fucking stop me?" His voice is low and icy, a sick smile appears when I don't answer, and he turns back around as his whole-body tenses under his leather like a bomb waiting to go off.

"In all the fucking years I've known him, he ain't ever been like this over a bitch." I jump at Sketch's voice, forgetting he was even here. I frown at his words. He doesn't say anything, just raises his eyebrow. We both turn to hear a growl.

"Shit!" I quickly push into my room. Ice is in the middle, his body tense, every muscle bunched beneath his shirt. His jaw tight and hands clenching as he watches the duvet move with an intense stare. Sketch groans, rubbing his face with a look of pity as he curses under his breath and glares at me. Before I can react, Ice pulls his gun, face void of any emotion. It takes me a second to respond, and I jump in front of the gun.

"Stop."

"Sketch," he snarls. Sketch walks over, ripping the duvet away and startling Red, who tries to cover herself with the loose sheet as she screams. Grabbing a gun beside her, one I didn't even know she had, lifting it up and aiming it straight at Ice. Leaving me in the middle of both guns. They both stare off, taking a second to realize what the other is seeing before lowering their guns and allowing me to let out a relieved breath. Her eyes widen as she scrambles to gather the sheet, whimpering as she notices Sketch.

"What the motherfuck!" his voice echoes off each wall in my apartment. Red doesn't seem affected by his reaction, like this is a typical day for her, rolling her eyes before grabbing the sheet as she stands.

"What the fucking hell? ... You smoke something this

morning?" she growls. So, it's a family thing. Ice looks between Red and me, then back at her. "What the fuck you are doing in Rae's apartment?" After a beat, he shrugs, then leans against the wall, pulling out a pack of smokes, pulling out one, he plays with it between his fingers as if he needs something to do. A way to dispel the tension and energy that seems to surround him.

"Came to fucking apologize for the shit last night." Her eyes widen, looking like a comic book character, you know the sort, whose eyes pop out of their head.

"You came to apologize... To Rae?" Frowning, she studies her brother, eyes narrowing.

"Yeah, ain't a total fucking asshole." Red bursts out laughing, a smile bigger than I ever saw. She jumps up and runs at Ice, where he catches her in a tight embrace.

"Yeah, you are, but I still fucking love you, always have, always fucking will." Her words are softly spoken, almost wistful. I look away, not wanting to encroach on their time. Sketch is looking at them. No, just her.

"Fuck! Get some fucking clothes on, Red... Don't need to see that shit." She turns at Sketch's hard voice, looking toward us, her cheeks a blaze as she quickly grabs the blanket back around her.

"If you're uncomfortable, I suggest you take your eyes off her." Sketch glances at me. I raise my eyebrow. Yeah, I saw you looking.

"Don't want to have to fucking remove your eyes, brother." Ice is back to growling. Sketch glares at him, his mouth opening before he slams it shut thinking better of it as if he can sense how close Ice is to the edge. He storms out of the room. There is a loud thump making Red and I jump. Ice looks towards the door, cursing under his breath.

Red dresses quicker than humanly possible, not looking anyone in the eye.

"I...um, see you later!" She bolts towards the door. Seconds later, we hear the front door slam.

RAE

The air in the room changes, becoming electric as I realize it's just Ice and me in my room. My fucking bedroom! I never wanted sex, especially from the man that wanted it from me. Ice has brought that side of me alive. My body reacts in a way I have no control over.

The same thing must be going through his head as he pins me with a carnal look. He stalks toward me, and with each step, my breathing gets heavier, my heart beats against my chest. He stops right in front of me. Eyes on my lips, he moves in closer.

"Fucking look at me, Kitten." His breath tickles across my lips.

His eyes hold me captive as he looks up at me through inky black lashes. I shake my head, closing my eyes tight as I try to block him, and the effect he has on me, out. Taking another step back. I cross my arms across my chest, hiding how harsh my breathing is and the way my nipples are like bullets. Not answering him. He reaches out, pulling his thumb across my bottom lip. Soft at first, then a little harder making my eyes spring open to see his focus on me and ablaze.

"Ice, you need to leave." It comes out as a breathy whisper.

"Your fucking body tells me something different, sweets," he growls. He runs his finger down my cheekbone, across my jawline, and down my neck to my collar bone. He follows the movement, and my breath catches, making him raise his eyes as goosebumps appear, making my whole-body shudder. "You fucking want me." He smirks. "Your fucking nipples are like diamonds, you're breathin' hard, your fucking pulse is racin', yeah, you fucking want me. I want you, Kitten."

Yeah, I wanted him. But could I give myself to him? Can I let my walls down enough to trust him with my body?

My heart is screaming yes! Which scares the shit out of me. But my head yells he would not want me if he knew the truth. If he knew that Rae was nothing but a cover, an illusion to protect the weak girl that lives underneath the surface. He would be disgusted with her. How she couldn't stand up for herself. She was so weak that she allowed them to destroy her world. That she didn't stand and fight, but she ran and still is.

How she believed their sweet lies like the naive, foolish girl, she is!

How the one time she did stand up, it cost her everything.

I don't ever want him to see the girl behind the mask. The girl who craves human touch. Desperately wishes to be held safely in someone's arms, protected, loved, welcomed, flaws and all.

Old instincts kick in as I arch my brow. "Sorry, I'll pass."

He can't hide the way my words surprise him. Standing to full height, he crosses his arms across his chest, tilting his head.

"You got an old man?" His words cool down some of the heat between us as I match his stance.

"And if I do?" I snarl back.

That smirk tilts up his lip, it's the one I've learned that he gives when he doesn't like something, and right before he's going to come out fighting.

"If he knows what is good for him, he will be gone by tonight, if not…" He leaves the threat hanging in the air between us.

"Psycho much?" My reply makes him smirk as if the words are true.

The past lingers right on the surface threatening to break through. No matter how much I changed the outside, those images lived in my head, dirtying everything. The darkness followed me as if it was my shadow.

I always hear his voice whispering, 'You will always be mine,' making me take another step back.

Ice points a finger between us. "This isn't fucking over."

I swallow, shaking my head. "It never started." Liar.

I've spent the last three years avoiding this sort of feeling. I thought I was defective, more than I realized, but one look at Ice has proved my theory wrong.

Rae wants him, as frustrated as he made her. Have him begging on his hands and knees, kissing her goddamn feet, and then fucking her like he promised. The scared girl still inside of me wants me to go to those places he promised. She wants him to make her forget everything. She wants him to consume her, tear down those walls that kept her insanity at bay. To replace the ugly.

It wasn't as if I could let Ice get close. I'll be moving on soon anyway. Maybe I could do the one-night thing. Let us both give in for one night, and then when morning comes, I could walk away. I was a pro at it, it's what I did. I wanted to experience what happens when we both let go. I knew I was playing with fire, letting the flames lick my skin. But I wanted it. For once, I wanted to feel what it felt like to burn bright in the darkness.

Lost in thought, I don't see him coming closer until he's right in front of me. Before I can blink, his lips slam down on mine.

ICE

I capture her fucking mouth, pressing my lips hard against hers, feeling her whole body lock up at my touch. I push harder as my fingers slide into her dark strands. Just as I'm about to pull away, it happens, her fucking downfall, her ruin. She submits to me. Her fingers cling to my leather as if she never wants to let fucking go, raising on her tiptoes as if to get closer. A small moan leaves her lips, that draws all the blood to my dick. As I lick her mouth, every fucking inch of it, I claim it as mine, our tongues stroking each other. I bite that fucking plump bottom lip, breaking the kiss. I know she is going to run. It's in those fucking damn violets. Full of fucking fear and desire, and the sight makes my dick throb. I don't miss the way her tongue pokes out, following its movements as it sweeps her lips as if relishing my taste. Fuck, at the thought it's like I'm energized, I could take on anything. She sees the male in front of her, senses the fucking red-hot blood pumping around me.

Fuck, I need to get out of here.

"I'll be seeing you real fucking soon, Kitten."

Her eyes flare at the name before she starts shaking her head, and I know she is going to start spouting shit. I place my finger against her swollen lips, stopping the shit that's about to come out. Rae blinks up at me through thick black lashes, giving me those fucking damn violets which I could fucking drown in, realizing I'm already obsessed with them.

"Got a party at the club tonight, be there, sweets." I can't help inhaling that smell that's all her. Vanilla and fresh air, it makes my mouth water.

I walk out of the apartment, grabbing my smokes. Sparking one up and taking a deep pull as I look back at the door. What the fuck is it about this bitch that's got me twisted up? I take a fucking seat on the step, and my fucking leg starts bouncing. Fuck I'm climbing. I grit my teeth, hating the feeling, knowing soon I'll be reckless. Restlessness will fucking claim me, irritability already flicks at my spine. The distant rumble of bikes has me jogging down the steps to reach the bottom, just as the guys pull up. Their faces tell me everything.

"What's fucking happened?"

Cas growls, his eyes lethal. "Foot soldiers, a few fucking miles out staying' in that run down motel." I'm on my bike before the last word is out of his mouth. Playtime. My demons cheer.

We race out of town, unlike them, we know this place as we turn right up Old Dust Road and park our bikes.

"How many?" I sneer. I made plans in my head on the way over, a few straying to the fucking female I could still taste on my lips. The one I didn't know what to fucking do with.

Rev looks at me. "Two." His raspy voice will never fail to surprise me. His eyes turn from golden to dark, and we know that his demon is with us. "Woe to those who call evil good and good evil, who put darkness for light and light for darkness, who put bitter for sweet and sweet for bitter." His words provoke my own demons, pulling them from the shadows.

He repeats it as we cross the field that will bring us up behind the motel. The rage starts to build as too many thoughts spin through my head. The bitch brought a new restlessness out in me, and I don't need to add something new to the manic phases I already have. The feeling she brought alive is stronger than the rest, overpowering. They cool the rage, quiet the thoughts, but make her stand out. I'm a possessive bastard and know she is quickly becoming my next fucking addiction.

We break through the trees to the motel. It had seen better days, paint peeling off the sides, and exposing its brickwork. Two floors, but the top is all boarded up. Overgrown grass layers the pathways, and an old sign, half hung off the side of the building, with the name Brandy's and a faded arrow showing the office's direction.

"You two wait fucking here, if you see anything shout." I point to Storm and Cas. They both nod. There's not a smirk in play, bodies primed and ready. Rev and I walk towards the office.

"You okay, brother?" he asks, I nod, pushing the door that's stiff on its hinges and creaks under the force. An older man sits behind the desk. If he's surprised to see us, then it doesn't fucking show. In fact, he turns around picking up something, and Rev and I both go for our pieces, then he turns back holding two keys out.

"You were never here," he says before he turns the page of his paper ignoring us as if it's normal behavior.

I frown at the keys. "We are not here for a room."

His eyes flick up from the paper he's reading. "Didn't think you were." He speaks in damn riddles. Rev's eyes narrow, looking at the man before he nods.

"Looks like he doesn't like the fucking guests here anymore than we do." I turn back to the man to see him putting the TV up louder and turning off the cameras, making my lips twitch.

I walk out, hold the keys, and four fingers up to let them know what room they are in. Not that we will need the keys.

Jogging down the pathway, we reach the door. Cas and Storm take up one side as I move to the other, nodding to Rev. He lifts a booted foot, kicking it, the door breaks like fucking firewood under his force.

We swarm into the room, guns raised. "Don't fucking think about it," I snarl. The one nearest to me scrambles across the ground, reaching for the fucking gun beside him. He barely manages to lift it in the air before a pop sound fills the room as Rev puts a bullet between his eyes. Cas leaps across the bed, lifting his gun up before he smacks the handle on the other guy's temple.

"Tie the motherfucker up." I walk outside, grabbing my phone. My father's voice answers on the second ring.

"Son." I grit my teeth from that word.

"We're having dinner." It's all coded words. You never know who's listening.

"Anything nice?"

I grin. "Steak, well fucking done but had mine rare."

A growl comes through the phone. "See you soon, kid."

I pull out a smoke, lighting up when Rae's face flashes in front of me. The taste of her fucking lips, so clean and fucking pure.

We've been at the warehouse for hours. A metallic rusty scent tickles my nose and the back of my fucking throat as the man in front of us bleeds profusely from Cas' handy work. He wouldn't usually be the one with the bloody knuckles, that's usually my outlet. But we all know he fucking needs this after the way they killed his father.

I squat down, looking at the mess of his face. A mask of fucking marred skin, eyes swollen, and the white underneath reminds me of the old fucking arcade game Pac Man. His lips bloody and swollen as crimson drips onto his bare chest, where black and purple spread like spider webs and takes up much of his torso. That blood thirst comes alive in me at seeing the crimson run down his face. I can barely keep it contained, skirting on the edge of reason.

"You fucking ready to talk?" I growl, moving to stand in front of him.

His head falls forward on a groan. "Fuck you," he spits, causing blood and spittle to fly from his mouth. I grin. It's playtime.

Grabbing the scalpel off the side, I start making a small little line down his chest, making him hiss. That's the thing about the thin metal between my fingers, you can control how deep you want the cut.

"Ever fucking hear of death by a thousand cuts? It can last days, fucking weeks." My voice is calm, cold, as I dig the tip of the blade in, watching as the skin splits open. The line of red follows its edge before it starts trickling like fucking tears. I smile because they are mine. I own them. I could have let Cas fucking finish him off. I didn't need to play tic tac fucking toe on his chest. My anger is now in control, guiding my hand over the bloody canvas, but each whimper that breaks, unties some more fucking rage. Every cut is like a rush through my veins, gratifying in its release.

"Who sent you, motherfucker?" I ask, making a longer cut in his stomach, knowing the soft flesh is unprotected and will cause pain but won't kill him. Yet. I watch in sick satisfaction as his skin breaks to release a river of blood as it gushes and pools around our feet. His painful scream fills the air as he shakes his head.

Grabbing the knife off the side, I slam it into his thigh, and a smirk crawls over my lips as I feel the blade hitting the bone. His cry echoes around the warehouse, and the sound of blood hitting the plastic makes my lips twitch.

"He'll kill me, please." Disgust rolls in my stomach at him

begging. It's something no Horseman would ever do.

I snort. "What the fuck, you think we won't?"

Motherfucker thinks we are soft. I growl, grabbing the pliers off the tray. A look of pure terror covers his face. Rev steps up beside me with a horse speculum as Cas holds his head tight. You would think removing teeth was easy, just a fucking few twist and they pop out. Nope. These fuckers are stubborn little things. I go for the front one first. His cries fill the air as I tug at it, and I relish the sound. After some pulling and fucking cracking, it comes loose as blood gushes into his mouth, making him heave.

He groans, "Please, mercy."

Mercy? I didn't fucking know that word anymore. My demons are so fucking dark, and I no longer have a shred of decency, or humanity, in me, let alone room for mercy. Seeing him in fucking pain and pleading for his death doesn't cause an inch of sorrow or guilt. I've been detached too fucking long for any type of feeling to register.

After all his teeth are fucking removed, sweat coats my skin, the motherfucker still isn't talking. I stand aside, blood coats me, my hands, and my shirt is now crimson, his blood, dark droplets shine like ruby's drying on my skin. This is who I fucking am. This right here, is the raw me. I am at one with my demon.

I nod to Rev to fucking finish, letting his demon have its fun.

Cas stands against the wall, smoking, his fucking eyes never leaving Rev and a smirk lifting his lips as the guy screams out. The agonized sound fills every fucking inch of air around us. Rev knows how to make someone suffer and bring a body the most pain without passing out. To hold you in your own hell.

Storm follows me out. As soon as the air cools over my skin, I take a deep breath as the adrenaline pumps around my body, more potent than any drug. I light another fucking smoke, pacing, thrusting my bloody hands through my hair.

"We are going to need a fucking grave."

"Got it sorted. Something's not right." I nod because my gut is screaming the same fucking thing. We turn as the door opens to see the others coming out, all of us coated in his fucking blood, and a feral look in our eyes. The truth of who we are laid bare to the world.

RAE

I pull up outside the clubhouse. It was harder to find than I thought. It's along the back roads, and most people would bypass the turning camouflaged with trees. Red had been blowing up my phone all day about the same party Ice had mentioned earlier. That is why I was here and nothing to do with Ice at all. That's what I keep telling myself.

I open the door to my car and get my first look around. The compound used to be a factory of some sort. Made of brick, it looks like it is three stories. Arched windows cover the first two floors, but the bottom level has been bricked up over halfway, leaving only semicircles of glass. I count ten on this side. A metal stairway coils itself up the building like a snake. There are massive steel gates that I had to pass through and tall walls, at least ten feet, with coils of razor wire along the top, making it look scary as hell from the outside. I don't know if it's there to keep people out or in.

A thin layer of sweat covers my skin as I look back towards the building I know they call the clubhouse. The music is blaring through the walls with some old rock songs.

I know Red and Sketch are here. I don't trust anyone, but they were as close as I ever got.

Voices carry through the air with laughter, and I turn to my right, seeing a field of grass with picnic tables and fire pits with men and women already sitting around. Their laughter changes into something more familiar. My mother's. Hearing it as if she is standing right next to me. Then I see her face more clearly than I ever have. She is smiling at me before looking back at the clubhouse as if telling me I am safe.

I walk towards the building's front door. The door is black with red and orange flames, the head of a red horse rising from them, as if I am about to enter hell itself. There's a young man with a cut on, but it hasn't got any patches, just the word prospect written on the bottom, so I know he's not a patched member like Ice and Sketch. His eyes snap to mine, taking me in lazily, biting his lip as he whistles low.

"Damn, sweets, the boys are lucky tonight." I home in on the name, knowing it's the one Ice has also been calling me, but now I have a feeling it means something completely different. I ignore him as I pull open the door. The smell of sex, leather, and beer invade my senses as soon as I walk through the door. The music is blaring. It's 'Sweet Cherry Pie' an old favorite of mine. Something about walking through that door has me frowning. Looking back and feeling like I have walked through it before, recognizing the smell and the sounds of it all.

Turning back around, my eyes widen at the sight in front of me. Men are standing by the bar, sitting at tables playing cards, or gathered around a pool table towards the back. Every one of them has a woman hanging off some part of their body. I thought the outfit I was wearing was daring. It appears that I came overdressed because most of the women are in tiny little black shorts, butt cheeks hanging out, and small red tank tops with their nipples playing peek-a-boo. Other women don't even have tops on. Their tits are out there for the world to see. Making 'Hooters.' look like a nunnery.

A strange feeling comes over me, and that's when I realize that while I have been watching everyone, a lot more eyes are watching me. There is not a man that's looking anywhere else. All of them have a look in their eyes that makes me want to run. I can almost hear David Attenborough's voice. *"As the lonely gazelle walks foolishly into the lion's den."*

I recognize some of their faces from the shop, but most of them I have never seen before. My heart beats, my hands become sweaty, and they start to shake when I see a few rise from their chairs. I dig my nails into my hands. No, I am not that girl ... I'm Rae.

There are a few women who are shooting me a look, wishing for my death as their lips curl up in a sneer. I hold my head high as I walk toward the bar that runs nearly the whole wall of the left side. Flags with the Horsemen emblem hang proudly. "Sweets" is muttered more than once. I look for someone I know when a head of red hair comes barreling towards me.

"Fuck, I can't believe you actually came." Red brings me in for a tight hug, and I give her an awkward one back. It hasn't gone unnoticed that she's been invading my personal space more and more. Red takes a step back, studying what I am wearing before smirking that smirk that spells trouble. "Fuck! Rae. You look incredible!" I laugh, feeling silly now. What was I thinking playing dress-up?

"I feel overdressed."

She rolls her eyes, making a face like she just sucked a lemon before holding her two fingers up at the barman, who is also wearing a Prospect cut. He puts down two beers. Red shrugs before bringing the bottle to her lips, taking a long pull.

"Sweets, or sweet butts." Disgust rolls off her tongue as she states it. Now I am interested. Ice called me that last night and then twice today and the guard outside and the few men in here. I'm really starting to think it's not something I'm going like.

"Sweets?" She nods, placing her empty bottle back on the bar before holding up another two fingers, and the bartender slides two beers towards us.

"Sweet butts, cum buckets, snatch, bed warmers. They are all different names for a whore. More specifically, the brothers' whores." She nods, pointing her bottle across the room.

A woman lifts her leg, swinging it over a man so she's straddling him. He smirks at her, grabbing handfuls of her tits. My eyes widen as his fingers disappear under her skirt. After a few seconds, they reappear. Going to his own zipper, undoing it before pulling his cock out, he guides her on to it and pulls her down. Her hips start to roll as I watch a different man come up to them. The woman licks her lips before nodding for him to join them. The second man pulls down her top, rolling her nipples between his fingers, causing her back to arch. She moans, starting to move her hips faster, when the man playing with her nipples stops, running his hands to his jeans as he unbuttons them, his hands disappearing inside, pulling his dick out! Yes, his dick is out. Holding it in his hands as he guides it towards the woman's mouth. She opens, taking nearly all of him in at once. I gasp at the sight as one fucks her and the other fucks her mouth. This is what Ice expects from me! No fucking way!

I narrow my eyes to fight the pain that is squeezing my heart. When he kissed me earlier, I thought…I am so stupid, still that fucking foolish girl. I need to leave. To escape. I can't be here now, not when I'm faced with this. My whole body starts shaking, I need air. God, I need air.

I push through the crowd hearing a few grunts as I pass and

hear Red calling my name, but I drown it all out as I see the door, and my escape.

I suck in a deep breath as the fresh air hits me, then Red nearly falls into me.

"Rae?" I see the questions in her eyes, wanting to know the answers I will never give.

"Are you?" I point inside. "Do they keep you here? I can get you out, come with me now, we will disappear," my voice comes out a whisper between harsh breathing.

"What? Fuck, no!" She frowns, then she turns to the prospect. "Bring out the good stuff."

"Yes, ma'am."

Red frowns. "I'm younger than you, stop calling me that, it's fucking freaky."

The prospect nods. "Yes, m--" He cuts himself off before racing inside.

She leads me over to a picnic bench, out of the way of everyone else.

"No, I'm not a sweet butt! I'm a virgin. You try being Luther's daughter and Ice's fucking sister. Everyone in town knows who I am." That explains Jameson's reaction last night. The prospect walks over with a bottle of whiskey and two glasses before disappearing again. Red fills the glasses, passing me one. "Down it." I do, coughing as it burns and makes her smirk as she refills them. "So, sweets or sweet butts, sleep with different brothers. Basically, they spread their fucking legs or fall to their knees whenever a brother wants...They are not held here against their will or anything fucked up like that. It is their choice... They are not claimed by the club, but it's their way to be a part of the life."

My breathing evens out as her words settle within me. It's okay. I am okay.

"They are not held here. They can leave at any time?" She tilts her head, pulling the empty glass out of my hand. I didn't realize how tight I was holding it until she tried taking it off me... Her brow raises as she pours me another one.

"Yeah! They can leave anytime they want. Some live here in the outhouses. They are the regular snatch and the ones you need to fucking watch out for. Others we call tramps and just come for a wild time before returning to their nine to fucking five lives. They usually come around a few times, have their fill, then never come back."

I nod as the last of my uneasiness leaves, but I still feel shaken.

"Rae, are you okay?"

I try to smile. "I'm trying."

Red watches me for a few moments before she stands. "Come on, let's get back in there, you're safe here, I swear." I want to believe her and feel the safety that she does, but this is her world, not mine.

RAE

I lean over the bar. "Two beers and two chasers." The bartender ignores me, serving everyone else. "Do I need a magic word."

Red's lips twitch as she leans over the bar. "Smithy, you gone deaf. Didn't you hear my girl fucking calling you?" Smithy swallows, and I see fear dance in his eyes for a second before he rushes our orders.

"Sorry, Miss Red, I didn't know she was with you."

"Anything my girl wants, you fucking get it." He nods his head, like one of them bobble heads. We both do our shots, hissing at the burn as we follow it with our beers. Using my bottle, I point back towards the girl from earlier, who is now sitting with another man.

"They don't mind that?"

Red snorts, her lips curling up to a sneer. "Nope! The brothers are good at fucking sharin' when it comes to club pussy. They all want a brother to stamp a claim on her ass. That will never fucking happen. Once you're a sweet butt, you're one for life. No brother will put his stamp on a whore." I grind my jaw together, cursing in Italian as I watch the women circle, and the men's eyes watching them, touching them.

My blood starts to boil. "I'm warning you that I might be wearing a new pair of earrings tomorrow."

She frowns as I slam my beer down. "Earrings?" I hold my fingers up and this time Smithy drops off two shots and two beers straight away. I do the shot and then Red's before chasing it with my beer. I turn, facing her, a sinister smirk playing on my lips.

"Your brother's balls...Three times he's called me sweets! He expects me to be like them?" I hiss, pointing to the girl and shaking my head as I bare my teeth. "Never!... You will have to kill me first."

My reaction doesn't seem to bother her. Neither does the fact I just told her I want to string her brother up by his balls. "It's what he's used to. They are all used to...Why go after a bitch when they can have it for fucking free? … Look, Rae, I love my brother, I fucking do, but he's not the commitment type. He won't call you back the next day, you hear me?"

Yeah, I did. If I gave into Ice, he would see me as nothing more than the girls here. Still, I didn't understand how it all worked. Even with Red saying they weren't held here, it made my skin crawl, made me relive my own dark memories of being used and kept as a plaything. I knew this life, and playing a whore was something I could never, would never, be a part of.

I wasn't someone to pass around, and I wasn't lying when I said he'd have to kill me first.

"He better get used to hearing it because hell will freeze over before I become one of them."

She frowns at my voice, studying me like I catch her sometimes doing, but doesn't say anything, just as a man begins to walk, no, swagger over.

"Want to introduce us, Red?" He isn't as tall as Ice. I'm

guessing around six feet. His skin is light mocha, with perfect azure eyes. His head is shaved, he is clean cut, which surprises me as most of the Horsemen I've seen have some sort of 5 o'clock shadow or trimmed beard. His lips are fuller for a man and are pulled into a sexy smirk. I take a glance at his cut, which I know carries their road name. Apparently, bikers didn't use their birth name. Instead, they all had nicknames, and he was Cage.

"This a Rae, she works at the shop." She chucks her thumb towards him. "This is Cage."

He lifts his chin in greeting before turning towards the bar, grabbing beers.

I realize Cage is whose party it is tonight. Red had said he had been away, and the party was in his honor.

When another one walks up, Flame, he is a bigger build than Cage, even though they are matched in height. Flame's hair is that dirty blonde you often see on rock stars, that hangs in his face and over his eyes. But he couldn't hide how hot he was. All these men were trim, showing how well they looked after themselves, and the power in each of them.

His eyes travel up and down my body "You busy later?" He winks playfully.

Red grins at Flame, slapping his stomach. "Stop playing with fire."

His smirk widens into a full smile as his blue eyes turn electric. "You know that's my favorite kind…Love that burns." She shakes her head in mock disgust, but you can tell she loves them. It's strange to see. I know Ice is her only blood brother, but she seems to have that same connection with all of them. The way they swung their arm over her shoulder and looked at her like she was an annoying kid sister, but their eyes softened as they watched.

Cage lifts two bottles off the bar before he turns back to me, his eyes full of amusement.

"Thinking of getting some ink." His lip twitches along with Flame's.

I know there is a smile covering my face. "Any idea on what you want?"

His smirk grows bigger as he lifts his top, showing a solid six-pack. I shit you not, an actual tight muscle, rippling, six-pack. No airbrushing insight. I honestly want to touch them to see if they are real. My tongue gets stuck to the top of my mouth as I take in all the defined lines, and a blush covers my cheeks because all I can think about is what does Ice's stomach look like?

"So, what do you think?" He laughs, it's husky, as he pulls his top back down. He asked me a question? I remove my tongue from the top of my mouth.

"Umm...What was the question?" I don't even pretend I've heard, which causes them to all burst out laughing. Even Flame can't hide his grin. He shakes his head, pointing his beer bottle towards his friend. "Don't come crying to me when the VP blows off your fucking dick and makes you eat it."

Cage frowns, covering his junk. "Shut your fucking mouth. He can hear you." He strokes his crotch as if his junk is offended before pointing his beer bottle at me. "No claim on her fucking ass or ink on her skin, and my dick hasn't seen action in over a fucking year."

I frown at them, hearing them confirm that Ice wants to fuck me, but he doesn't want me. I wave in their faces.

"Excuse me, still here!" Cage lifts his eyebrow. He seems to be looking at me differently.

"You've got spunk...I like it. You fucking need it around here."

This makes me snort. "My family, well, my father's family, loathed it. They prefer their women to be weaker, controlled." I hate myself for letting my guard down, for giving a piece of my life away that should have stayed buried with my other demons. I'm not supposed to get close. Sharing my life.

His eyes widen at the anger in my voice, though his expression tells me he understands. Flame's body changes as he studies me, rubbing his jaw.

"Thought you said your fucking daddy ran off." Suspicion fills his eyes, regarding me more closely. I shrug. I was too young to recall the man that took part in making me. I used to dream of him out there, and how he would love my quick tongue and wit. That dream disappeared over the years.

"Yeah, my sperm donor did, but my mom remarried when I was two, and he's the only father I've ever known." He hadn't been a bad man, not really. Treated my mom good. He couldn't give her children because of an accident when he was younger. He despised the man that managed to get her pregnant, even if it was before him. By hating my father, I was a byproduct of that hate. He never physically hurt me, but a relationship never formed.

The drink is flowing, and I find two things out about Cage. One; it is a welcome home party from prison. Yep, he had just got out after doing a year. Two; Cage is close with Ice from the stories he's told. And Flame, as his name suggests, loves anything to do with fire. He continually runs an oil lighter down his leg, catching it alight and moving his hand through the fire. Flame grins as he winks at me, handing me another beer. He's nowhere near as intense as Ice, but you can't ignore the undercurrent of danger coming from him. The air seems to pulse with it.

Cage got his name because he was good at driving cars. In biker's language, a vehicle is called a cage, and although he could ride a bike well, he kicked ass at driving vehicles. If I ever need a getaway driver, he is my man. He's a biker brat like Ice, Red, Flame, and Casanova, who I've yet to meet, and someone called Rev.

Cage's father, a man named Relic, had died a few years back in prison. Flame came from the Ohio chapter, run by a man called Rags, and he came back here to prospect with the rest of the biker brats after his father had moved up there. You can see in his eyes that he was ready to return to the Ohio chapter. The banter between them is hilarious, and the stories they tell have Red and me snorting our drinks, which didn't displease either of them. In fact, they seemed to find it amusing, which caused another round of laughter.

I've got to admit, considering I'm surrounded by some of the most intense men I'd ever met, and I'm an outsider, I don't feel threatened. Do not get me wrong they aren't fucking teddy bears that shit rainbows. They all wear a sense of power and danger about them like a lethal aftershave. But I don't feel unsafe. I am not sure if it's their no bullshit attitude, and that they say what they think, no holding back or sugar-coating their words, no matter how fucking crude, they say it without apology. If you didn't like it, you could fuck off out of their club, which I strangely liked about them. It was freeing to be yourself without judgment, or under a watchful eye. I understood them more and the way they lived.

Like another world inside our own, they didn't mess with the outside world unless it broke into theirs. A world of lost souls who had found each other, it was almost poetic. Red was right; they loved as they lived, hard and fierce. I was jealous of it. To me, love was something you should hide from, never expose it and make yourself weak, but not here. Here it was what held them together. You could see it in the way all their eyes softened as Red walked past, how their voices changed when they spoke to her, and how they watched me with curiosity and hesitation at someone new being around her. The way the brothers laughed and joked, and the stories they told was like a fairy tale where the villains had found their place. Instead of being banished, they were accepted, celebrated even.

RAE

For the first time since I can remember, the feeling of wanting to run never surfaced, instead the thought of leaving made my chest hurt. Had I finally found a place I belonged? Was this the reason my mother had sent me here? How would she have known?

"You okay?" I turn to Red as she pulls me from my thoughts.

"Yeah! I think I am." She kisses my cheek, and a smile spreads across her face like she understands.

"Come on, we're going to play some pool before the party starts." My eyes widen as I glance around. Does she not see the same as me? Men hollering and cheering as they drink beer, hugging as new men come in. Women dancing on tables, doing body shots at the bar.

"What do you mean, I thought it already did?" Red laughs behind me, shaking her head as if I haven't got a clue.

"Trust me, you will know when it's fucking started." She holds my hand as we walk through the men and every one that steps in my direction Red gives them a look that has them moving back. There are two men already standing by the pool table. The one nearest to us is tall around six feet four, with a buzz haircut, and the way he stands tells me he was military. There is no denying it. It is like it lived in him.

He looks at Red before me, lifting his chin. "Storm," he introduces himself. He is an intimidating bastard as he looks down his nose at me before turning back to the pool table.

"Rae." He doesn't look up and doesn't say anything but takes his final shot. He straightens and leans on the pool stick.

"Bitch that's got VP's dick hard. You were meant to do my ink." A lopsided smirk plays at his lips. Ah, he's the one that was hugging the rum the other night.

"I'm going to get some drinks." Red grins, and then must see the look on my face because she smiles. "You will be fine, just stay with him." She points in Storm's direction, which doesn't make me feel any safer. I watch her until she disappears into the crowd. I feel a shiver crawl down my spine. It isn't the sort that Ice gives me, and I swallow before I turn, coming face to face with the most unusual eyes I have ever seen. They are a kaleidoscope of golds and browns.

I take a step back but can't stop the gasp that comes from me. It isn't because he's big, even though he's around six-feet-five, and built like an MMA fighter. Ink trails from his neck down and covers both arms and knuckles. Dark raven hair hung like a veil, covering his face. The danger rolls off him, so thick it wraps around me like a pair of hands. This man is death. None of that's what makes me gasp. It is what I see hidden inside his eyes. Demons that live so close to the surface, they are looking right at me. Some of them smirk at me like they recognize my own.

He frowns at my reaction and tries to hide his eyes by looking at the floor and pulling his black hood up until it covers his face. I want to beg him not to hide.

I want to scream at him that I recognize that pain. That darkness. It lives in me. Instead, I walk towards him until we are a breath apart, waiting until he lifts his head, acknowledging me. When he does, the look in his eyes nearly has me backing away, but I stick out my hand.

"I'm Rae. Your eyes…They are beautiful." They widen, looking almost frightened, as he glances anywhere but me before he nods.

"Rev." It comes out a rasp like he doesn't use his voice much, if at all.

"It's nice to meet you." I keep my voice soft.

He licks his lips as if they are dry. "They fucking hurt you, I see it." There's that husky tone again. I nod, feeling my eyes mist.

"They did. Somebody hurt you too." He watches me for a bit, and then his eyes flick over my head before returning to mine and nodding.

When I turn around, everyone is looking between us. Knowing we were speaking too low to be heard. I know Rev wants as little attention as me because I can feel the tension and see his muscles tense with everyone's focus on us. Dragging the focus away from him, I place my Rae mask back on and chuck out my hip, strutting to the pool table and picking up a stick.

"Are we playing pool? Because I've got a fifty that says we are going to whip your ass." Red grins, back from the bar and handing me a bottle of beer. Storm nods his head in respect and gratitude, but for what, I am not sure.

"Oh! This is going be the easiest fucking fifty I ever made." He grins. Red stands next to me, and we click our beer bottles together. "Double or nothing?" His grin widens to a smile, and his eyes are full of amusement as he looks past us.

"What do you say, Rev? Ready to whip some ass." Rev takes slow steps, glancing at me out of the corner of his eye before he nods.

They won, and I knew they would. At the end of the game, Rev has lost most of the tension, and his muscles seem to relax slightly. I could feel him watching me, studying me. He saw my demons; you can't hide them from a man like Rev. We were mirroring each other.

Just as we are finishing up, another man comes walking up. I should say strutting because this man walks with a cockiness, I've seen in most of them, but his is more in your face. His body dipping to the left as he walks, and his eyes pinned on me before dropping to my feet and grinning when he sees my shoes. He slowly drags his eyes up my whole body, lingering on my breasts before his eyes meet mine. He reminds me of Thor.

"Damn, fucking, sweets, I bet you taste as good as you fucking look, baby." He gives me a smoldering look, dragging his teeth over his bottom lip as he continues to rake his eyes up and down my body.

All the others are handsome, rough, and rugged in their ways. He looks angelic, gorgeous. I growl. A pure animalistic growl. It seems like they are rubbing off on me. Before I can say anything, Rev stands in my way, blocking the man from my vision. Bending his head, Rev says something low that I can't catch. Then he moves away, and the man scowls after him before turning back to me. He looks at me through dark lashes.

"Didn't recognize you, Rae, the bitch from the shop." His eyes running over my body like he cannot help it. "Cas." His voice is smooth like an expensive whiskey. I can't help the way my lips twitch.

Cas or Casanova is exactly what I expected. He is cocky and arrogant, but he's also a joker, almost like he was making fun of himself. I wasn't sure if it were to deflect people from looking deeper. From really seeing him. I know Cas is a biker brat, but no one has mentioned his family. I watch as he walks over to Storm and grabs a bottle of whiskey with a smirk on his face. Then when no one is watching, I see the hurt and anger flash briefly underneath the surface. When you have been running like me, you tend to watch people, see what they are not saying.

As I watch them, I realize that Ice, Sketch, Cage, Flame, Rev, and Cas and even Storm are close. They are their own little family amongst the bigger family. It didn't mean they didn't love the rest of the men, just that they had something more robust. Brothers, amongst brothers.

A blonde girl walks up, strutting and making her hips sway from side to side. I don't miss the glare she gives me as she walks towards Cas, and then drags her nails up and down his shirt. Leaning up on her tiptoes, she says something that has him grabbing her ass before he looks around and pulls her into a dark corner. She gives me a smug look over her shoulder before they disappear. Storm's eyes follow them before he looks out into the crowd, smirking when he sees what he's looking for, then walking off. Soon Rev disappears into the shadows, taking a bottle of Jack with him.

Red wasn't wrong because I can't believe I am standing in the same club a few hours later. The women who had been wearing clothes are now only dressed in red thongs, Horsemen colors. Some were giving lap dances and others pole dancing, while some kept the beers flowing. The women outnumber the men, and apparently, that isn't an issue as I had seen Cas walk up the stairs with two girls! He had been up there an hour before he came back. Now he is smoking and playing cards as another girl straddles his lap. Cage is also in a dark corner with a woman grinding on his lap. Sketch turned up an hour ago and is currently kissing some girl's neck, while groping her tits. It's the same woman another brother was feeling up an hour ago. So, I guess this was my crash course on what sweet butts really are. This pisses me off even more, knowing this is what Ice wants me to become. I'd never admit it out loud, but it stung more than I want to let on. Thankfully, Ice is yet to show his face tonight.

Red is on karaoke, and I know she is the president's daughter, she isn't pawed over, the men aren't insulting her, and is treated differently from the sweet butts. Red is respected and loved like a little sister. The sweet butts keep their distance from her and their eyes down when she walks past them. This place brought her alive.

Not so much as she is on stage singing. 'Pour Some Sugar on Me.'

A version that I never heard or want to again. Shit, the girl can't sing. But the men cheer her on, whistling like she is the world's biggest rock star.

Cage told her she had to get on as her present for him. They have been listening to Red do this since she was five.

I put my fingers in my mouth and whistle, causing heads to turn my way, but I don't care. I'm cheering on my girl.

"A lot to take fucking in, isn't it?" I jump at Storm's voice. He drinks his beer, keeping his eyes on the stage.

"Yeah. Red said you were military." I deflect the question, but his lips curve like he knows what I am doing.

"Yeah, didn't have a fucking clue what I was going to do, but I ran into Sketch the day they told me I couldn't go back. Honorable fucking discharge," he snorts. "Joined two years ago, the best fucking thing to happen. Now I get to wear this patch." The pride in his voice is evident. When his eyes slide to mine, he says, "You are taking all this in your fucking stride. For a civilian and first timer, you're missing that fucking wide-eyed fear look."

I shrug. "I know the Horsemen are dangerous..." I hold up my own beer. "Maybe this helps."

He watches me a beat longer. "You don't need to be fucking scared, not unless you cross them..." He leaves the remainder of the answer in the air as a warning.

Ah, so he's been sent over to sniff me out, and my own lips curve. "I'm leaving in a few weeks, so don't worry, I'm not here to cause trouble."

He turns toward me. "Might not be, but you're not fucking telling the whole truth, you have secrets."

I nod, no point in lying. "Don't we all?" I raise my own brow, watching as his lips curve.

"Fair enough. I like you, Rae and Red will be sad to see you go." He points the top of his bottle to the crowd of brothers. "You need any fucking help with any of this, come find me."

He slides away, just as Red takes a bow, glancing at me and smirking as her eyes twinkle with mischief and making mine drop.

"Tonight, my girl Rae is an honorary Horseman, so I want you to show her some fucking loving." The whole crowd cheers and hollers, deafening me. I shake my head, smirking up at her. "Get, that juicy ass up here. Show these fuckers how us girls do it." My eyes widen. Taking a step back and holding my hands up as I shake my head. No fucking way am I going up there. Before I can make my getaway, Cage walks towards me, grinning, then picking me up fireman style and jumping up onto the stage as if I weigh nothing. Depositing me on my feet in front of everyone. I throw out some curse words in Italian, which makes him grin, teeth and all.

"Did you just curse at me in fucking Spanish?" I shake my head, no, trying my best to glare. His grin widens as he adjusts his junk. "That's fucking hot!" I shake my head as Red hands me the microphone. I am about to tell her hell to the fucking no when she whispers in my ear.

"Look to your right." When I do, I see him.

Ice is sitting there in a relaxed pose as, not one, but two sweet butts' paw at his shirt and kiss his neck. His eyes are on me, and his brow raises with that smirk I want to slap as much as I want to kiss, covering his face as he slowly slides his hand up one of the girl's legs. His eyes never leave mine.

I smirk--Oh, game on.

ICE

I stand in the shower, resting my head on the tiles as the water turns pink around me. After everything that went fucking down, I wanted to go back to Rae, fucking taste her, have her nails dig into my skin, and let her pureness wash away my sin's. Instead, I came back fucking here. I had no right tainting her with my touch or staining her pale skin with my motherfucking filth. Tonight, I gained another fucking mark on my soul. How many did you reach before there's no motherfucking soul left? Nothing about her made any fucking sense. Yet for the first time, I wanted to work a bitch out. Wanted the secrets in her damn fucking violets.

Anger still vibrates through me, now in time to the harsh beat of the rock song. Cage is home, I should be down there greeting my brother. He did a year's hard time for this club; we all owe him.

Instead, I'm standing in my shower with my dick in my fucking hand, thinking about a dark-haired beauty. I needed to fuck her, get her out of my motherfucking system, and burn out the liquid fire in my veins. Walking out the shower, I tie a towel around my waist, all my scars bared in the light. Wiping the steam off the mirror, I lean on the sink looking at my reflection. Would her heart beat frantically and her lips fucking part if she knew the truth? Could she fight the demons, or would they rip her a-fucking-part? Did I want to fucking know? She is just a fuck, a nameless snatch. It's all she could be. I'm too fucking dangerous to let a female like her close. She is safer staying away from me.

Feeling bone-tired, the adrenaline fading, the side effect to my fucking high. I always came fucking down. How fucking far would I fall is anyone's fucking guess. I lay down, closing my eyes.

"Baby." Her voice circles around me, and my dick fucking throbs as I feel her lips on my neck, causing me to growl as she moves across my chest, biting slightly on my fucking nipples, wrapping her tongue around the bar in a direct line to my fucking dick. I thrust my hips, showing her where I want her. The first lick of her tongue against my dick and I nearly fucking explode. As she nearly bottoms out, her movements too staged, not sloppy like I expect, it makes me frown. "I love your dick." Her voice is quirky, too high pitched, none of those deep, husky tones. Sharp nails against my thigh. A sickly perfume tickles my nose, it's fucking all wrong.

I blink, the room is now draped in darkness. I frown down at blonde, not dark hair, bobbing on my dick. "What the fuck!" I roar, making her pop off. Barbie. She is one of the better-looking sweets, and one of my regulars. Her eyes widen as she scurries backward in fear. I push her off the bed, making her yelp as my dick slaps against my stomach. "What the fuck you are doing? Coming in here sucking my fucking cock!" I sneer, sitting up. "I know you fucking heard me, answer my fucking question before I throw your fucking bony ass out."

She shakes her head, moving backward until her back hits the wall, and a little squeak escapes her.

"Y…you never minded before," Barbie whispers, standing on shaky legs. She is right, but something about it now twisted my gut. I'm pissed that it isn't fucking Rae.

"Get the fuck out, and never come in here without being fucking asked." She nods before running out the door. I take a deep breath, grab my jeans, and pull them up before grabbing a shirt and my cut. As soon as I open my door, the music hits me. Fuck! I'm not in the mood for all of this tonight. For the first time in my life, I don't want to be here. Smithy sees me and hands me a beer.

"Prez wants you."

I should have fucking checked in with him as soon as I got back, but I was too raw. Everything I felt and tried to numb lived too close to the fucking surface. Loud laughter catches my attention, and I look through the guys all hanging about to see my sister. Hawk moves out the way, and I suck in a breath when I see her. I would have bet my motherfucking bike Rae wouldn't have turned up tonight, but here she is. I feel a pull towards her grow in my gut as I watch her. A dark mane of hair falls down her back like a silk sheet. Her eyes are wide, and there is a smile on her face that captures more than one fucking brother's attention. She laughs at something Cage says, and I watch as he stretches his arms over the back of her chair. The bottle in my hand smashes, just as Flame looks up to see me staring. I go to take a step forward.

"Son." I take my fucking eyes off her because she is just another nameless snatch, right? The other brothers aren't as fucked up as me. Rae would be better suited to one of them, so why the fuck did I want to kill all the brothers looking at her. Gritting my teeth. Beating back the feeling to go to her, I follow my father, just as I'm programmed to do. Club comes first always. The sounds of the party fade to a dull hum as my father shuts the door behind us and moves behind the desk.

"You're bleeding." My brows pull down at his words, I

scrubbed in the shower. "Your hand." He chucks me a cloth, and I look down to see three cuts, I didn't register were there, then wrap it.

"It's fucking nothing." His dark brows raise, but he keeps his mouth shut. Taking a seat at his desk.

"So, the motherfucker, he didn't talk?" My anger starts bubbling under the surface.

"Only a fucking mumble, nothing made fucking sense. Something ain't right." Even his brows raise at that before he strokes his jaw.

"Recon?"

I shrug. "Could be, but my fucking gut is saying we haven't got the whole picture." I watch him, waiting for the anger, but it doesn't come, like he isn't surprised. I narrow my eyes. "You need to fucking tell me something?"

"No, but no other chapter has had any fucking problems, and they are not stupid enough to mess with this fucking one."

"Motherfuckers are sniffing' around. It's enough," I say.

"Only two and you've got rid of the fucking problem. I called you in to talk about the run tomorrow."

He is right, it was only two, but that doesn't fucking explain why they were here. I hated loose ends as much as I hate the fucking Mendez.

"What's the deal?"

A smirk covers his face. "Got talk on some handmade guns, no fucking trace numbers, nothing."

I lean forward, everyone had heard of guns that were made from fucking scratch, but they were like a myth.

"You're talkin' about ghost guns? No fucker can get a hold of them!"

"They came in from the fucking Philippines, but the buyer fell through." I whistle. If this isn't someone yanking our fucking chain, the payment would be big.

"I'll take the guys up, see if he's not fucking blowing smoke up our ass." He nods, and I stand, walking out the door. We didn't do small talk, not anymore.

Walking back into the main room, my eyes go straight to where she was sitting. Cage and Flame are still shooting the shit, but Rae is missing. Storm comes into the room, heading for Barbie, but he turns direction when he sees me.

"Fuck, man, your girl is a fucking riot." I raise a brow, my gut twists as a red-hot poker feeling comes over me. Something telling me the motherfucker ain't talking about Barbie.

"Rae?" I hiss, making that fucking smirk drop and his brow to raise. If anyone deserves a girl like fucking Rae, it would be him. Storm is motherfucking Grey Adamson, the fucking war hero. Saving a bunch of civilians after going into the heart of the fucking war. He grew up in the trailer park just outside of town with Sketch. He would treat her fucking right, put a ring on her finger in a couple of years and get her fucking ripe with his baby. Knowing how soft her fucking lips are and what she fucking tastes like, unexplained anger flies through my veins at the thought of him touching her. My fingers tap against my piece, drawing Storm's eyes there.

"Yeah, do we have a problem?" The group of brothers around us moves out the way. "Keep your hands off and your fucking dick away, if you want to keep breathing'." It's a gut reaction, the words out before I can fucking stop them.

"She ain't the type that's going to be happy being a bed warmer for you." I knew it. Did he think I was fucking blind and didn't see her? But I couldn't make her fucking more. He knows how messed up I am. I would fucking destroy her.

That's how two hours later, I ended up sitting in between two fucking sweets as I watch Cage carry Rae onto the stage, and her eyes finding me. The asshole I am, I move my hand up one of their thighs. Which one, I couldn't tell you because my eyes were on her.

Always fucking her. They flash with a challenge that draws the blood to my dick.

ICE

Rae turns to face the brothers. "My girl Red, tells me you Horsemen know how to make a woman feel welcome."

There's an extra purr in her voice as those blood-red fucking pouty lips caress the microphone. The whole room erupts in hollers, and yells, and curses, everyone is in good spirits. Having a brother back home is always a fucking good feeling. Sketch also told me Red had warned every brother with their fucking dick that they better be nice to Rae. She would have never invited her if other chapters were down, but I knew it was my interest that kept the fuckers away. Rae shakes her head at Red, sitting on the edge of the makeshift stage, swinging her legs. Rae smirks, biting her lip before pulling her phone out and handing it to my sister, who chucks her head back laughing as she presses play and Avril Lavigne's Bad Girl kicks in.

The room goes fucking quiet, silence compared to the commotion that was just happening, even Cas has detached his mouth from a sweet butt to breathe and has his eyes on her. I watch her every fucking little movement, the way her hands clench together, the way she's running her teeth over her bottom lip, she's fucking nervous. Then her eyes find me, and I raise my brow as if knowing what she needs. Are you going to choke Kitten?

Then it fucking happens, anyone else would've missed it, but a change occurs. This here is the real Rae. She starts singing, swaying those damn motherfucking hips as she walks along the stage, and her breath catches as the adrenaline kicks in. Surprising the fuck out of everyone, she shouts, jumping off the fucking stage as she heads straight for Cage. As she places her back to his front, leaning close, she continues to sing. Oh, Kitten, you'll fucking pay for that.

She pushes away from him, her eyes searching as the brother's cheer, and then she smiles, heading towards Cas, who is already grinning and shaking his head. I relax, realizing she is going to the brothers she knows. Feels fucking safe with. Rae circles him, continuing to belt out the song. I see a few brothers going to step fucking forward, their eyes flick to me, but I shake my head to tell them to stay fucking back. I don't know why, but I know it will fucking spook her. All I can do is fucking stare. Her cheeks are flushed, lips in a smile, and the way she moves her fucking body? Fuck, she is beautiful.

The crowd breaks, just like it did the first night. There she is. My nostrils flare, and my dick hardens as our eyes fucking lock. I watch as her mouth circles around each of the lyrics and sweat glistens on her skin. At the last second, she bypasses my table and heads for Sketch, who grins like a fucking proud older brother. He leans in, saying something that makes her laugh.

Red helps her back up, swinging her arms over Rae's shoulders as they both finish the song together. When it ends, they are both grinning like fucking crazy at each other as the brothers whistle and holler. Time's fucking up, Kitten.

I jump up on stage, and Rae turns just in time for the shock to register before I lift her in the air and over my shoulder like a fucking caveman. The brothers all start cheering and laughing. I don't give a fuck.

"Put me down!" she shouts, dragging her nails down my back and making me fucking hiss, which ends with a sharp slap to her ass.

"Calm the fuck down, Kitten." I smirk as she freezes.

The noise fades as I walk into the first room, the kitchen, and I place her against the steel worktop. Before Rae has a chance to fucking recover, I bury my head in her neck, inhaling, like I need her scent to fucking breathe. Her body shivers under my touch. I need her god damn taste and attack those lips, holding her head so I can fucking control the kiss. My teeth dig into her bottom lip, causing her to gasp and giving me the perfect amount of room to fit in. Our tongues fight against each other like exotic lovers, both fucking wanting and greedy. It's all teeth and rushed. I can't get close enough to her, and it's like she's in my blood. Fuck, I want to fucking devour her. Never knew a fucking bitch could taste as fucking pure as her. She pulls back, looking at me with those goddamn violets, making my fucking gut twist as her chest heaves. For a few fucking minutes, the voices in my fucking head go quiet, the anger simmers down, leaving me staring at her, and a brand-new fucking feeling takes over. What the fuck has she done to me?

RAE

I take hold of his face, running my fingers through his beard, and then leaning in, I kiss the side of his lip before doing the same to the other. Then I kiss his lips, licking and biting them and causing him to gasp as our tongues meet. Each swipe of our tongues makes the fire between us grow. When the kiss breaks, his eyes are wide, his tongue comes out running across his lip before his brows slam down, and he lifts me up. Before I have time to wrap my legs around him, I feel the coolness of the steel bench through my pants. The difference in temperature to my hot body, sets the fire inside me blazing. His lips slam back down on mine, and not breaking the kiss, Ice rips the zipper on my jacket down. Pulling away, we study each other, gasping for air.

"You're a fucking bitch," he hisses as he yanks my bra down. His words should make me want to slap him, but that look in his eyes as he takes in my breast sends shocks through my body. His body at total war, raw want and desire, anger, and something more. I can't yet decipher. Before attacking my chest, Ice sucks air through his teeth, sucking and biting using his hands like he can't get enough. It causes the right amount of pain, and the pleasure it causes has my back arching, offering him more. All thoughts evaporate. The darkness and demons in my mind are kept away by the feral look in his eyes. It shouldn't excite me the way it does. It screams danger, telling me his words from earlier were the truth. He is going to consume me until I am entirely owned by him. Hooked on him and unable to escape. I've been in that position before, and I know what that sort of owning can do. What it means, but this time it will destroy me.

As I watch Ice devour my breast, I know this is different. He is different. Ice's touch caresses; doesn't harm, his words crude; but not destroying. He believes he is cruel, a monster. His actions speak otherwise.

With that final thought, I submit to him. To his mouth. To his touch. To his taste. Unequivocally.

"Fucking perfect," he growls, twisting me quickly, so my bare breasts press against the cold steel, making me hiss as my body shudders. Using his hot body to hold me down as the difference in temperature rips a moan from my throat.

"You want me, tell me you fucking want me," he growls before I feel his teeth dig into my shoulder, causing a wanton moan to escape, and then he yanks my pants down enough to give him access to me. He grabs my ass tight, kneading the globes. I know he's leaving bruises, and the pain mixed with the pure pleasure I'm already feeling is a lethal mix. I press back into his hands, doing something I never thought I would do. Asking for more. Submitting.

He rams his thick fingers into me, and my body clenches them tight. The other men who had sex with me were nothing like this. The way Ice is playing my body with his fingers like a maestro, as if I'm his own personal instrument, and my body bows to his every touch.

"You're fucking wet, all for me. Yeah, you fucking want me."

He sounds pissed, disgusted by the fact. I would be ashamed if it weren't for the fact that my mind can't hold a single thought, but the last doubt is erased as he pushes himself against my backside. The outline of his thick cock evident as his breathing becomes heavier, betraying his own words. He's just as affected as me. Moving his fingers in a come-hither motion that sends me to a place I never knew existed. The intense feeling continues to build, and I'm right there on the edge of wherever he's taking me. As he continues touching that spot over and over, making me gasp for air, my whole body tightens as a feeling I've never felt before comes over me. Ice rips his fingers out of me before I have a chance to fall or fly. I'm not sure.

My body is tight in an almost painful way. I try to turn my head, but he wraps my hair around his wrist, making my body arch towards him. I feel the wetness of his tongue drag up my neck, towards my ear. Licking the shell before biting on my ear lobe, causing another moan to escape.

"Beg for it," he says, continuing to assault my neck. I shake my head, trying to form the words. He pushes the outline of his cock tighter against me, making me shiver, and I feel his smile on my neck. The bastard knows what he's doing.

"Fucking tell me you want it. Say it!" His fingers rim my entrance as my body tries to grab them. Ice makes sure they're just out of reach, teasing me. My body is burning bright because of the need for him. I am positive that I'm about to burn in this Horseman's flames. The torture of his fingers touching me, the feeling of him all around me, invading every sense is too much, and a sob breaks through me as a tear rolls down my cheek.

"Please." My breath catches. "I want you, please." He wraps a thick arm around my waist, holding my hips tight as his fingers enter me, and this time the force of him hitting that sweet spot sends me over the edge. My body burns brighter than I've ever felt. His name is ripped from my throat, and blackness fills my vision. Aftershocks continue to assault my body as the ecstasy slowly starts to ebb away.

My eyes flutter open to see light blue pools staring down at me. There's an animalistic hunger shining bright, but there's also a softness about them. Sitting up slowly, I notice how brilliant they are, and the shadows that usually swirl there aren't so close to the surface.

He rubs my lips with his thumb, almost angry as he stares at me. I lean in, undoing his buttons and pushing his jeans down as the urge to touch him, taste him, takes over me like I am starved for him. I'm not sure if I'm ready for this to go all the way, but this I can do. I want this. His cock stands proudly like the man himself, and the thick head starts to leak. My eyes widen at the size and the Jacobs ladder.

The other times I've had sex, their dicks were nowhere near his length or thickness. I know that thought should frighten me, but the craving to take him pushes everything else away, and I lick my lips at the sight. I didn't generally like sucking cock, but there was something about Ice's. It was almost beautiful. I wanted to hear him panting and begging me. Watch him come undone as I had. To know he was just as desperate as I was.

"On your knees." He's back to growling, and his authoritative look should have me running as fast as my heels can take me. But I am ashamed to say how quickly I end up on my knees. His heady smell surrounds me, making the tightening in my stomach return with a force as I feel wetness cover my thighs.

I lean in to smell him, to take in all that masculinity when I see it: the ring of smudged red lipstick. Lipstick that isn't mine. And like someone chucked cold water on me, all my senses come back; flashes of my memory invade me so much, that I find it hard to breathe. Staggering to stand. This is what he wants, me on my knees, his little whore before he moves on and chucks me away like I'm disposable.

No matter how much I want this, I can't do it; I can't become someone nameless.

I'm not like those other women, and I can't let that happen
again. I can't destroy myself for him, no matter how much my body
craves it.

"What the fuck!" I do my jacket up and looking him right in the
eyes, I use the last bit of strength I have left.

"I told you if this ever happened, you'd remember my name.
I'm not one of your damn playthings." He looks bewildered. I walk
past him with as much dignity as I can muster. The dirty feeling is
crawling against my skin – little fucking puttana. I cringe as his voice
invades me, memories I can never escape.

Just as I get to the door, I turn. "By the way, that shade really
isn't your color. I'd say you're more of a mauve." I look directly at
his cock, which still stands proud, and then walk away.

I walk back into the room when a blonde comes and stands
in my way. "Stay the fuck away from Ice," she sneers, crossing
her arms over her string top. "He's mine," she growls when I don't
answer her.

"We both know that's a lie. Does he even know it's you when
he's fucking you? That is all you want? Your big fucking dreams."

She takes a step closer to me. "I'm going to be his Ol' Lady one
day, everyone here knows it." I shake my head, she is delusional, but
the stars in her eyes tell me she believes it.

"If he wants you so damn much, then I'm not going to be a
problem." Something crosses her face.

"You're nothing special. He'll get bored of you soon, then Ice
will be crawling back in my bed. I know how to look after my man."

"That's the difference between us, though. I won't ever let a
man treat me like that. Ice can fuck who he wants, but it won't be my
bed he crawls back into."

"You're a fucking cunt," she hisses. I shake my head, looking
her up and down, and a little laugh escapes, which makes her frown.
I walk past her, not even giving her a reply, before going straight to

the bar, where Smithy looks at me.

"Keep them coming." He nods, handing me a glass of amber liquid, and I down it before handing the glass back, which he refills quickly, and this time, leaves the bottle. I feel someone slide up next to me, glancing, I see Champ. He's one of the men that's come into the shop. He looks like Father Christmas, well, if Father Christmas was nearly six feet and covered in ink. But we haven't officially been introduced.

"He's not a bad man." His voice is grave. I down another shot before nodding.

"I know." I did. I wasn't under any illusion and knew they were criminals that walked on the dark side. I wasn't blind and had seen the danger in them, especially Ice, and I also saw the fight in him. Something had changed Ice, altered him, and it held onto him, and he struggled constantly to fight against. I knew he had a good heart, even if he didn't believe it himself. It's why the brothers loved him.

He holds his hand out. "Champ."

I hold mine out, smiling. "Rae." His grey brow raises. I'm sure he's smiling, but I can't tell with his beard.

"Okay, if that's what you're saying." I instantly frown.

"It's who I am." He studies my eyes before looking into his own glass, nodding as he takes a swig, and then glancing back at me.

"We can all be who we choose to be, ain't fucking saying any different, but what we are inside? That's who we really are. That is something we can't escape." I bite my lip, he knows. He might not know who I am and what I'm running from, but he sees the lost girl inside of me. He sees what no one else has.

"What brought you here?" I ask, and he smiles, but doesn't answer, just takes a long drink.

"You make him feel good." I go to speak, but he shoots me a glare that has me slamming my mouth shut. "He did something that should never have been placed on his shoulders. That shit eats at him.

Messed him fucking up, so he locked down." His words mix with the ones Red told me. The reason that changed him, and why they call him Ice. But I can't help remembering his eyes. The light blue with almost sliver shades that look like glass. How clear they are.

"He doesn't know what to do with you. What you make him feel. He will fucking fight it." I snort when a sound like thunder comes from him as his shoulders shake. He glances at me. "He'll fuck up no doubt, this life will make sure of that." He rubs his jaw, glancing around. "These men, they protect what is theirs, you hear me." I heard Champ's words.

"I'm not theirs. I don't belong here." He shoots me a look.

"You feel it, girl, don't bullshit an old man like me, you belong here. You feel that shit deep down." I don't know if I'm willing to accept his words. Too scared of what they could mean. He nods as if understanding before turning back to the bar. I turn to lean my back against the bar, and I look for Red, knowing I've got to get the fuck out of here before I have other words of wisdom thrown upon me. Or Ice makes an entrance and carry's me off to the cave I am sure he lives in.

I spot her with an older man standing by the door. He is in his early fifties. Raven hair falls to his shoulders in a messy style, that is weirdly attractive, and his body is in good shape for his age. He looks more like someone in their late 40s than 50s. As I get closer, the air changes and electricity fills it. Not the same way it does with Ice, but a way that makes my step falter. I know whoever this man is he is powerful. I can feel his dangerous current from here, and it's like a forcefield that surrounds him. Feeling me, he lifts his head, and this time I stumble. The man looks exactly like Ice, the same chiseled cheekbones and strong jawline. The only difference is his eyes are a darker blue compared to Ice's light ones.

I don't need any introduction. I know I'm standing face to face with the president of The Red Horsemen. Luther himself. He crosses his arms over his chest, his legs widen, giving off an intimidating stance.

"I heard you've made quite an impression" Every word is slow, laced in danger.

I grin, hoping it's coming out playful as I bump Red's shoulder. "I am not a wallflower." Luther lifts an eyebrow studying me, turning to face me more, his eyebrows pulling down.

"What did you say your name was?" There is no way he didn't know my name. I worked in one of Horsemen businesses, where his daughter worked,

"I didn't. But it's Rae, and I work at the ink shop, but I guess you already knew that." His eyes widen. I swear I see amusement in them as he nods his head, confirming he knows exactly who I am.

"Oh, that reminds me, I've got to see Sketch about a client," Red says, smiling before disappearing into the crowd and leaving me alone with her father.

Luther's lip twitches as he nods his head. "Not a fucking lasting impression, I see." I follow the direction he's looking to see Ice and a sweet butt walking up the metal stairs next to the pool table, which leads to fifteen private rooms that used to be offices.

I try tamping down the rage that boils inside as she looks over her shoulder at me, smirking. Who the rage is directed at? I'm not sure? Me for thinking what happened would make a difference, that the connection between us is real and Ice could feel it as strongly as me. Or Ice, who had done exactly what I knew he would when I walked out the door and found the closest sweet butt to fuck. I school my features before shrugging, my lips lifting into a sweet smile.

"She's just like the rest." He rubs his chin as he watches me.

"That so?" He asks.

"Yeah, I'm not some club ass. I'm not a sweet butt."

"You got a fucking mouth on you, can see why my daughter likes you." He tries to cover his mouth, but not quick enough that I don't see his lips twitch as Red comes over.

"I think it's time you left, let the brothers finish the fucking rest of the night." Which means before they really do get wild. She frowns, crossing her arms, I know she is about to open her mouth and disagree, but I jump in.

"Come on, girl, I've got a night with Channing Tatum booked for us." Luther lets out a noise that I swear is the sound of nightmares, and taking a quick glance at him, I flinch back at the look in his eyes. A look that makes me swallow hard. It is like the devil himself is looking at me, and what's even scarier is it's directed straight at me.

"Dad, fucks sake, she's talkin' about a movie! I ain't some kid." She rolls her eyes, letting out a breath. I know she's pissed that she is being sent home like a little girl that's not allowed out past her curfew. His eyes lock on mine.

"That right?" He's watching me like a goddamn lie detector.

"Yeah." He watches me for a beat longer before nodding as his whole body unwinds in front of me.

"Okay, I'll have a prospect take you home."

ICE

As soon as I reach the top of the stairs, I drop my hand from Crystal's waist. I pull out my wallet, handing her a few bills. "Keep your fucking mouth shut and make yourself scarce for the rest of the night." She frowns.

"Is this about that bitch?"

I shoot her a look. "What the fuck are you talkin' about."

She shrugs. "Barbie's been talking about the new bitch that's got you by the fucking dick."

My anger flares. "That fucking cunt doesn't know anything."

Crystal's lips curve. "We all know that she's got stars in her eyes, that you'll make her yours."

I shake my head. "Ain't making' no fucking bitch mine, especially that motherfucking cunt. Tell her to watch her fucking mouth." I walk into my room, slamming the door behind me as I pace back and forth, anger pumping through my body like another fucking heartbeat.

No one else winds me up like Rae, nobody else has ever gotten under my fucking my skin like her. Fuck! I want to kill her and fuck her all at once. "Fucking motherfucker." The pain from punching the wall does nothing to tamper down the fury. I light up a smoke, running my hand through my hair. Never kissed a bitch before, but fuck, as soon as I tasted her I knew it would never be enough; I wanted it fucking all. The feel of her skin, that hot cunt, and the sound she made as I brought her closer to the edge. The way those fucking eyes turned violet, widening like I was the only fucker who made her body react that way. It's like a shot of fucking pure adrenaline.

The banging on the door makes me wince, and the empty bottle rolls, hitting the floor. My hand is still around my dick, and thoughts of fucking Rae still linger under the surface.

The banging gets louder. "What the fuck?" I growl getting out of bed, chucking my jeans on. Grabbing my smokes off the cabinet, sparking one up and letting the smoke claim my lungs as I swing the door open to see Champ, Cas, and Cage all standing outside.

"We've got a fucking problem." I narrow my eyes at Cage's voice, feeling every one of my muscles bunch under my shirt and take another drag.

"What sort of fucking problem?" I blow out smoke as Champ narrows his eyes, and a dark look passes over his face.

"Prez wants you." I walk back to my room, grabbing my shirt and cut and sitting on the bed, reaching for my socks and boots, and putting them on before picking up an extra piece.

"What's fucking happened?" I ask, sparking up another smoke.

"Motherfucking Marco got his throat slit this morning." Champ growls. This has me stopping. Marco is the head of Mendez, and the same one who sent the motherfucking foot soldiers.

"None of this makes fucking sense? How the fuck did Prez find out so fast?" A few days ago, we had his fucking men sniffing about, we got rid of them, and now Marco turns up fucking dead?

"Rags had some understanding with the fuckers." I turn, nearly giving myself whiplash.

"Prez fucking know?"

Cas shrugs, his eyes full of anger. "Fucking sounds like it. They are on a call now."

He walks off, the rest of the guys give a look before following him over to the bar. I don't know why he wanted only me and not all the council. This affects us all. He ends the call just as I walk in.

"Boys fill you in?" I take the seat.

"Champ said Marco had his throat slit. What I do not understand is why it matters to us?" He lets out a breath, his eyes fixed on me.

"Spoke to Rags, but he seems to be dealing with his own shit. He's trying' to find out if the word on the street is true. That Marco is dead."

"You know about this deal he had with Mendez?"

He nods. "Yeah, it was with Gino. It happened years ago when he first moved up there. Rags gave him access to the road for shipment." This makes me frown. We don't mix with those dogs, we're like oil and water.

"He was butchered a few years back with his family, so how the fuck can you have a deal with a dead man?" I hiss.

It was meant to be a bloodbath, they killed Gino and his family in his own house. Butchered the fuck out of all of them. Even his wife and kid, all killed like animals.

"When Gino was murdered, the deal was kept with Marco." He shrugs.

"What about Carlo? Rumor is he deals in the type of shit

the Horsemen shouldn't be," I growl out, trying to keep a hold on everything.

"He's nothing to worry about. He is a fucked-up daddy's boy."

We had kept close recon on the Mendez family, especially after they killed Cas' father. Gino was the sanest of the brothers. His wife had been the perfect little fucking trophy wife who threw parties at the country club, and their daughter had gone to private school until she was fifteen, done ballet, and had been the perfect little princess. The intel we had on Carlo said he's nothing but a spoilt brat, an old spoilt brat. He'd never married, never had a girlfriend, likes the kind of women you have to pay for. He lives in a luxury penthouse in New York, goes on vacation every few months, and loves to party in Vegas.

"Something's not fucking right. First, their footmen come sniffing, and now Marco is fucking dead. We need eyes on that motherfucker Carlo. We could end up in the middle of a fucking damn war. Are we going on lockdown?" I ask, knowing how quickly it goes bad.

"No, we got ears to the fucking ground, and I'll get a prospect to cover Layla." I sit straighter.

"And the other bitch that works there?" His brow rises as he looks around the table before back at me.

"Something you gotta tell me, son?" I relax in my seat, stopping my leg from bouncing, making my eyes cold.

"No, but I'm guessing Red ain't going to be fucking happy with her friend full of bullet holes." It was total fucking bullshit, but I knew that if he didn't put men on Rae, I fucking would.

"Yeah, you're right. Layla seems to like the bitch. I'll get Smithy to cover her. Pop into Rags and getting a week of fucking intel on that motherfucker Carlo ain't going to hurt. You'll be gone a week, so get your shit together and get going."

"What about the guns?" I shoot back.

He shakes his head. "This is more fucking important. Something's happening." I nod, getting up, rolling my shoulders to try and work out the tenseness. "I spoke to that bitch last night, she seems ...Nice. Layla seems to be friends with her." I slowly turn, crossing my arms across my chest. Feeling all my muscles wound up tight.

"Too nice for a fucking messed-up fucker like me. Scared I'll fucking corrupt her? Since when did you give a fuck about club snatch? I've seen Barbie creeping out of your fuckin' room plenty of times. Good to know what you think, Prez" I spit at him, he opens his mouth, but I'm out the fucking door before I take a swing at him and he can say anything. Walking into the main room, I'm wound tight, itching to get on the road. I'm surprised to see Sketch there waiting.

"We'll be gone for a week. Are you sure the shop will be fuckin' okay?"

His lips lift as he nods, a proud look crosses his face. "Yeah, Rae's got it under control, and I'm feeling fuckin' good to join the ride."

At the mention of her name, each of my muscle's bunch together. She is a fucking torment in the worst and best form. Sketch had missed riding the last couple of months. The shop needed him, so on the longer runs, he'd had to stay back. I knew he fucking hated it. I feel a twinge in my gut at the idea of her back here, alone.

"Are you sure that bitch will be okay?"

"Yeah, she's got balls bigger than most fucking men."

He was fucking right. Rae did, but she also had this vulnerability about her that she hid from everyone else. I turn to the brothers. "Everyone grab your fuckin' shit; we are leaving in fifteen."

ICE

We pull off instantly, falling into formation with Sketch and Cas pulling along beside me. As we near the shop, I can't fucking help pulling in. Like a fucking junkie I crave my hit. I jump off my bike and ignore the fuckers behind me. I push through the door, and Red frowns.

"Ice, what's up?"

I lift my chin, not fucking answering but hearing the gun in the room opposite to Sketch's, I shove the door open. The full eyed look and the way her mouth parts when she sees me makes my chest tighten. I don't stop my stride, not giving her time to fucking speak as I grab the back of her neck, tighten my hold and crush my lips to hers. I push my tongue into her mouth, letting her fucking taste consume me. I break the kiss just as fast and walk back out of the shop, not even stopping when Red calls my name. All the brothers are smirking as I join them. I toss them the finger before swinging my leg over my bike. Just as we pull off, I look back in my mirror to see Rae standing in the doorway with her fingers touching her lips before raising a finger, flipping me off, and my lips twitch.

We pull into Rags' chapter, getting off our bikes and stretching our backs as I roll my shoulders. I grab my smokes, sparking up as a few brothers come over, all wearing grins. Most head straight for Flame as this was his chapter before he asked to be transferred back to us. He meets and greets, and Fuse, Flame's old man, comes out wrapping him in a tight hug.

"Good to fucking see you, boy." Rags comes out looking older than he did just a few weeks ago.

"You okay, old man?" I ask as the rest start walking to the clubhouse.

He seems to let out a deep breath. "Yeah, the fuckin' years are catching up with me."

I snort, he'll most probably fucking outlive us all. Right alongside my father. They're tough bastards. Everyone jokes that not even the devil wants them.

"Where's Bolt?" I ask, searching the crowd. I was pissed he wasn't here last time...Something fucking dark passes over Rags' face.

"On a job." I guess he's dealing with the shit my old man was talking about. We walk into the club, music is blaring, and the club pussy all raise their heads. "Enjoy your night, boys, got some girls in. We will meet in the morning."

"Wait, I need to talk to you all." Flame speaks up.

Fuck! I knew this was coming as I'd seen him become restless the last few months. I knew he had been waiting for Cage to get out so he could make his fucking move. "I want to transfer back up here."

Fuse steps forward. "Son."

Flame shakes his head. "Ma is fucking sick, and I know you're not being straight." He turns to me. "It was fucking great prospecting with you all, always meant to be that way, but this fucking place is where I belong."

I nod. "Yeah, I get that fuckin' shit." Squeezing his shoulder, I turn to Rags, he nods in agreement.

"I'll talk to Luther in a bit, it will be good to have you home, boy."

Rags slaps my shoulder one more time before he walks away. I watch him as he does, shoulders fucking tense, and a phone to his ear. The news isn't what he fucking wants because his whole body seems to sag before straightening, and then nodding at the motherfucker on the phone before hanging up. He walks to the end of the bar, and the prospect hands him a whole bottle of the dark stuff before disappearing into his office. I feel something on my chest, turning, I'm met by dull, brown eyes, looking at me through mascara caked lashes.

"Hey, want some company tonight?" I skim my eyes down the length of her body. She is a good-looking bitch, and I usually wouldn't think twice about dipping my fucking dick in her. But my dick doesn't twitch. Not even at her fucking tits.

"Maybe later...yeah." She tries to cover her frown with a smile before walking away. Sketch slides up to next me and passes me a bottle.

"She got you fuckin' tied up." It's not a question, and I pick up my bottle taking a swig, ignoring him, giving him a cold silence but the fucker continues. "She's a good bitch, but she ain't no fuckin' club ass."

I frown, glaring at him. What the fuck! Did he even think I would let some other fuckers touch Rae? She was fucking mine. I would kill any motherfucker who even thought of touching her.

"I fuckin' know."

He nods, takes a long swig of his beer, and holding his fingers up at the bitch behind the bar who is smiling at him like the fucking

Cheshire cat. He rubs his jaw as he studies me.

"You putting your mark on her?"

The thought of Rae with my mark on her skin makes my fucking dick twitch at knowing the fact, she belongs to fucking me, and that every motherfucker will know I've fucking claimed her, that she's fucking mine. I drag my hands through my hair as the anger the whiskey had calmed was back with a vengeance because I did fucking want her. Fuck, I craved the bitch. The way she felt, that damn look in her eyes. The fucking way everything inside me calmed down around her. The moments of peace she gives me, I already crave. I knew fucking better than to let someone get close. For fucking years, I had pushed every other fucker away to keep them safe. I would fucking protect her, even if it were from myself. I'd make sure she fucking hated me by the time we were finished. How the fuck would Rae feel if she knew the hands that touched her were painting her fucking skin in crimson? The same fingers that brought her fucking pleasure had ended more than one life and would end many more.

Rae would want a man that takes her out on fucking dates, dances with her, buys a house with a white fucking picket fence, and has a dog called fucking Rover that would give her the happy ever fucking after. That would never be me. I would never be that motherfucker.

"No, I'm not the motherfucker for her. Fuck, I would destroy her." Sketch pours a glass of the dark stuff.

"I get that man, but Rae ain't no normal bitch." I turn to him, and he smirks, holding his hand up.

"Don't fuckin' forget I work with her; she gets that shit. She's been to the club and took it all in her fuckin' stride. Fuck, man, she even spoke to fucking Rev. She didn't run away fucking screaming, even club ass runs in the opposite direction from that fucker. But Rae, she walked straight up and offered her fuckin' hand, and then a game of pool."

He was right. Rae was rare for a bitch, last night was her first night at the club, and she fit in like she always fucking belonged. Not many bitches could handle this fucking life.

"She wants dating', flowers, fucking cuddles, and shit. Not a fuckin' man coming over covered in blood. Not her man to be fucked up in the head."

The fucker's lips twitch. "Most bitches do."

I shake my head and light a smoke, inhaling before letting it out. "This is all I've ever fuckin' known; the club fuckin' owns me. It's a part of my motherfuckin' soul ...I ain't ever fuckin' going be that man. If I had her, I wouldn't ever fuckin' let go. I would want to fuckin' control her, every inch of her. I'd kill any fuckin' bastard that messed with her."

His eyes widen. "Fuck, I forget how much of a psycho you can be." He stands, slapping my back, when Champ slips into his seat.

"Heard what you were fucking saying." I slam my drink down.

"When the fuck did our dick's runoff, and we grow a pair of fuckin' ovaries?" Fuck! What is it with everyone wanting in my motherfucking business and acting like a fucking girls locker room?

Champ moves, grabbing his dick. "Mine's here, boy, not surprised you lost that fucking maggot of yours."

I let out a gruff laugh and watch as Champ's shoulder shakes as he pours us another drink. We hold them up, clink glasses, and down our drinks.

"Spit it out, old man, cause I know you want to spread that fuckin' wisdom. And I respect you enough to sit here and motherfuckin' listen."

Champ is the kind of man that if you give him a fish, he'll eat for one day, but teach him to fish, and he will eat forever.

"She doesn't stay long; she's a fucking runner." His words feel like acid in my gut, every muscle bunches as he watches my reaction, and then he nods.

"That twist in the gut like some fucker is digging a knife in? Not one other fucking bitch ever made you feel that. Could you give her a motherfucking reason to stay, VP? You let her go, and you'll be a more miserable fucker than you are now. Let her fucking prove to you that you deserve her. Let her fucking in, boy." He stands to squeeze my shoulder. "It wasn't your fuckin' fault, boy, no one knew. Let it go before it fuckin' destroys you."

It already has. None of these fuckers know how deep I've fallen. How fucking messed up I am. How much it fucking hurts, the feeling of this rage so close to my skin, you can taste it. That I'm out of fucking control. The way my mind fucking swaps. Some fucking days it takes everything to get out of bed, other times I'm living on a fucking high. Like some motherfucker has injected something into my fucking veins. That I am losing it, my mind is so fucking messed up that only a bullet would save every fucker around me. The one I carry around in my pocket, the perfect sliver that I polish, even holds the Horsemen insignia on it. It will end me one day. Soon. That I can guarantee. Even as Rae threads hope around me, I know it's a fucking illusion because there's no hope left for a fucker like me. I know, I'm getting too restless, too dangerous, and my time is on a countdown, it's just a matter of when.

In the morning, we all walk into fucking church, dropping our pieces and phones in a box. I notice Bolt's seat is still empty. So, I take his place, and Rags nods his head. Foxy, his enforcer, is a mean fucker who sits opposite, and I lift my chin in acknowledgment. As soon as the last brother enters the room, the gavel goes down. Rags rubs his beard, looking like he hasn't fucking slept. His body is even tenser than it was yesterday.

"First, thank you to the boys for coming up here." We all nod, and I lean back in my chair.

"We know you got something in the pipeline with the fuckin' Mendez'. Any news on that fucker Marco?" I get straight to the point.

He glances out the window, looking like he's a million fucking miles away. "Marco is fuckin' dead. Motherfucker was found with his throat slit in a hotel room, and no one seems to know anything or they're keeping it close to their fuckin' chest. Only a handful of people even know the bastard is dead. My guess is the originals in Italy are keeping it under wraps to keep everything ticking over. Got a few guys looking into it, but nothing back yet."

The originals are four of the most powerful families in Italy and controlled most of the families on this side of the pond. Nothing big happened without their say so. They were ruthless.

"You think something is brewing'?" Sketch asks, and Rags frowns.

"Don't fuckin' know. Nothing has gone bad with us, but we all know fuckin' gangbangers can't be trusted." Everyone agrees.

"We cut the motherfuckers off. No more usage of our fuckin' roads. We are not working' with Carlo," I growl. My eyes skipping over the rest of the brothers from the chapter.

Rags stares at me before sighing and nodding. "My deal was with Gino. With him being dead, we let it carry on out of fuckin' respect as he never brought trouble to our door, but I agree, we pull the plug on that shit." I frown at that. I thought that Rags would be more for smoothing things out, but the way he's talking, he wants their blood.

We both stare each other down. "Could Carlo be starting' a fuckin' war?"

He breaks our stare-off. "Carlo's not one for getting his hands dirty, too much of a fucking pussy. He gets others to do his fuckin' dirty work, so if he's in town, then there's a fucking reason. It's finding out what that motherfucker wants." He stands and starts pacing. Bolt is the same when things aren't adding up, and they fucking pace until they come at it from all different angles, ripping it apart before putting it back together again. He sits back down, dropping the gavel.

"You boys staying tonight?" I shake my head. Prez called this morning, wanting us to sort out some business in the next state over. Duke Mason skipped state from the state while still owing the club $20,000. Python, the best damn hacker around, has found the little fucking snake. Then we go up to New York and see what that motherfucker Carlo is up to.

Rags follows us all out. "See you soon, boy. Ride free."

I grin over my shoulder. "Always."

But I don't miss the way my fucking gut twists and the look in Rags' eyes like he suspects something. Nothing concrete, but I fucking see it. I hate doubting a brother, especially someone like Rags. He is a president, and one of the fucking greatest men I know. He is fucking family, so I ignore the fucking twisting in my gut.

I'm fucking pissed. We've been in this run-down motel for the last five days waiting for Duke. The floral wallpaper peeling off the fucking wall, blinds yellow from nicotine, bed sheets dirty with stains, and the carpet wore marks that you knew meant more than one fucking person met their end here.

Cage moves the curtains. "Eagle is landing."

Who the fuck uses lines like the fucking eagle is landing? The door begins to open, and Cas leans against the wall, so as soon as it opens enough, he grabs the fucker by the shirt. Duke squeals like a fucking girl, and his eyes widen as he takes the sight of us in.

"I-I-Ice, ma-man," he stutters as his fingers twitch, his pupils are wide, and a thin layer of sweat covers his greyish skin—he's fucking tweaking. Cas pushes him down in the chair.

"You left without even a goodbye," I snarl before landing my fist in his jaw, which breaks like it's fucking made of glass, and as blood spurts out, I'm sure there's a fucking tooth in the mix.

Not that the fucker needs them where he's going. I wipe his blood on his own shirt, not sure what I'll fucking catch. He mumbles something that no fucker can understand. Tears mixed with snot run down his face.

"Have some fuckin' dignity," I growl, kicking him.

"Awe fuck, man! Every fucking time," Storm growls, and we all take a step back from the piss running down Duke's leg. Rev starts mumbling.

"As we walk through the shadow of death." He recites the Psalms 23 fucking prayer. Pulling out his piece, lifting it, and by the time Duke realizes what's happening, there's a bullet between his eyes. He is low on the totem, nothing worth our trouble, and we did the fucker a favor taking him so quickly from his pitiful life. We had already ransacked the place and found the couple thousand he had stashed under the mattress. He was just a loose end. No one gets away without paying the debt they owe us. He's fucking lucky it was quick.

We slip out of the building. I guess it will take a few days for anyone to find him. We get on our bikes, and Sketch grins. "Let's go home, boys." Hell fucking yeah!

Sketch races in front of us before waving to pull fucking over. We are still miles from home and are staying another night out. Prez called this morning to say that Rags' boys had pulled fucking through and found out Carlo is leaving the country for Italy this evening. Rags' boys even had eyes on him arriving at the motherfucking airport.

Sketch grabs his phone, cursing as he holds it to his ear. His eyes widen as his body tenses.

"Was anyone hurt?" he asks down the line.

Those dark eyes find me, and I'm off my bike, jogging next to him.

"Shop window was fucking put through. Red is okay as she was in the back." I know my first thought should have been my sister's safety, but it's fucking Rae I'm thinking of. As if realizing, he hands me the phone. Rae is still speaking as I put the handset to my ear.

"Some of the brothers have come around. It was three kids, I saw them. I'm sorry you trus—"

I cut her off, "Kitten." There's a gasp down the line.

"Ice?" The way she whispers my name pulls at my balls.

"Anyone fuckin' hurt?" My ice fills my veins as my legs bounce, I wait for her to answer the question. I won't ask if she's hurt. I can't admit it.

"We're all okay. We were at the back." I let out a breath, kicking a stone.

"I'll see you when I get fuckin' back," I growl before hanging up. Times up, I'm coming for you.

RAE

It has been a whole week since Ice walked into the shop, gave me a kiss that left me gasping for air. Most of the club rode out, something to do with club business. Red says it takes the men away sometimes, but it's strictly need to know. This means only the brothers know, and not even Red gets that sort of information. She accepts it without question. I don't know if I could blindly accept their rules the way Red does.

They got back late last night, and she left mine around midnight to meet them. It took everything in me to wave her off and not follow and make sure they were all back and okay. I didn't know how to feel about the brothers hiding where they were going and what was going down. It reminded me too much of home. The secrets, lies, and deceit, and the illusion and false security they built in the world that surrounds them.

It makes me feel unsettled, but as much as it scares me, it doesn't make me want to run. I'm more worried that they could get hurt. I want to be there, making sure they all walk through that door.

After hearing his voice asking if everyone was okay, I needed to know if it was me he was asking about, but when Smithy turned up saying Prez told him to cover me until they were home, I knew it wasn't Ice.

It gave me time for my senses to come back and hide away from the intense feelings that he brought out in me. I couldn't regret that night, no matter how or which way I put it. I needed to box up my feelings and put my mask back on because I realized that Ice gave me something that no one else had before. Hope. Hope for a future and that is the most dangerous feeling of all.

That's the reason I'm standing in my kitchen surrounded by dirty dishes, covered in flour. When I had something on my mind, I cooked or baked. Red had found this out last Saturday night after the party. I didn't tell anyone what happened in that kitchen; that Ice had not only given me my first proper orgasm, but that he appeared in dreams, and had me waking up, gasping, and needy for his touch or that my body blushed every time I thought about it.

When she asked me to make a cake for the cookout the club was having, I was more than happy to help. Red failed to tell me until two days ago that it was Ice's birthday, and the cake is for him. She said they didn't usually have cakes as no one could bake, and there was no way they were visiting a bakery. Apparently, big bad bikers didn't do that.

A part of me couldn't help thinking of Red, the brothers, even Luther, never having a proper birthday cake. I know I am leaving soon, but maybe I can leave them with a special memory. That's why, instead of the chocolate cake I was planning on making, I am looking down on a huge Harley Davidson. The exact double of Ice's bike, including the Horsemen colors.

I make my way to the club, second-guessing myself the whole way. I decided on a short denim skirt and a red shirt. My hair is tied up with a red ribbon, and even though Red said it was casual, I couldn't help it, and I'm wearing a cute pair of red peep-toe heels. As I pull into the club grounds, it seems a lot busier today, and there are more children than I ever have seen here.

I see Sketch walking out of the main doors as I push open my car door. I jump out, putting my fingers in my mouth and whistling. This has him turning, a scowl in place until he spots me and grins.

"Hey, sweetheart. You miss me?" The bastard smirks, making me roll my eyes, but I did miss him. I couldn't believe he trusted me to run Branded. It meant a lot knowing he had that sort of faith in me. Some kids had smashed the window in, and before I knew it the shop was full of prospects that had the place cleaned and the window repaired. I had stayed late to catch up on the appointments and make sure all the glass was picked up.

I missed them all because it was kind of dull without them. I missed Cas' cocky comments, the back-and-forth banter between Flame and Cage, Storm brooding around the place, and Rev lurking in the shadows. Those beautiful eyes of his constantly watching us like an avenging angel.

"I need your help." Darkness crosses his face, and his whole body becomes tense. His eyes glance around the place, and when he looks back, I nod my head as I walk to the back of my car. His eyes widen, looking around even more as he sees me going to open the trunk. I press the button to open it, but he slams it shut, the darkness he hides covers each of his features.

"What's in there?" he growls, holding my arm as he searches my face.

"What the fuck, Sketch? It's a cake for the cookout, not a dead fucking body. Why are you acting so shifty?" His whole body seems to relax. He lifts his chin as I pop the trunk, still staring at it like something is going to jump out. Gasping as soon as he sees the cake, and his mouth opens and closes in shock.

"That's fuckin' ... where the hell did you get that?" I shrug, glancing away and knowing heat is touching my cheeks.

"I…umm, I bake, it's nothing." I wave my hand dismissively. His eyes widen as he looks between me and the cake.

"You made that?" I grab the trunk, going to close it. What the fuck was I thinking?

"Forget it, okay! It's too much. Red said you don't get cakes, like ever, and before I knew it that was staring back at me." I point to the offending cake. Sketch pulls me into a one arm hug.

"It's cool, Rae…You do that shit, it means something around here, okay?" I smile, leaning into him. We've become close over the last few months. He has taken on a protective big brother role, where some of the others such as Storm, Flame, Cas, Cage have become annoying brothers. They piss me off most days, popping into the shop just to mess with me, but you miss them when they're not there. Rev is different, though. He is always there in the shadows watching me, but not in a Freddie Kruger sort of way. It was more protective. Sometimes he'll come out of the shadows and might say a few words, but it isn't long before he disappears again.

"Shit, that's the cake?" I jump at Red's voice, who comes and stands next to us. I hadn't even heard her approach. She has the biggest smile on her face. Sketch reaches in, grabbing the cake before heading towards the grass area. I reach in to grab three of the other containers, and Red takes the other two.

"What's this?"

I shut the trunk while trying to balance the containers. "My mother's pulled pork." It was one of my favorite meals. It's pork, simmered until you can pull it apart.

"There's also some homemade bread rolls and some coleslaw and salad" I don't miss the way Red's eyes go glassy and her breath hitches. Has no one ever done anything nice for them? We walk over to the grass area. There are a few other men around a massive grill, and against the club wall runs a long table full of food. I follow Red, putting the food down. I can't help looking around and noticing how different the place is. Children run around, and their laughter fills the air. There are women around the men, but they seem different from the normal girls I've seen at the club. For one, they're dressed. There are also a lot of men's faces I haven't seen before. Red hands me a bottle of beer.

"I can see your mind trying to work it all out." She smirks.

"There are a lot more people," I reply as we walk through the sea of people and Red points to an older man with a cut on; it's got Nomad written on it.

"Nomad means you're still related to the club, just not in the everyday running of it, but they come around on big occasions." We walk over to where I see the guys are sitting. They all smile, bringing Red in for a hug and kissing her hair. I'm shocked when they all do the same to me, apart from kissing my hair, and I try to swish down the warm feeling that happens when they do. It's been a long time since I was a part of something that felt like family, and this is what the club is becoming to me. I hate that I let my guard drop enough to let them in, but part of me also needs to belong.

"Good trip?" I ask. They all narrow their eyes before lifting their chins but not saying anything. Red rolls her eyes, taking a seat on the bench. "Where's Flame?" You can normally hear him clicking his lighter. All the guys' shoulders fall.

"Gone back up to Rags' chapter, his mother is sick," Cage says, and I frown, but when a woman walks past with a man, Red smiles, waving, which surprises the shit out of me as she usually doesn't even bat an eye towards the club woman.

"That's Suki. She is Bear's, Ol' Lady." I elbow her, Suki is still in hearing shot.

"Shh, she can still hear you!" Insult a woman's clothes, hair, makeup, they get over that shit. Call them old, they plan your death in their heads and never forget!

There's complete silence before every one of them bursts out laughing, tears and fucking all. Cage smirks, slinging his arm over my shoulder.

"Ol' Lady Means that Suki is Bear's property. You make a bitch your property, stamp your ink on her, that shit, it's big around here."

I frown, watching Suki. Is she happy being someone's property? I know what it felt like to be a possession, a trophy they wanted to show off, and the power they hold over you.

Storm smirks. "Same look I had on my face when I heard it for the first time, but it's not a bad thing. When a brother lays claim to a bitch, he is responsible for her and her actions. She reflects him. Not just any bitch can handle a brother, the club, and this life." Red nods, and so does everyone else. She grabs my hand.

"It's a big deal to be claimed, and to have a brother declare she is his. To be given the property cut, it's like a marriage. It means no men can touch her. She is completely off-limits."

So, an Ol' Lady is different from a sweet butt, which explains Red's reaction. Cage sits next to me.

"It shows the club, and any other clubs, that she is taken. She is given respect, and no one messes with an Ol' Lady ever! No one messes with the Horsemen's property." All the guys' body language changes. Their eyes grow dark as they nod with Cage's words.

I could hear the passion in Cage's voice, see the truth shining bright in their eyes, and as the afternoon went on, I couldn't help watching the Ol' Ladies. There was a big difference between how the men treated them to how they handled the sweet butts.

The Ol' Ladies were treated with respect much in the way Red was. Every brother greeted them with a hug or a kiss on the cheek and smiled at them. The Ol' Ladies themselves seemed to be a club on their own, and they gravitated to each other, laughing and joking like best friends. They had the same obvious dislike of the sweet butts that Red did.

My throat tightened as I watched Bear and Suki, and the way he always kept her in his sights when she was near, pulling her to his side. It was like swallowing a razor when the realization hit me like a hard slap across the face.

Ice didn't see me in that way. Didn't want to lay claim to me or for me to wear his mark. He would never surprise me with his cut that told the world I was his. That I was enough.

I felt a shiver go down my spine, and my eyes scanned the space as though fingers trailed over my skin. I'm being watched.

I didn't freak out because I knew the man watching me was Ice. Don't ask me how, I just did.

He hadn't made himself known yet and had stayed away, but I shifted, feeling a little uncomfortable with the heated gaze I could feel directed at me. He is playing a cat and mouse game. Only he didn't know that I was bowing out of it.

Hands come around my waist, making me jump as their arms tighten and pinning me to their body. My breath comes out in harsh gasps as darkness fills my vision, and I'm sucked into nothingness...

"Hold her down." I shake my head. Why is he doing this to me? "Uncle?" He wasn't my real uncle; we weren't even blood. My mother had married his brother, and ever since I can remember, I've called him uncle as a sign of respect. He comes over to me, his steps slow and steady. There is a look in his eyes I don't understand, but it makes my stomach turn. He runs his hands down my hair as if trying to soothe me. Only it makes me want to pull away as they travel down my jaw, across my face to my lips. Why is he touching me this way? "Uncle?" I try again. Pain radiates up my cheekbone, my head whips to the side from the force of his hit. His strike sends waves of pain down my jaw and neck. His family ring slices my lip, causing it to split.

"You will no longer call me that! Your mother protected you,

but she is no longer here because of you." Pain wraps around my heart at the mention of my mama. It's still too fresh, too raw. The last of my strength disappears. I give up the fight because he's right; they died because I found out what he was planning and disobeyed. They paid the price. "I want you; I've wanted you for a long time." Bile rises in my throat. I try breathing deep, keeping my eyes on him. "Don't look at me like that, you know how beautiful you are." He pushes my hair behind my ears. "You call to men like a siren luring men in."

He runs a finger along my collarbone. I press my lips together tightly, keeping my body still and holding my breath.

"You gave yourself over like a whore, and now you will be punished." I don't know how long the beating goes on for. Every inch of me aches and metallic scents tickle my nostrils as inhuman sounds fall from my lips. I curl into myself as everything trembles, even my teeth chatter. My muscles clench, trying to make myself smaller as every bone vibrates with pain. His voice is hard to hear over the beating of my own heart. "My men will make sure you are ready for me." What does he mean ready? He can't mean what I think. I am fifteen. He picks up my blood-soaked hand and kisses it, and then I feel something cool slide onto my finger. I gasp when I see the diamond on the gold band. "In three years on your eighteenth birthday, we will marry... You will be mine, Arya."

"Rae! What's the matter with her?" I could hear my name being called, but it was like a tunnel, a vortex pulling me in deeper. Was that Red's voice? I cling to the sound, but it isn't enough. The darkness is all around me, clawing at my throat as a hand clenches around my heart, squeezing it. My chest contracts as I struggle to breathe. Pins and needles race through me. My body feels like it's on fire. Someone touches me, making me cringe, and I want to scream but I can't. I can't do anything. I am helpless. I'm safer in the darkness.

No, he's gone, I killed him.

Get out of my head! Please leave me alone.

"Come back. Don't let them fucking win!" I hear the deep, gruff voice reach out to me, as the darkness evaporates. Tears wet my cheeks, and my whole body vibrates from the shaking. My breathing slows down as a kaleidoscope of golds look back at me.

Rev nods as I grab on to him to keep me steady, grounding me once again. I feel the way his whole-body tenses, and the arm I'm touching visibly shakes under my touch. It's as if it's taking all his will not to move his arm, and my anchor, away from my contact. I stand slowly, glancing around at the different expressions on each face. I didn't want them to see this version; no one is ever meant to see her. Arya is meant to stay hidden away. Where is Rae?

Red grabs my arm, making me flinch and drops her hand as concern blazes in her eyes. She pushes some of the hair behind my ear, smiling.

"Are you okay? What happened?" The concern in her voice feels foreign when I hear it. Like a distance memory. When was the last time someone worried about me? Cared enough to be concerned? I smile the brilliant Rae smile and paint lies on my face for the world to see, the mask is firmly back in place.

"Nothing, I'm fine...We needed cups, right? The red ones?" My voice shakes, but I ignore it, focusing instead on Red, who nods slowly as if I've lost my mind. Maybe I have. I peer around at everyone before I force a smile.

Slowly, Red says, "Yeah, I'll come with you."

I didn't want her to. I needed time to get myself together and get Rae back in place. Rev must recognize it in me because he holds Red back slightly. Gently.

"Rae, all good?" Her eyes widen between the two of us, and I give a nod to let her know I'm fine. She nods back before taking a seat back on the bench. I give Rev a grateful smile.

ICE

Fuck my life! I watch from the shadows like a fucking creeper as Rae laughs at something Cas is saying. Her head kicked back, a smile gracing her face, but it's not a hundred percent genuine, something is up with her. I can sense it. Her body is tight, holding tension. I get closer, making sure I'm still hidden. She smiles at my sister and taking a seat on the bench, when her eyes go to the left. I look to see Bear and Suki. He's smiling down at her and holding her face. Rae frowns. Her shoulders seem to sag, and her lips pull down at the corner, I step forward before catching myself and taking a step back. I want to go over there and demand what the fuck is wrong so I can fix it for her, but that would be a mistake. I can't let her see what she makes me feel, it would sign her death warrant, place a mark on her head.

I watch as she gets up, those hips fucking swaying, and I take a quick glance around, noticing how I'm not the only fucker watching her. My brothers watch her like she's some magical fucking creature, causing my grip on my beer to tighten. I'm surprised it doesn't crack under the pressure.

Rae doesn't even know what the fuck she does to men. How she has this light about her that you can't help being drawn to like a lighthouse when you're lost at sea. And how it lights up the darkness inside of us like the moon in the midnight sky.

After she left me in the kitchen last week with the biggest case of fucking blue balls, I wanted to fucking strangle the bitch. But after I calmed down, I did something I haven't done in years; a real fucking smile broke across my fucking face.

Rae causes every emotion to come to the surface, to battle, and to win. The bad, the darkness, and even the fucking crack of light that she found in the deepest darkness of my fucking soul.

Every fucking mile we made on the way home; a fresh wave of anger came over me because she was all I fucking thought about. It left me all weak, with my dick in my hand as I remembered how fucking perfect those tits where. When I got back, I'd walked straight in grabbing Sadie, the nearest snatch, and I planned on taking her hard and fast and fucking that violet-eyed beauty out of my system. I could feel the recklessness starting to build, needing to be let loose. No bitch is worth this much fucking hassle, that's for sure.

Only, as soon as she touched me, it felt wrong. It was like Rae had already branded herself on me with a red-hot fucking poker. Sadie didn't smell of fucking vanilla and that elusive something that was just Rae. Her hands weren't fucking smooth, and it felt all fucking wrong. Rae was the first kiss I had given a woman, and when I kissed her, fuck, her taste exploded on my tongue. A sweetness that no fucking one should ever taste like; like she was my favorite piece of fucking candy. I lick my lips, just at the memory.

As thoughts of Rae, her taste, her sounds, invaded me, my dick turned to stone only for it to shrivel up when Sadie touched it as if the fucker were trying to get away.

I sent Sadie away with the excuse of club business and spent the night with my dick in my hand jerking off on the memory of Rae's touch, taste, the way her greedy cunt grabbed my fingers, and the wetness that covered her thighs.

It was because of me; all me because she is fucking mine.

The Mafia was becoming braver or fucking stupider. They weren't careful. With Marco dead and Carlo out of the country, something was still off. We were all on the chessboard of life, waiting to make a move. It was all a fucking waiting game. We didn't back down from anyone, and if death came, then we would meet the grim reaper and tell him to suck our dicks.

That's why I couldn't make a move on the only fucking bitch I'd ever wanted. The one I fucking wanted just as much as I hated her for making me want her.

All my life, I thought the club, the brothers, the open fucking road with my bitch between my legs was going to be enough. I wasn't rich, but we made enough that we lived the way we liked.

Then she walks in and turns it all on its fucking head. Made that piece of fucking meat in my chest start beating again. Ripped me apart until I was raw. She drove me crazier than I already was. My mind was at constant fucking war to take her as mine, to make her hate me and keep her far away.

"Okay, son?" My father looks at Rae before raising his eyebrow. I don't say anything. We were not the fucking sharing and caring kind of father and son that spilled our secrets over a beer. That died with me ten years ago. He nods when I don't say shit. "Smithy, what are you thinking?"

Getting back to the club business was a safer area to talk about. Smithy is a prospect, one that had been around about thirteen-months. He was good, had shown his loyalty.

"Yeah, he seems on the up."

My father rubs his jaw. "We'll call a vote in church on

Monday." He slaps my back walking off, and I watch him. He thinks we are going to war; he's preparing to bring in more hands, and he expects blood to be shed. Shit.

That's why I was going to fuck Rae then walk away. I might be a fucking bastard, as cold as my name, but I couldn't ask her to be a part of all this. Not when we were on the edge of war.

I turn back and realize Rae has gone. My stomach twists as I search the crowd for her, catching a glimpse of her as she walks into the clubhouse alone through the back. Something I've been waiting for all afternoon.

I follow her slowly, not to give myself away yet, watching as she walks into the kitchen. Perfect. Where it all started, and where I'll end it. Saving us both from the pain ahead.

When I push the door open, she has her back to me leaning her hands on the counter, her head hanging low. Being this close, the craziness in my mind somehow slows, the tension in my muscles falls away, but I can see the tension in her body, and I know one of two things could happen; she'd either fucking open her mouth and start spewing all kinds of shit or kick me in the balls. Either one was a strong fucking possibility with this bitch. Everything leaves my fucking mind as my eyes settle on her naked legs. Legs that seem to fucking go on and on, and legs that I've pictured all week around my waist as those fuck-me heels she always wears bite into my ass. My dick presses against my zipper, and I am fucking sure there's going to be a permanent imprint left there. She looks over her shoulder as if sensing me. Smirking like she knows what she's doing to me.

Memories of the way she tasted that night slam into me. Did she fucking know I'd never kissed any bitch? Is that why she is smiling?

"Did you tell anyone?" My jaw ticks, and my hands clench into fists as she raises her brow before turning fully around. She laughs, fucking laughs. But the laughter holds something underneath. It isn't carefree, it holds darkness. Her voice cracks as the laughter drains away.

"There's nothing to tell." Her chin tips out defensively.

Anger burns through me at how quickly she dismisses it, when I haven't been able to escape that night. Even fucking drunk, the thoughts of her find me. I take slow steps towards her.

"So, it wasn't you begging, *please*? Calling my name when you came over my fingers as your cunt squeezed me?"

Her breathing hitches, and the place at the bottom of her neck beats as wild as the wind as her chest rises and falls harshly. Those fucking eyes turn from navy to violet, and my lips lift into a smirk. Yeah, she can pretend all she wants, but the bitch is affected. Rae is fighting the same fucking battle I am, and she hates the power we have over each other.

My eyebrows draw in as a delicious smirk covers her lips. "Ahh, so you remember me? So, not so nameless?"

The fucking bitch! Did she fucking play me? Leave me with blue balls on purpose? Was that her plan from the beginning? I cover the distance between us in just two strides. My breathing is unsteady and harsh, and before she can blink, I bury my nose under her ear, taking in that smell that melts the coldness away. Kissing from her ear down her jaw to the corner of her mouth.

"Fucking bitch!" My lips crash down on hers, attacking her mouth, pushing my tongue in as she gasps, and I use my tongue to fuck her mouth, growling as her taste invades me. I lift her, those fucking legs I've dreamt of, automatically wrap around my waist. I push her up against the wall with a thud, and with her heels biting into my ass, just like I imagined, it sends desperation through me. Thanking every fucking god that she wore a skirt as I lift it, not breaking the kiss, instead I let it consume us both. I find her ass bare and growl in approval as I find the thin piece of lace. I break the kiss as my lungs scream for oxygen, both our breaths heavy and ragged. I look in her eyes as I pull the thin material, ripping it, and letting the fabric fall between us. A moan leaves her ripe lips. Lips that I swear could start a fucking war.

I run my fingers over her bare lips, finding her wet and ready. That's all I fucking need, and everything inside of me snaps. I undo my buttons, getting my dick free and enter her with a harsh thrust. Her eyes brighten to a vivid violet color, half-closed and filled with lust as I continue my punishing speed. As her cunt squeezes around me, her mouth opens on a silent scream. Fucking beautiful.

"Yes, make me forget." Her words and the way she said them, strikes something in me. Later I would fucking wish I had asked her, gotten all those secrets hidden in her eyes. But I'm too consumed with her to think about it. The way her cunt fits around me like a fucking slick glove, the sounds she's making, everything, was driving me wild.

I pull nearly all the way out before slamming back in, feeling my balls slap her bare ass. She's getting close with the way her greedy pussy wraps around my dick, squeezing it like a fucking vice, and the way her juices cover us. I feel the familiar tingles race up my spine, and my thighs shake as my balls draw up tight. I lean in and bite her shoulder, marking her.

As the most intense orgasm takes over my body, an animalistic growl escapes from me. My breathing is uncontrollable, and the aftershocks leave my legs weak. I pull out, hissing at the loss as I lower her. I'm unable to look her in the fucking eyes because the feeling of what we just did is different from anyone that came before her. I never want anyone else. It's like her cunt is crack, and now I'm fucking addicted.

I want her again, already, even with my dick still covered in our juices. Like someone just fired bullets at my chest, it hits me. All of it fucking hits me.

I know without a fucking doubt she's mine. There is no fucking war because it's already been won. I risk looking at her, her breathing is still heavy, lips swollen, but those dam violets are narrowed. They are darker than they were a minute ago; she's pissed. She tries to push me, but I don't move a fucking inch.

"Really!" she hisses, and my dick twitches as her hellcat comes out. My lips pull up on the side, making her eyes narrow even more.

"Payback's a fucking bitch!" Her mouth falls open and words pour out. Is she cursing at me in fucking Italian? She looks me dead in the eyes glaring at me.

"You're a fucking bastard."

I pull my cigarettes out of my jeans, bending my head to light one and shrugging as I study her. To keep from reaching for her again.

"Never claimed to be different, Kitten." Fuck! I was back to calling her Kitten. I know she doesn't miss it when her eyes widen and look at me as if she is trying to work some shit out, but she quickly shakes her head, pulling down her skirt.

"Now am I free to be passed on for the next brother to have a go?" Her words break something free inside of me. A possessiveness that I never knew was part of me screams through my veins and anger roars in my head. Did she think I would let another man touch that sweet body? Experience what her cunt feels like as they sink into her, and taste those fucking lips? I would rip any fucker apart that even thinks that shit. She isn't club ass; she never would be.

I was a bastard for even saying it, but I knew this was how to keep her away from me and at arm's length. I keep my mouth shut from saying that she is fucking mine, and that I would destroy any fucker who dared to touch her. That I would protect her from anything… including her greatest ruin; me.

Instead, I shrug, and something passes through those damn violets, but she blinks it away too quickly for me to read. Walking past, her spine straight, her little chin poking out, she stops suddenly, turning on those fucking heels.

"Thanks for asking. I am on the pill! You asshole." My eyes widen as her words register, just as the door slams shut. Never, I mean never, have I not covered my fucking cock. It doesn't matter how pissed or how fucking high I've been, that shit is always covered. The fact I didn't put one on shows how much Kitten fucks with my mind, and how totally screwed up I am around her.

The door opens, and Red walks in. Halting my steps and stopping me from going after Rae, which is a good thing because I didn't even know what the fuck I was going to say. Sorry for chucking my muck up you when I really wasn't?

The thought of her with a ripe belly and my kid growing inside her did something strange to me. The chunk of meat that people called their heart, pounded in my chest as it beat wildly. The unaccustomed feeling stirring my gut.

Red looks around the kitchen and frowns as she leans on the counter opposite me.

"Have you seen Rae? She came in for cups, but she hasn't come back." I shake my head. I had one of the best poker faces.

"She was around a while ago." She narrows her eyes trying to read me, and her shoulders fall like she knew Rae wouldn't be here. Grabbing her phone out of her pocket, she types out a quick text before putting her phone back away, and I'm guessing she is messaging Kitten as she is her only real friend.

"Oh! I nearly forgot something in the garden." I groan. I don't want to go out there and make small talk. Fuck! What I need is a fucking ride to clear my head of that violet-eyed beauty. She looks up at me with that fucking look in her eyes that she knows I can't refuse.

"Come on, brat!"

I follow her into the garden, with my thoughts still stuck on Kitten. She completely knocks me off kilter. The brothers love her, and I've seen all the guys letting her into the circle, hanging on her every fucking word. Fuck, I even caught Rev watching her from the fucking shadows like her own bodyguard. The fact that he is watching her is a first, making everyone else more intrigued. Sketch has taken on a protective big brother role, and their relationship is tight with her working in his shop and the business she brings in. Fuck, any of those fuckers would make her theirs.

They weren't the VP. She wouldn't be as big of a fucking target with them. The thought makes me murderous. I already had the blood of one innocent on my hands, if something happened to Rae, I know I would drown in her bloodshed.

I could own her body, give her pleasure for the rest of her life. I could even keep my dick for only her, but I'd still walk away after it. I wouldn't play fucking house or pretend it was more because it couldn't be more. This war with the could go on for years, and even after that, there will always be another enemy or another war. It came with this life; tomorrow was never promised. My own recklessness and craziness stood between us. Something deep inside me told me she is the last of my humanity. If I lost her, I'd lose any remnant of the man left inside me, and the darkness would win at last. It would finally claim me fully. Leaving behind the monster to escape and thrive.

I look up to see everyone gathered around with shit-eating grins on their faces. What are these fuckers finding so funny? It's like a grandmother's fucking meeting. Red is standing in front with the biggest smile, her eyes shining as she moves, and my eyes land on the biggest, badass cake I have ever seen. It's my fucking bitch, Horsemen colors, and all. What sets it off is the black background and the red and yellow flames.

We were celebrating my thirtieth birthday like we did every other birthday, with a cookout for everyone, and then the brothers would party through the night. We love an excuse for a party, and we partied as we live; hard. Birthdays are fucking big in the club. You had survived another year. Beaten the reaper just that little bit longer. This cake meant shit around here. The last cake any of us had was from my mother, who had died when I was nine. I grab Red, bringing her in for a bone-crushing hug, and kissing her hair as I whisper, "Thank you."

She shakes her head, pulling back so she can look up at me.

"It wasn't me …I knew Rae baked and was expecting a chocolate cake, but today she rocked up with this."

My mouth falls open, and I turn to my brothers who all nod, confirming she is telling the truth. Sketch lifts his chin.

"Ain't bullshitting, brother. I was here when she arrived with this fucker in the trunk. I even carried it for her... The girl did good, really fucking good." His eyes narrow, never leaving mine.

I nod, looking at the cake. Kitten had done this for me, and no matter how much of an asshole I was, she still came through for me. For fucking me.

I look around for her face as Cage walks over. "She left." He raises his brow, tone tense. I knew he liked her, but it better not be any fucking more than he likes Red. "She was as pissed as a baptized cat." His eyes search mine looking for an answer, but I just shrug.

"Most probably on the fucking rag." He frowns. He knows I'm lying, but there's a pecking order, and Cage knows better than to call out his VP with everyone around.

RAE

I was pissed. Fucking fuming! Ice had left me wanting and needy. My body was strung so tight I was having trouble walking. The bastard was smirking that smirk, and I wanted to slap it off his face.

I couldn't stay around and watch as he moved on, chucking me away like yesterday's trash. Like I knew he would.

The truth was, I had no one to blame but myself. I let Ice use me. I let him fuck me in that kitchen and use me as his own personal whore because I had used him too. I needed him, I needed to feel just one last time.

For once, I'd let the walls down and took something just for me.

Ice had made it clear that he only wanted to fuck me and nothing else. He didn't mind sharing because I was no one special to him.

As much as I hated to admit it, I had opened myself up to Ice. I listened to Champ's words, and I thought I could scale his walls.

tear them down. I could burn with him in the heat he held in his eyes. Together we could burn the darkness away. I saw the manic side and how it calmed around me, and the finger tapping stopped when I was near. I'd seen his demon's retreat. He was an enigma. I thought he felt the same. I thought he saw me the same way I saw him. I thought it was real.

I got swept away in Red's beliefs about how the men loved each other. Thinking he could maybe give me a small part of the love I saw him hold for his brothers and the club. I got swept away believing I was accepted into a world I didn't know existed but somehow I needed. The only place that had truly felt like home, like I belonged.

I was angry with men that held respect for me, would now see me as free pussy, club snatch, and just Ice's discarded plaything.

Walking into the bathroom, I turn the shower on before stripping out of my clothes. The reflection from the mirror catches my eye, and I study the girl looking back at me with her cheeks still flushed, lips swollen, hair a mess, looking like she's been up to sinful things. But it's those vivid violets staring back at me that makes me take a step closer. They have never been so bright.

I shower, letting the water wash away the tears I wouldn't let fall. Once I'm finished, I leave my hair wet as I start to gather my stuff, placing it in bags. It's time to go.

There is a sharp knock on my front door, I don't want company, and I assume it is Red as she messaged me. And she's the only one who would bother to check on me but standing on the other side is the last person I expect.

"Ice."

When he looks up, something is different in his eyes. "I am an asshole. It's not fuckin' news. I'm a bastard."

I lean against the door wondering why he is here. He looks at me for a beat, rubbing his jaw before nodding. Standing up straight, he places his arm above my head, leaning his face towards mine.

"Ain't going to apologize for that shit at the club, 'cause, Kitten, that was going to happen and there's nothing we could do to stop it." I snort, yes, fucking snort. Crossing my arms over my chest.

"We're not fucking teenagers. We can control ourselves." His lips twitch as he shakes his head. My body heats at the memory of being pressed against the wall as that heated look passes through his eyes, and it's still a shock to see how the color can turn from ice to heat within seconds. "Look, I don't want things to be awkward, I work in your shop, so can we just be civil?" If Ice agrees, I won't have to leave straight away. At the shake of his head, my stomach drops. Thinking about leaving the shop, Red and the guys. It might just break me.

"Can't, Kitten."

Before I can think, my hand connects with his cheek. The sound echoing around us. I can't believe I let him in, fell for his games. How dare he treat me like a fucking whore! It wasn't just his face I saw; it was all of them. His eyes pin me as he grabs my wrists holding them above my head, in just one of his. The other hand grabs my jaw, forcing my face towards his. I wait for the punishment, the harsh words, the violence. Before I can say anything his lips land on mine, silencing me. They're not demanding like all the times before. This time is almost a question, like he's unsure. He breaks the kiss before licking my lips, releasing my wrists as he grabs my hips and brings our bodies closer.

"Don't kiss, Kitten, never fucking have...love your taste."

My heart starts beating as wildly as the wind. Is he telling me that I'm different? I try to squash the flicker of hope because hope only brings hurt and pain. I know how dangerous that emotion is. His big hand engulfs my face, and I can feel the coolness of his rings, showing me how hot my skin is.

"Need you, Kitten." I nod, unable to speak. I'm not even sure of the words for what is happening, but something is changing between us. The chaos between us evaporates.

He grabs my ass, leaving my only option to put my legs around his narrow waist, holding on to his shoulders. He looks up at me.

"Don't cuddle or sleepover, ain't never going to brin' you flowers or do any romantic shit. I'm a fuckin' selfish bastard, and I should walk away…But I can't."

I understand what he means. How that pull is between us. He stops any train of thought as he steals my breath in the slowest, most sensual kiss I've ever had, making my toes curl as I moan into his mouth. His words come back to me; I'm the only one he's kissed. I've been given something from him no one else ever has.

I land on the bed with a bounce as he crawls on top of me, but it is not rushed like every other time. It's predatory. You can see every muscle bunch underneath his shirt.

I sit up and rip it over his head, taking in his chest and stomach, and holy mother of God! Ice is sexy with clothes, but without, he's complete sin. Chiseled chest and with the ink and scars mixed it is almost too much. Holy shit, he has his nipples pierced and a full rippling six-pack. My breathing picks up as I try rubbing my legs together. His whole body covers mine, dipping his head, licking my lips, he really does like my lips, before he claims them. Lifting my hands to his face, I place them either side, and as I take the kiss to the next level, he has no other choice than to accept what I am giving him. I slow the kiss down, breaking it by biting his lip, dragging it through my teeth. I watch his reaction, and the way his eyes widen like he's surprised before the color darkens right in front of me. His nostrils flare as he rips open my towel, leaving me utterly bare to him. I instantly try to cover myself, but he grabs my wrist in one hand, pinning it to the bed above my head. His other hand runs up and down my rib cage.

"All fuckin' pale skin with pink fuckin' nipples... begging for my touch." His finger circles my puckered nipple, moving across my chest to the next one, but he doesn't lift his eyes. Then he starts running his fingers over every tattoo as if he knows the pain behind them. "Fuckin' beautiful."

I've been told I'm beautiful before, but never have I believed those words. But the way Ice takes me in, the way his touch makes my body heat, and my back bow as the wildfire from his words spreads through my veins.

"Please." He raises his eyes, and the stark difference makes me slightly gasp. They are bright as if the darkness that lived behind them has disappeared. My own needs are forgotten as I lean up, planting soft kisses across his chest, up to his neck, to his lips, licking them the same way he did mine. Then I kiss him as if this is my first and last kiss. He pulls away, looking at me as he rubs his finger over my swollen lips, his eyebrows pull into a scowl and darkness flashes across his face.

"Do you know how many of the brothers want you? How many times I caught them watchin' you and know what they're thinking." I watch the approaching storm in his eyes. It's like standing at the beach, watching it approach on the horizon.

I kiss his lips softly and whisper, "I'm here, with you."

He grunts, letting my hands go, and I miss his body as soon as he moves to stand. I frown, wondering where he is going, but then he smirks before taking off his jeans, no boxers. His dick stands proud, and the light just catches his Jacob's ladder. I lick my lips as my mouth dries, and his smirk turns devious as he picks up one of my shoes I had chucked on the bed.

"Fuckin' love these." He smirks before chucking it to the floor. He trails his finger along the arch of my foot, bringing it to his mouth. His tongue comes out, licking my ankle before slightly nipping and causing me to gasp. A smirk pulls at his lips, but it's not that cocky one he usually wears, no, this time it's playful and more boyish. He does the same to the other foot before kissing, licking, and nipping his way up my leg. And each touch of his lips, lick of his tongue, pain from his teeth, sends my body higher.

I hear him inhale, and I look down with wide eyes when I see him staring at my most intimate parts, and I try to close my legs as he shakes his head.

"Don't ever hide this pretty pink cunt from me." He scents me again, making my cheeks heat. It's so dark and forbidden, but my stomach twists in pleasure.

"Fuck, no bitch should smell this good," he growls before parting my lips with his two fingers as he drags another finger through my wetness. "So, fuckin' wet. All for me, Kitten?"

I don't answer, but I feel my cheeks blush even darker when I feel a sharp slap to my thigh, making me yelp,

"Answer me." I nod, unable to answer. He looks at me, studying me, trying to work out if I'm telling the truth. Can he honestly not see what he does to me? How my body reacts when he's around. After a beat, he nods, leaning in and taking his first lick.

"What are you doing?" His eyes rise to mine from in between my legs.

He smiles before taking another lick, making my back bow off the bed. I heard the girls talk about this when their boyfriends had done it to them, but never did I think for a moment this is how it felt. He devours me. The sounds of the wetness sends me spiraling to a place only Ice can take me.

"Let go, Kitten, I want to taste you." As if my body hears his words, I break apart, and the whole time Ice doesn't let go of my hip or let up as he licks me clean. His face glistens with my need, and it's the sexiest thing I've ever seen. Leaning over, he captures my mouth, kissing me.

The taste of me on his tongue causes another moan. Breaking the kiss, he reaches for his cock, stroking it in long, hard, slow strokes. I bite my lip as I continue to watch him pleasuring himself.

"As much as I want those fuckin' lips tight around my cock, hitting the back of your throat, I want your cunt more...Yeah?"

Crudeness isn't something I considered a turn-on before, but coming from him, all the dirty words make goosebumps cover my skin.

"Yeah, darlin'." His eyes widen at the name, and his throat moves as he swallows hard. He doesn't say anything, lowering himself over me so our naked skin meets, and I can't help running my nails over his back. The feel of his skin, just like him, is a complete contradiction; his skin is as smooth as silk, yet the muscles are hard underneath and feel like steel. I feel him at my entrance, but instead of entering me like I was expecting, he rubs himself against my clit. It is an agonizingly slow torture that has me moving my body and trying to capture him and push him where I need him.

"Please." His head lifts at my plea, and I'm starting to think he loves torturing my body and making me beg, when a smile, not a smirk, covers his face. Hot fucking shit. He has dimples! Kill me now!

He enters me slowly, inch by glorious inch, making my back arch off the bed, and my eyes flutter closed. A loud smack stings my thigh, causing my pleasure to climb.

"Give me those violets."

I open my eyes, trying to focus on his face. He starts moving slowly, so slowly, pulling out almost all the way before entering just as slowly and dipping his head towards me.

"Want your taste." I lean up, giving him my mouth as soft moans leave me.

"Harder." His eyes look directly at me as if he is looking into my very center.

"Not this time, Kitten. I want to feel you, yeah?" How can anyone argue with that?

"Yeah, darlin'."

I wasn't under the illusion this was making love. Men like Ice didn't make love because they lived how they fucked; hard. But with our eyes never leaving each other and our hands touching, the rest of the world faded. We were in a perfect bubble where our lives and our past did not define us, and futures didn't matter.

My orgasm hits me out of nowhere, sending my body arching as I scream his name. Darkness claims my vision as the orgasm shatters my body, and in the distance, I hear Ice growl my name.

I open my eyes feeling hardness under my cheek, and I look up to see Ice looking down on me with that same look I saw earlier. The lightness in his eyes, and a smile on his lips.

"Thought I lost you for a second." His fingers run-up and down my back and heat touch my cheek, but I can't help the goofy grin breaking out.

"I think you broke me."

His whole body starts to shake, and I see him holding in a laugh. I realize he is absently playing with my hair between his fingers, and I swoon. Yes, fucking swoon as I let out a soft sigh and snuggle into his side. His body is tense, every muscle bunched, and I glance up and see a strange look appear on his face as his brows pull in and his lips thin—his words from earlier hit like bullets. I lean my head on my hands that are over his chest, plastering on a fake smile.

"Won't they be missing you? It's your party." He lets out a deep breath, and I am not sure he realized he was holding it. He nods before getting up, and I do the same, suddenly feeling vulnerable without clothes. We steal glances at each other, but dress in complete silence, and I walk him to the door. He stops at the door, hesitating, but I know he's not going to feed me full of false promises, it's not his style. I don't want to make him awkward or taint the moment, so instead, I slap his ass, one that you could bounce a quarter off. "Get out of here before they send a search party." He hesitates a bit longer before he starts to walk away without a word. When Ice reaches the top of the steps he stops, turning and making my heart start to beat.

"You made me a cake?" I nod, unsure where this is going but knowing Red has obviously told him it was me, and he nods, looking away before his eyes return to me. "That shit? Nobody ever does that." He gives me another one of those rare smiles. Before I can say anything else, he jogs down the steps. I make a secret promise to make him all the cake he can eat.

I learnt long ago that a phone ringing before the sun was up, never brought good news. The phone ringing continually is even worse. When I answer, all I can hear is the hiccups and sobs coming from Red, and my thoughts run wild as the most sense I get from her is that she is at the clubhouse.

Tears burn my eyes, and there's a lump in my throat as panic grips me and I put my foot down on the gas, breaking every road law there is. I can't imagine anything getting to Red. This kind of distress the men would never allow. Which leaves one thing that's out of their hands. Death. A Horsemen's death.

The concern it might be Ice has my tires peeling as I enter the Horsemen's compound. I don't care as I jump out, not even remembering if I turned the car off as I run for the entrance. When the door opens and he walks out of the shadows, my breath catches at the sight of him, and not caring or thinking, I fling myself at him. He catches me with an 'oof' as I wrap my legs around him and bury my head in his neck. After a beat, his arms come around me before he rubs my back absently.

I feel silly when I realize he's okay. I slide down and look up at him, but his face is a mask of coldness. This isn't the man in my bed yesterday. This is the Red Horsemen's VP. He's shut down. His demons are battling for dominance. I watch as his fingers tap the chain hanging from his belt at a speed I've never seen before.

"Red rang," I say, to explain why I was trying to climb him like a damn tree. He lifts his chin but doesn't look at me, instead looking across the compound. He grinds his teeth so hard I can hear them, and his hands clench into fists. I don't know what makes me grab his hand and rub my thumb over his knuckles, but as soon as I do, he looks down at our hands before looking at me.

"Shit's bad, Kitten." I look him over to make sure he's okay; did I miss something? When his thick finger pulls my chin up.

"Ain't me. Champ got killed last night." The darkness in his eyes terrifies me, and my breath hitches, taking a step back.

Champ was like a father to the guys, and I spoke to him every time I was here. We only sat in the shop a few days ago, joking about. I still see the way his shoulders vibrated with the gruff laugh that escaped his lips.

He even had his own seat at the bar. Cage had explained that Champ turned up a few months after the Horsemen were first founded. Turned up at a party one night and never left. He never talked about his family or his past life, and I can't help the sadness that takes over. Tears fill my eyes, threatening to overflow. What about his funeral? Will people care?

"He had no family, but what about a funeral?" As soon as the words leave, I know I've made a mistake. Ice's face turns harder, shifts like granite and his eyes arctic cut through me like a sharp shard of Ice.

"What the fuck you talkin' about? He had family; the Horsemen are his family! He was my fuckin' brother…He will have the best funeral we can give him," he sneers, shaking his head, looking at me full of disgust and disbelief. "Just go, you don't belong here." He sneers.

I nod, feeling stupid because they had shown me how much

they meant to each other. It was taking me time to get used to it, for it to sink in. Red was right, death wasn't even strong enough for these men. And though it had taken their brother, their friend, it couldn't take their memory.

It couldn't take Champ's legacy. Champ's memory would live on and be told around campfires in stories passed on to those who get to wear the cut and are brought into the brotherhood.

I could see the pain flash briefly in Ice's eyes as he tried to mask the effect of Champ's death. I understood that pain. I place a soft hand on his arm, making him flinch, but I take a step closer.

"I'm sorry, Please, is there anything I can do?" He watches me unsure as he rubs his jaw. "I know I don't belong here ...but I liked Champ. Please let me help."

His brow pulls in even more, and I am worried I've said something wrong again, when he nods.

"The clubhouse. There will be a lot more brothers coming in the next few days from other chapters and friendly clubs, and they'll need somewhere to sleep, and we need supplies too. Anythin' you can help with. Just ask Red, she'll know." I nod making a mental list of all Ice has told me, and he walks off without another glance. I know he's off to do something dangerous, I can't leave it at that.

"Ice." He looks over his shoulder, and I let out a deep breath. "Take care...Yeah?" His scowl comes back before he walks to his bike, and I watch as he throws his thick leg over before starting it. The roar of the pipes vibrates through me. He has his head down, then he looks up, and something in his eyes makes me run towards him, not caring how I look. As soon as I am in reach, he grabs me, kissing me until my body begs for oxygen. He leans back with a lift of his chin. As he pulls off, the ground vibrates, and the roar of pipes fills the air. I still hear my heart as it whispers, he's the one.

Then I realize I did the one thing I swore I would never do.

I broke my own rules.

I stayed here longer than in any other place.
I made friends and cared about the Horsemen.
I fell in love with Ice.

ICE

As soon as I walk in the clubhouse, the brothers are on my ass like they are flies on shit, talking about the bedrooms, the upstairs games room, and how clean the main hall is. I swear they turn into bitches more each day. After a day like today, the last thing I need is a bunch of men acting like teenage girls. So, I ignore each of the fuckers. I also can't get Kitten out of my head. Last night changed something between us. I wanted to stay. Like a dumb fucker, I had stayed outside on my bike for an hour trying to convince myself why I shouldn't break my own rules. Why I didn't chain her to my fucking side and never let her go. Before I ran back up those steps to retake her and claim her as fucking mine, I got on my bike and peeled out of there like the devil himself was on my tail, driving for hours. That's until my phone rang, and everything went to fucking shit. I should have been there. Not wrapped up in Rae, who fucked with my head.

Nothing could stop my foul mood this morning. Losing a

brother? That shit never got easier. The pain was sharper than a knife to the gut, and each one of us would take on Rev and his blades in the meat shed to bring that old fucker back. The mood in the club was fucking bad, at an all-time low. Red was trying to be brave, but her swollen fucking eyes and tear-stricken face was too much. I needed to escape it; I needed to get the fuck away.

When I opened the door this morning, I didn't see her running towards me. Rae took me back a step as she landed against my chest before climbing me like a damn fucking monkey and burying her head in my neck. Her smell surrounded me, bringing me back from the darkness, and letting my demons sink back down for a time as I nuzzled into her throat. Drawing her scent into my body and pulling me from the chaos.

When she let go, I wanted to pull her close, but the look in her eyes when she explained Red had called her stopped me. She was worried about me. It was there in the way her eyes took me in. Fuck, I was a total bastard who was going straight to hell. I was letting this woman care for me, and her words confirmed it when she asked me to be safe. No one apart from Red worried about my ass returning home. I should have driven the fuck away, but I couldn't.

I needed to taste her. Fuck! Just how much I needed her was like a gun butt to the head, and it hit me how much I cared about this bitch.

Instead of punching the guys, who were acting like the dumbest fuckers I've ever met, I take my ass upstairs to see what got them so excited.

I reach my door, hoping to get five minutes peace to escape the noise in my head and the racing thoughts that are fucking draining me. I've been gone over eight fucking hours trying to find out everything that went on last night. How my father did this shit for so long, I don't fucking know.

I push the door open and realize immediately that something

is very wrong. All my shit is in the same place, but it feels different, so fucking different. I walk back to the door, checking the plate that says VP.

Turning back to my room, I notice what's different. The floor is fucking gleaming, no rubbish or clothes, the bed has been changed and made, the small desk has been polished, the window washed, and the smell has gone. What the fuck is happening?

I pop my head in the bathroom, and it shimmers the same way my room is, even the toilet. I can see through the shower screen, and the towels are folded. I never gave a shit about my room at the clubhouse. It was only used for two things: sleeping or fucking. I had my own house, twenty minutes away, which I kept the way I want. But fuck, whoever did this deserves a medal.

I make my way downstairs to the games room, which is usually trashed. We used it for private parties, poker nights, and for fucking if you couldn't be bothered to make it to your room.

I stop dead as I push through the door, my eyes must be comical in size because I'm sure as shit that the room wasn't like this when I left. The floor has been cleaned, there's no trash around the place, no empty beer bottles or discarded food. Instead, there are sleeping bags laid out, all with pillows. What the hell is going on?

All the brothers are gathered around the bar, and I turn, taking in the room to see the floor is spotless, not a mark on it. All the tables and chairs are placed tidily and have been cleaned, even the sofa has been moved, opening the place up, and the frames of brothers' past and present are all gleaming and hung correctly. The flags hung proudly on the wall behind the bar now look like they've been ironed.

I turn in a daze to the bar, and notice how shiny the wood looks, how the bottles are lined up neatly, and have no dust, and even Smithy's shirt looks like it's been ironed too.

I grab the beer he puts down, taking a big swig. "Okay, what the fuck is going on?" Sketch slaps my shoulder, is the fucker grinning? I've seen nothing but that lopsided smirk on his face in years.

"Trust me, brother, you wouldn't believe us if we told you." I raise a brow when the rest of them just nod, but Cage nods towards the kitchen.

"Answers are in there, bro," Cage says.

I put my beer down, heading towards the kitchen. I push the door open and suck in a breath at the sight. Kitten is stirring a big pot of something that smells fucking amazing. Her hair is pinned-up, showing off her slender neck, and she laughs, turning her face slightly, and I see a smudge of something on her face. Fuck, she looks beautiful. Ah fuck, this woman has captured me.

A deep laugh makes my head whip to the side, and that's when I spot Cas, who's leaning casually against the counter smiling at her. Rage flares in my belly, and my veins turn to ice as I take in the scene. My lips peel up into a snarl as I roar at Cas, "Out now!"

Rae jumps at my voice, turning to face me. Her eyes crawl over my face as she wipes her hand on a towel before starting to undo her apron. That's when I realize Rae thinks I am talking to her.

"Not you, Kitten." Those fucking eyes of her soften and turn a vivid violet color.

I'm starting to notice that when she is mad, they are slightly darker in color, but the violet still shines through. When she is happy, they glow brighter, but when she is with me, they turn entirely violet. That's my favorite color.

Cas looks at me like I just kicked his fucking puppy.

"But the chili is nearly ready." He pouts, making Kitten grin.

"As soon as it's done, I promise you'll get the first bowl."

He smirks at her, then walks past me with a look so smug I want to punch him in the gut. I elbow the fucker hard as Kitten looks away, smiling when he grunts in pain.

Slowly, I close the distance between us, wrapping my arms

around her waist, and I bury my head in her neck, taking a deep inhale, scenting her. This is starting to be one of my favorite places.

"You're cooking for us?"

She bites that damn lip, nodding. "You've been out all day and Red is upset, so I sent her to your dads to rest. I finished everything else you asked, so I started on the food." She rushes through it as if trying to explain. She's joking, right, and going to burst out fucking laughing at any second? When she doesn't, I spin her around, so she is facing me.

"Let me get this right, Kitten. It was you who cleaned those rooms, put out the sleeping bags and those extra blankets, scrubbed the fuckin' floors out there, and now you're in here fuckin' cooking for our asses?"

She nods, looking unsure. It's something you don't see a lot, and only when the mask she seems to wear falls slightly. I'm starting to think it's only around me.

"Red explained that you need to show a good appearance when the other clubs turn up, and you gave me the list and said it would help. I wanted to help."

Fuck, was this bitch even fucking real? She must have slaved all day.

"Damn, girl. I didn't mean do all the things on your own. I meant fuckin' pick one."

She shrugs. "You were busy, and I didn't want to let the brothers down. They all accepted me, besides I liked Champ too." Her bottom lip trembles, eyes turning almost navy. That's a new color. I realize I don't like this color at all.

"I'm sorry. I didn't mean to make you mad."

I grab her face, leaning my forehead against hers. "I ain't mad. Shocked as shit, yeah. Surprised as fuck, but not mad...there's only one other woman who ever done shit like this for the club, for the brothers." I swallow past the lump in my throat. "My mother, you hear that. She was the queen of this place. Seeing you making chili..." My words drop away. She bites that damn lip again, and my cock throbs.

"I made fresh bread too." I can't stop my mouth from quirking up at the corners into an almost smile.

"That blows my mind. You fuckin' blow my mind." I kiss her slowly, but when a buzzing sound goes off, she pulls away too quickly.

"Get everyone ready, it's done now." Like a fucking bitch, I listen.

ICE

I walk into the main room and survey all the brothers, most looking down at the table, the somber mood so thick you cut it.

"Rae is bringing food out. Anyone not sitting, get your ass down," My voice booms. Cas practically runs to the table, and the rest of the brothers stand still, watching as Rae walks out pushing a giant trolley. Walking straight over to Cas like she promised, she gives him the first bowl and two bread rolls. The brothers watch wide eyed.

When no one moves, I bark out, "If you want to be fed, sit the fuck down."

Every brother runs for a chair like they've never been fed.

My eyes don't leave Rae as I watch, what is she? She ain't my woman but it's changed between us. She hands out bowls and bread, smiling sweetly. Rae glances up from serving and catches my eyes. I give her a look that I hope tells her how fucking happy this shit makes me. She smiles and winks, and my cock twitches again. I feel my chest widen, with fucking pride. Proud she's mine?

We all stop eating when we see her heading to my father's office. She knocks before entering with a bowl and bread. A few minutes later, she walks out, still smiling.

Storm rubs his stomach. "Fuck, man, that's one hell of a good chili."

Cage and Cas agree. "Fuck, yeah."

Sketch turns to me. "Every brother in here sees her." Anger and something else nips at my heels as my hands clench, ready to lay him out.

I lean over the table. "Want to fuckin' explain." Any calm I'd felt with a good fucking meal in my gut turns sour at his words.

He crosses his arms tight across his chest just as Rev grunts, and Cas raises his bottle of beer before taking a deep pull. It hasn't gone unnoticed how much more he's drinking, and how that smirk and cocky attitude is disappearing under a wave of anger.

"She's fuckin' rare," Sketch says, and all the brothers around the table nod as Sketch leans in. "Don't know what the fuck is happening between you two, but she deserves good in her life, man."

I narrow my eyes. He, of all people, should be keeping his mouth shut. He still feels the pain of his bitch leaving when she couldn't handle it—a fucking preacher's daughter.

"Me and Rae ain't none of your fuckin' business. What? Did you all grow fuckin' pussies overnight?"

Cage shakes his head. "You don't get it." He opens his arms wide. "Look around you; today she kicked ass. Losing a brother, that shit touches us more than anythin', and she went out of her fucking way to help US!"

They all fucking agree when Cas chirps in, "She doesn't even truly belong. Rae is what legends are made of. What every brother dreams of capturing."

I know what they are saying. Kitten would be a good Ol' Lady.

She will make her man proud. Has sass that means she can hold her own, but she has a pure heart beneath that. Today, she proved that she would go out of her way, not just for the brother that claimed her, but the whole club. A woman like her is the perfect mix of fierce and pure and is hard to come by in this world. The fact she is all sexy and sinful is a bonus.

"Ain't disagreeing with you. You think I don't see all the fuckin' shit you all do! That life ain't for me."

Sketch sighs, and Storm raises a brow.

"I'm telling you, that girl, she is fucking strong. She can take you on, brother, we all see that alright." I shake my head. Yeah, she had a strong shell, but undeath she was soft and pure, something she hadn't shown the guys.

Rev puts his bottle down hard, the glass slamming against the table. "Then you need to be prepared to lose her," Rev says with a shrug.

I stand pushing my chair back. "What the fuck does that mean?"

Rev cracks his neck, not intimidated by me, and he's the only fucker who isn't. Because of the hell he escaped from, nothing does.

Cas shakes his head. "He ain't stepping on any toes. You ain't claiming her ass. That means she is free pussy. You know the rules as well as I damn well do. As every fucker here does. You are really sure she will wait for you to pull your head out of your ass?" He leans forward in his chair. "I am telling' you now, Rae ain't the hang around type. She's better than all the women here by fuckin' miles. The brothers already respect her, and that takes a fucking lot. Ain't seen them like it with anyone else who's not family, and if you don't hear us, hear that."

His words all hit me like a direct punch. I fucking know the shit he's spewing is all true. What, does the fucker think I'm fucking blind? I stare at them all. If anyone knows what I'm capable of, it's this lot. How cold I can be.

"Don't love. Ain't never going to love. You all know how fuckin' messed up this is." I tap my temple, shooting them all a look. "Yeah, she is a fuckin' good bitch. We will keep having' fun while it lasts... but I can't claim her ass."

I hear a small gasp, and my head snaps around to see Rae standing there. Hurt clouds her features for a moment before she pulls up her mask of indifference. I don't like fucking seeing it, not on her. She forces a smile before handing Cas a wrapped container.

"There was some leftover."

Cas grins at her, and I want to wipe that smug fucking look off his damned face with my fists.

"Fuck, girl, marry me?" She laughs at the same time I growl, which makes Kitten tilt her head.

She lowers her voice so only the ones closest can hear her. "Just because you don't want to claim my ass, doesn't mean there isn't a man who would."

Cas and Storm both slam their hands on the table, laughing. Fucking pricks.

I get up to show her just who exactly that pussy belongs to and who those lips crave, when my father's booming voice stops me.

"Church, now."

Everyone gets to their feet, a little bitching and whining over having to leave the food but they move over to the room we use for church. My eyes seek out Rae, and when she raises her eyes to mine, I don't like what I see. Indifference. Cool. As if she's put something between us again.

With no choice but to follow the brothers, I push up from the table and make my way to the room, but my eyes stray back to hers as I see her push back into the kitchen. Fuck. I'm screwed.

I bring my attention back to the box outside church and empty my pockets into it-- cell phone and gun go inside before I stride into the room, ignoring the unpleasant feeling swarming in my gut.

I take my seat next to my father on his right, Rev takes his left, and the rest drop their asses into the wooden chairs. Prez drops the gavel on the old oak table that bears the scars from men before me, and I know it will have those marks after me. It shows different names carved into the wood. Some old and some new. I search the table until I land on the name I know everyone will be looking at. 'Champ'. Anger boils through me as I look at the deep carving of his name.

Prez looks around us. "Called you all in because it was the Mendez boys."

"What the fuck? We are sure?" Rev roars. His voice as lethal as the demons that live inside him, as he slams his hands down on the table. I swear a crack appears from the force.

My father nods. "Seen the footage myself, and no fuckin' mistaken' it's them. Ralph and two of his boys. A shot through the eye is a message. They're watchin' us."

When he looks at me, I see his eyes full of hunger. That lets me know he wants blood. About fucking time too as they have been screwing us for the last couple of months. They started this fucking game, but we were going to show them how the fuck it is played.

My father turns to the rest of the table, his eyes ablaze. "I've already spoken to Rags. He told me he wants a week before we send our own reply to their message."

I jump up, sending my chair back. "What the fuck? You forget we got a brother with a fuckin' hole in the eye, and that we've got to plan that brother's funeral? What do you expect us to do, just sit around with our fuckin' thumbs up to our asses while they are fuckin' laugh at us?"

The brother's eyes ping-pong between us. No one has ever stood up to my father, not even me. But this wasn't right. The need for revenge swirls inside me, growing and clawing as my hands clench into fists. I feel my control slipping.

"Sit down, boy. Before I fuckin' put you down." My father's words are deliberately slow with venom in each letter, and we stare off for another beat before I sit down. "This is what the fuck is going to happen. We are going to welcome the brothers that will be down over the next couple of days. Rags isn't coming, but he's sending Bolt."

A grumble of surprise goes around hearing that. First, he wants to fucking wait and now he ain't coming to the funeral! It's fucking bullshit.

"Then, we are going to give our brother the send-off he deserves and have one hell of a fuckin' party. We'll meet next week with Rags to find out what the fuck is going on. Then, we will call everyone in here. We'll go on lockdown before we send our message, are we fuckin' clear?"

Everybody nods when my father's eyes land on mine. I grind my jaw before nodding.

We all walk out of church with hunger in our blood. I head straight for the kitchen, expecting her to be gone, but I find Rae cleaning up. Before she can run off, I have her sitting on the counter and myself between her legs. I bury my head in her throat, inhaling that smell, and when I lean back, I find violets full of questions that I can't give her answers to.

"Need your taste." She watches me, defiance stares back, but there's hurt circling those violets, making them darker as she slides down from the counter making me take a step back. "You're pissed about what I said?" My tone holds bite, making her brow raise before she turns to finish off the cleaning, but then she lets out a breath as she spins back towards me.

"No, I know what this is, Ice, you've made it clear." Her words are strong, but I don't miss the tension in her body, and the look in her eyes slays me.

"I hate that I want you like I do." It's no more than a whisper against her lips, her eyes staying on the ground.

I grab her face, giving her more than I've ever given before. "I'm the VP, and I can't be seen to have a weakness. The shit you feel, so do I." I rub my thumb over her lips. "I can't love. I've seen too fucking much." I tap my temple. "Too fucked up, but you make me want things I should never want. Have no right to want. You don't know what I've done, what I will do, and I should walk away, but I fuckin' can't. I want to tell you to walk away, but I'll come after you." Those violet flecks brighten. "Champ is dead, and things are going to get really rough around here, really fuckin' quick."

"You don't need to protect me."

"Yeah, Kitten, I fuckin' do. I'll protect you against anythin'…. Including me because…" Her soft lips cut off my words by landing on mine. Opening as soon as I run my tongue along the seam, and the first taste of her on my tongue has a growl vibrating in my chest as I pull her tighter. My hand, travelling over her perfect curves. We draw back from the kiss gasping for oxygen. Those violets shine bright as they take me in. Like she's looking right into the very depths of my soul and seeing all of me. Her back straightens, and her chin tips out as if she knows I need her strength.

"Take me. Use me. I'm here." Her words break something loose. I lift her up onto the counter, moving her skirt over her hips. I don't get her prepared, hoping she's ready. I slam straight into her, causing her to hiss and her back to arch, rubbing those perfect fucking tits against my chest. I take her so much harder than I've ever fucked anyone before. Still, she takes all of me, rage and all. Rae's head falls back, mouth partly open, and her cheeks slightly flushed. Fuck, if I were to die right here, right now, I would be a happy man. Dragging the wetness around to her tight bud, she freezes and holds her breath.

"Trust me?" She nods as I continue to play with that forbidden hole in an opposite thrust to my dick. I breach the hole to my knuckle as she whimpers.

"Oh, God, Ice." Driving into her deeper, when her whole body shakes from the orgasm that lays just underneath the surface. I push a finger into her ass deeper, and her body desperately grabs it. Rotating my hips, prolonging her orgasm as another wave washes over us and her pussy clamps around me like a fucking vice. I bite down on her shoulder, growling before I bury my head in my favorite place.

Rae stands, trying to straighten herself out, but nothing will take that freshly fucked look from her, and the way her eyes are the most vivid violet. Her bee-stung lips are even more swollen as she smiles sweetly before undoing the apron that I didn't even realize she's still wearing.

"I've finished the prep for tomorrow, but if it's okay, can I come back and cook again? I know the other clubs will start coming in from noon." I nod my head, speechless that she is talking like I didn't just fuck her seven shades to heaven. Her walls are back up. She's doing what I want, keeping the distance and leaving. I grab her hand.

"Stay." Rae's eyes widen before a little frown appears. I see the confusion in her eyes, but instead of calling me out, she nods.

I wake up with the sun filtering through the window, and I rub my hand over my face. Fuck. When have I ever slept through the night? Fuck, not in ten years.

A small groan has my eyes flicking down to Kitten, with her raven hair spread around her. Her dark lashes rest on her cheeks, and her lips are still swollen from our kisses throughout the night or early morning. I reached for her twice in the night and both times she surrendered without a word. The first time, hard and fast, the second was slow, and I mapped every curve, memorized everything about her. Hearing her breath catch, the taste of her skin, and the feel of her nails dragging down my back. With a look in her eyes that told me more than any words could.

Looking at her face free of makeup, she seems more innocent, younger, and vulnerable. Reminding me how much of a bastard I truly am.

I untangle myself and make my way to the shower, knowing I need to be ready for when the brothers start to arrive.

When I step under the spray, I let the water travel down my body as my head rests on the tiles. Champ didn't deserve to go out like that and getting revenge will only go some of the way to fix this hurt. Seeing their blood flow, the sound of their screams, and them begging for mercy will satisfy my demon's lust for blood even more.

A small hand wraps around my waist, placing kisses on the ink that covers my whole back. The ink that claims me to the club. Gradually, my body relaxes as the tension seeps from my pores. Rae doesn't say anything as she reaches for my body wash and squirts some in her hands before rubbing it across my shoulders and down my back, rubbing my muscles as she goes. Over my ass, down each of my legs, and then she comes around the front, rubbing my shoulders, my chest, my arms, and my stomach. She falls to her knees in front of me as she washes both my legs, then her hand covers my thickness, softly at first before using more pressure, and I close my eyes.

"What are you doing to me?" I whisper, but she doesn't answer and instead, continues to wash me, massaging all the knots out of my muscles. I lean in taking those fucking lips and bringing my hand up to cup her. "Fuck, you're soaking." A low moan pulls from her as she steps away, shaking her head no.

"That was for you…you only." She smiles sweetly before leaving me in the shower, and I stand there watching the door she walked through until the water runs cold.

I am so fucking fucked.

RAE

walk into the kitchen and start making coffee, along with bacon, sausage, and egg rolls. The brothers pile in one by one, their eyes widen as I hand each one a roll with a large mug of coffee. Some smile, while others lift their chins.

We all burst out laughing when Cas runs in, nearly running into the door, and I hand him his roll.

"I've put some extra in," I say with a wink. He's one of my favorite brothers, but I have seen the change lately. He doesn't smile as much anymore, and he isn't flirting as much. And yesterday, a sweet butt walked past him, and he didn't even notice. It seems like the light has disappeared from his eyes, and it guts me to see that. Cas has always been larger than life, but I can't put my finger on what's going on with him.

For a moment, I see a brief flash of his old self as he mutters, "Fuck, yeah." Then smirks. It's not quite his usual level of cocky attitude, but it's getting there. I think everyone misses him.

I tune into Storm telling a story about when he was a prospect. The brothers sent him for a glass hammer, thinking he'd never find one. When he realized it was a joke, he had one made and walked into the club holding it up.

I burst out laughing at the story, imagining the brothers' faces when they realized he'd played them as good as they'd played him.

We're all still laughing when Ice steps into the room. It's like the air is sucked out of my lungs as my eyes find his. He leans against the door frame, forearms resting on the top plinth as his eyes roam over me from my toes to the top of my head. Something has changed since yesterday, only I'm not sure what. I just know we are both in uncharted water. Going to places we've never been, never wanted to before. I feel his eyes on me as he makes his way to a chair and sinks into it. With slightly trembling hands, I pour his coffee as he likes it and grab a roll.

As I cross the space between us, I can feel the weight of his gaze on me. I stop at the edge of the table and hold the coffee cup in his direction, placing the roll in front of him. I squeal when thick arms come around my waist. I land in his lap before I can say anything. One hand grabs my nape as he brings my head down to meet his icy blues. They search mine before his lips crash down in the most sensual kiss. When he pulls back, a smile is tugging at his lips, showing his dimples. I don't get to study it for long before he buries himself in my neck, inhaling and kissing my throat. I look around the room to see surprise on all their faces.

"Smithy, grab Kitten a coffee." He's up and has a coffee in front of me before I can say anything. Ice keeps his one arm around me as he picks up his roll, taking a bite before carrying on the conversation around the table, and my body finally relaxes as he squeezes my hip.

The brothers rode out earlier for a few hours, but not before Ice left me breathless, with a knowing smirk covering his face and making all the guys grin. He winked at me before he disappeared, after promising me he would take care. I know they went for clues to who'd killed Champ. They want revenge, and you can taste their need in the air, and the anger and danger that circles the club.

Brothers from other chapters start arriving throughout the day, but Red still hasn't come back to the clubhouse. I try to stay in the kitchen as much as possible because the way they are looking at me is making me feel uneasy. I know I'm not Ice's property, which leaves me as only one other thing: a sweet butt. Sleeping with Ice confirmed that. He'd told me enough times.

Even though things have changed, I don't know where or how these rules work. The thought of being passed around by the brothers makes my stomach roll and bile rise in my throat. Red said they can leave. But if they came for me, could I really walk away? I know that I'd kill them or let them kill me before that would happen. I swipe angrily at the tears that fall down my face as I knead the dough.

When I feel someone watching me, I turn my head to see a man I've never seen before. He matches Ice in height and muscles, but his head is completely shaved. His jaw is chiseled, but what startles me is the hazel eyes. They're the perfect mix of green and brown, and a severe contrast to his golden skin.

"Who are you?" His voice is soft like a whisper as he grabs on to the counter, unsteady.

"No one. I should really be going." I tug off my apron before heading towards the door, but a hand latches onto my wrist.

"Wait, please?"

I stop at something in his voice, it sounds like a plea, and one thing I've learnt is Horsemen don't beg for anything. I bite my lip. There is something about him. I look into his eyes and hope he can see my plea.

"Please. I'm not like them. Please, let me go. I shouldn't be here."

I fight as memories of my past try to claw at me. I'm getting sucked down the rabbit hole, and I'm helpless to stop it as another tear falls.

A frown covers his face, making him look more deadly than earlier.

"Who's upset you?" his voice rips out of him in a harsh whisper. I bite my lip and look out at the room to see if I can see anyone I know before returning to the man. My back straightens, and my chin sticks out.

"I won't be passed around. I don't care what the rules say! I'm not a fucking whore, sweet butt or whatever else you want to call them."

The man's eyes widen, surprising me when a chuckle escapes him. He grabs hold of my hand like he doesn't want to let go, pulling me deeper into the kitchen. He opens a few cupboards before he smiles when he produces a bottle of Jack.

"Come on." He nods his head. I stand solid when those hazels hit me.

"I'm Bolt. My old man is Rags...Not going to make you do anything, I promise you. Trust me."

I don't trust, but if there's one thing I've learnt it's to read people, and he isn't lying. I also remember Red talking about Bolt. My feet move as I nod and get a breathtaking smile in return. He's good looking, seriously hot, but my body doesn't react that way, and my heart doesn't jump. He's not Ice.

Bolt leads me out a back door, across the grassy area. A few brothers give us sideways looks, but no one says anything as he pulls me behind the garage. It's where I know some of the brothers work on their bikes.

He slides down the wall, taking the top off the bottle before chucking it back, and then he hands it to me. I stand watching him for a beat before I sit opposite him and take a swig, wincing as it burns my throat. We drink in silence, sharing the bottle before he turns to me.

"So, want to tell me what's got a pretty girl like you upset?" I frown, taking a deep breath.

"It's my own fault. Ice the um…VP here, you know him?"

Bolt chuckles. "Yeah, we know each other."

I pucker my lips. Of course, they do. "I mean, I'm still learning, and all this is new to me."

"Yeah, I guessed that and don't take this the wrong way, but you don't seem like a girl that wants to get into a club by lying flat on her back." There was a bite to his tone.

I shake my head, frowning. "What, no, I don't! I'm not… I'm a tattooist. I work for the club's shop, Branded, with Sketch, doing most of the ink."

His smile widens. "Now that fits you. Though you look a little young? How old are you? And want to tell me how you ended up a sweet butt?"

I don't miss the dark undertone in his voice, and the darkness that passes his features as he waits for an answer.

"I'm twenty-two," I lie, and it falls artfully from my lips. I look young because I'm a lot younger than my ID says. I don't look at Bolt knowing he might see the lie. So, I continue. "Ice, that man, he infuriates me and pisses me off so much that I want to shoot the moody asshole..." I let out a deep breath. "The man behind the layers. From the moment we met, it's been..." I try and think of the right words. "It's like pouring gasoline on the fire. I've tried to fight it."

He studies me. "You love him?"

I nod. Bolt is the first person I've admitted it to.

"It doesn't matter. From the beginning he told me I was just another nameless snatch. So far, it's worked out that no one else has tried. The brothers here respect me, and some are even my friends…I think. Now other clubs are coming in. I'm not an Ol' Lady, and Ice isn't going to lay claim to me." I hate showing weakness.

"They won't fucking touch you. I swear to you." I don't know why he's promising me things, but I feel my body unwind at his words. He takes another sip of the Jack, his eyes going across the compound, distant yet alert. "You like it here?" I see genuine curiosity there. He is not just sitting here hearing me. He's listening.

"Yes, I do. I've never stayed anywhere, no place longer than a few weeks anyway. When I ended up here... let's just say it was the last place I thought I would come to feel safe."

The truth came to me as I spoke. I always associated this place with pain, but now I feel that lost girl inside of me and hear her pleas of wanting to belong. Where she will be accepted and grow roots. I feel her pain and loneliness. I see how much they really did break me, how much I lost at their hands.

"I want my sun back. I don't want to be in the darkness anymore. It's cold and lonely." I let the truth come out.

Bolt reaches out for me pulling me close. "Fuck, you're killing me pretty girl." He smooths my hair, not in a sexual way but more comforting. "Why did you move so much?"

I didn't move. I'm running. They couldn't find out who I was, or what I'm running from, or the truth of who I am, and that Rae is just an Illusion; a mask I had constructed. That she is many of the roles I have had to play, made up from my imagination, to enforce steel walls around myself. Walls the Horsemen have torn down.

I rest my head on the wall behind me as I continue my story, almost robotically, like someone else is speaking.

"I followed my mother's last wishes for me to come here. I don't understand why. Maybe she knew I'd finally find peace here." I shrug and snag the bottle from him, taking another drink. It's giving me a good buzz, and I kick off my shoes so I can stretch my legs and wiggle my toes.

"But my mother couldn't know, could she? She couldn't know

that I would find Red, Sketch, and the brothers? That I would find Ice?"

Bolt smiles, taking the bottle off me and taking a drink himself.

"Maybe she did. Maybe she knew you belonged here, and what you would find here. Seems like a smart woman. What's her name?"

"Rose." I don't miss his sharp intake of breath, but I continue. "She was sharp as a tack, but trust me, when she told me to come here, me being another nameless snatch for the Horsemen wasn't anywhere on her radar."

He clenches his jaw. "You're right about that. You're not like them." The threat of his words should have me worried as I've only just met him, but the whiskey makes me smile instead.

"Oh, I'm Rae by the way. Did I tell you that?" He laughs, shaking his head. I join him as I grab the bottle back, taking another swig.

"Rae. It's nice to meet you." He says my name as if he's trying it out. The idea he knows the truth makes its way through my muddle thoughts, but I dismiss it. There is no way he could know.

"I sent Sketch my profile, and he wanted me because I'm a total badass." This makes him snort out laughing. "I walked into Branded, and it was like I already knew the place. Everything here feels like I've seen it before, and I feel safe. Do you know, the last time I felt safe I was fifteen years old. Fifteen," I whisper. Remembering that carefree girl who loved to draw, had friends, and danced to music. Who slept peacefully through the night without monsters haunting her dreams.

"It's not his fault. He warned me if I slept with him, he wouldn't be laying claim and kept calling me sweets. I hate that name. And I let my fucking pussy take the lead and boom! Now I'm on the train to bucket-ville." I pull a pretend train chain.

Bolt looks at me before he bursts out laughing, causing laughter to erupt from me too, when a shadow lands over us. I look up to see

Ice, and he looks pissed.

"I think we might be in trouble," I try to whisper, but my voice comes out loud—Bolt's lip twitches.

"What the fuck, Kitten?" His face looks as hard as stone, and eyes as cold as he is.

I stand, swaying as I do, but Bolt is by my side in seconds, holding me steady.

"This nice man is Bolt, his father is Rags, and he's a VP like you," I sing the last bit. "He's nice. Told me I don't have to be a sweet butt and took me away from all the men in there." Ice turns a different shade of red. Pushing me out the way, he picks Bolt up by the neck, slamming his body into the wall.

"You better fuckin' start talking," his enraged voice echoes around the whole place.

ICE

No fucker will tell me where Rae is. I know she is here because her car is still outside, but no fucker seemed to know who the fuck I was talking about. Which is my first clue that these bastards are hiding something because no one misses a female like her. I noticed Bolt is also missing. He's the complete opposite to me; laidback and always wearing an easy grin. I know the fucking women love him. My hands clenched as I searched every room, coming up empty, and then Cage comes up to me.

"She's outside. Look, brother, you need to cool this shit." I don't listen to the rest before I'm out the door. Hearing her laugh carry over the wind does shit to my chest. It makes some of the pain there tighten. I remember how she laughs with the guys and now that fucker Bolt, but she never laughs like that around me. Jealousy rages through me, and I want to rip whoever made her laugh apart. I have an idea who it fucking is.

I storm across the grass. No one sees me as I take in the scene.

and the only thing stopping me from tearing Bolt apart is that they are both dressed, and it doesn't look like anything is going on. As if she senses my presence, her head snaps my way.

"I think we might be in trouble," she tries to whisper.

I watch as his lip twitches, and the way he's watching her in total awe. A possessiveness like nothing else breaks loose inside of me, and it seeps into my veins.

"What the fuck, Kitten?" I hiss between my teeth, my fists curling into balls at my sides.

She stands, unsteady, swaying a little. Automatically, I reach out to steady her, but Bolt gets there before me. He must have a fucking death wish.

"This nice man is Bolt, his father is Rags, and he's a VP like you." She almost sings it. That's when I notice the half-empty bottle of Jack beside them, but Kitten isn't finished. "He's nice. Told me I don't have to be a sweet butt and took me away from all the men in there."

I watch as a single tear falls. That's it. I grab Bolt by the neck and chuck him against the wall.

"You better fuckin' start talking." He starts turning a different shade of red, when I feel someone kick my shin, making me lose my grip on the bastard.

"What the hell?" I roar as Rae frowns and pokes me in the chest.

"Get off him, you pig-headed bully. He was nice to me," she growls, as Sketch walks up to Rae.

"Not helping, Rae." She notices Sketch for the first time. A breathtaking smile takes over her face.

"I've missed you." He holds his hands up, trying to hide the smirk.

"Fuck, girl, you trying to get me killed?"

Rae frowns, her lip trembling. "No, why would I do that? I like you, I shouldn't, but I do. I like all of you." His eyes widen, taking a step back. Chuck anything at us, but crying bitches is something none of us know how to deal with.

Sketch points to me. "You need to sort out your woman."

Rae frowns deeper as tears hang on her thick lashes. "I'm not his woman. Everyone knows that! He told me. Told everyone." She hiccups. "Now, there's a bunch of new brothers in there who look like they want to eat me and not my dinner." She sniffs, looking back at the clubhouse. Those violets turn to me, but they are a shade darker than usual. "This is your fault! I didn't want to be one of them." She comes towards me, raising her fist and punching my chest as tears stain her face. "I told you I couldn't be like that." Pain lances through my cold heart. "But you made me one. You made me a puttana." I grab her wrist, pulling her close to my chest, needing to fucking feel her close.

Bolt stands forward, anger radiates off him as he turns to Sketch. "Take her home."

I open my mouth to tell him this shit is my problem to deal with, but Bolt glares at me, breaking the distance between us so we're foot to foot.

"I'm going in there and having a fucking drink to cool my ass down. When you are done, we are going to talk," he sneers before walking off, but not before whispering something in Kitten's ear. She nods her head.

I pace back and forth, wondering what the fuck happened? I leave Rae with swollen lips and a shy smile and return to her with another brother and tears falling down her face telling me this shit is somehow my fault. How I made her into a fucking puta! What the fuck even is that? I make Sketch take her home. I couldn't risk something stupid coming out of my mouth. I hear the truck pull in, and when Sketch opens the door, he nods letting me know Kitten is home and safe. I cross the yard to the clubhouse, and as soon as I enter, Bolt looks up before standing. Ripping off his shirt and nodding his head towards me.

Yes, fucker, this is what I need. The men crowd round us in the bar, forming a ring. We both circle each other.

"She is fuckin' mine," I growl, and he just fucking smirks.

"Didn't seem that way to me, brother," he taunts, that grin mocking me.

Before I say anything else, he lands a hit on my jaw that snaps my head to the side as pain radiates through my face. I don't react, spitting out blood. His green eyes turn almost brown. I know now that this is Bolt, the VP of the northern chapter. This isn't friendly. We land punch upon punch on each other's skin, but neither of us goes easy on the other. He gets a few good shots in, but I repay them with hits of my own. When a high whistle comes through the air, we break apart, both breathing heavy, blood, and sweat glistening on our bodies—ribs hurting like a bitch. My father steps into the ring, glancing between us with a confused expression on his face. Bolt and I always got along. We fucking grew up like brothers. Right now, we don't look like brothers. We look like fucking enemies.

Bolt gets inches from my face and sneers at me. "You better sort your shit out, or I'm going to, and that is not a threat, it's my fucking promise. You make Rae cry one more time, and I'm fucking taking her with me."

I lunge at him, another wave of anger raging through me, but my father grabs my shoulder, stopping me.

"Enough. She is not your Ol' Lady, there's no claim on her and you know the rules." I shoot my father a warning glare.

Bolt gives me one more look of disgust, shaking his head, and I'm glad to see he looks as bad as I feel.

I am about to open my mouth when the sound of glass shattering fills the air. Before I can react, gunfire explodes around me. I flip a table, trying to grab my piece as shots fire up the wall beside me, punching through the plaster like its hot butter. The air filled with yells and screams and the rain of bullets. Rev jumps in front of Prez to protect him. I don't miss the fact Rev stumbles, a red patch blooming over his t-shirt from beneath his cut. He growls, and his eyes flick to mine shaking his head, telling me it's not life-threatening. I push up from the table and rush towards the door. Hearing my name being screamed as bullets fly past me. I push open the doors just as it ceases. Bolt and the others follow on my heels, our spat forgotten. We come together to fight as a club.

Hitting the compound, we see two black vans pulling off. Running towards the gate, I raise my gun and fire, the shots pinging off the van's rear metalwork. Knowing I can't take them that way, I sprint for my bike. I don't need to turn around to know that my men are behind me because they'd follow me to hell if that's where I ended up. The engine roars beneath me as I take off after those fuckers at high speed.

I keep my eyes locked on the vans as we follow closely with the sound of Harleys loud behind me. We chase the black vans to the end of town, where we lose them in the traffic.

I pull my bike to a stop. "Motherfucker."

We ride back to the clubhouse, heart still pounding and adrenaline fueling my body. When I step back inside, I find Rev sitting on a chair, blood over his chest as doc sews him up, and a blank look on his face. A few of the club girls huddle together, seeing a body on the floor, Amber. Her soulless eyes letting me know she's gone. Cage pulls a body from behind the bar. It's Marty, one of the prospects, Cage shakes his head to the room. "Fuck!"

My father stands in the middle of the chaos. "Church." His tone is as lethal as the look in his eyes.

We all pile in the room, our brothers along with Bolt and five guys he came down with from the northern chapter. Everyone voices anger when my father drops the gavel.

"This came through the window attached to a fucking brick." He chucks the piece of paper on the table, and I pick it up.

"You have what's ours, hand it over or we start a war, and you'll end up like your friend."

Fury burns in my stomach as I read each word before passing the note along. Tormenting us with Cas' dad's death and Champs and now the two dead bodies in the main room.

"What the fuck do they think we have that belongs to Mendez?" Cage asks, my father shakes his head.

"That's what we need to find out. I guess whatever they think we got is big enough to start a fuckin' war," I growl, racking my brain with what the fuck the Mendez think we have. None of this makes sense. It was as if all the pieces belonged to different puzzles.

"Could it be set up?" Cage speaks beside me.

"Sounds fuckin' right because we ain't got shit that belongs to them," Cas growls, then his eyes land on the paper, and he slams a hand down, letting out a roar. "We are going to fuckin' kill them. Every one of those bastards will bleed."

Each of us nod, letting him know the club and his brothers are all behind him.

"Need to say something, Bolt?" All eyes turn to him. He stops and looks at my father.

"Pacing the same way your old man does. Swear between the two of you, you could burn your way to hell. It means the same fuckin' thing, that fuckin' magic mind of yours is connecting the dots quicker than club pussy can open her legs."

His eyes skip to each of the brothers before going back to my father's eyes, and he nods his head.

"My old man should be here in a few hours." Then his eyes turn to me, trying to work something out before he speaks. "You care for Rae?" I feel all eyes on me and all waiting for my fucking answer. I keep my mouth closed as I stand, my chair falling back. What I feel for Rae has nothing to fucking do with him. It is my business.

"What the fuck does Rae have to do with this?"

"Trust me, brother, we have been friends for years."

I search Bolt's eyes, and he is fucking begging me without words to listen to him.

"Fuck!" I turn to look around the table, knowing my next move shows everything I've tried to hide. "Cage and Sketch go get Rae, but don't let her know what's going on, just that we're on fucking lockdown," I growl. Both get up, racing out the door.

Prez turns to Bolt. "Layla?" He shakes his head no.

As soon as Rae arrives, I cross the room, taking her in my arms. I bury my nose in her hair before grabbing her face and kissing her like my life depends on it. Showing the club and my brothers exactly what this female means to me.

I pull away without a word. I watch as confusion fills her eyes, and as Bolt walks up to her that frown deepens. "Ice?"

The way she says my name has my knees buckling. I can't speak. Too scared that I'll fucking tell her what I feel. She makes me feel scared that if I say those words, I'll give them life, and the power to destroy us both.

Do I love Kitten?

I don't know what love is.

Everyone talks about falling in love. Rae doesn't make me feel like I'm falling but rising from the darkness.

Around her, the chaos calms.

She captures me.

I slip on the mask before she can read me because I can't be weak. If this is a war with Mendez, then the Horsemen need me to be Ice, the man that men fear, and as cold as the name.

This will be her biggest test. If Kitten really can be in this life, then she needs to accept me. Not just as the man she sees, but as the Club's VP. They are one and the same.

For an hour I watch the stairs where Bolt took her, everything in my gut screams to go after them. I lean elbows on my knees resting my head in my hands when someone nudges me. I lift my head to see Bolt storm down the steps, his fists landing in the wall one after another as blood smears the plaster. Fury burns off him in waves as he roars to the ceiling. I go to step forward, when the doors open, and Rags walks in.

"Boy?"

He turns to his old man. Who looks nothing like the man I saw a few weeks ago. Bolt turns his whole body and sinks to the floor. In a room full of brothers, he's on his knees, head in hands, shoulders shaking. Never in my life have I ever seen him shed a tear, not even after the shit his mother put him through.

He lifts his head and whispers something, and Rags staggers as he holds onto the bar—Bolt nods.

Then we hear the cry that breaks from one of the strongest men I know. Bolt runs to catch his father as he falls to his knees. We all watch on as Rags' loses it right in front of us. Fuck, this is one of the hardest men I have seen in my life, on his knees, crying like a lost and broken boy.

I look at my old man whose eyes are glassy. He walks over to Rags, bending down and whispering something in his ear. Rags shakes his head. I see his mouth mutter something, and my father flinches back from his words before helping Rags to stand. My father turns looking directly at me, and I feel something tighten in my chest. The guys all coming closer to me as if they feel it too.

"Prospects, swap with Cage and Sketch." Both nod their heads as the rest of us walk into church.

We all sit around the table as Bolt, Rags, and my old man walk in. I stand giving up my seat to Rags, and he hits my shoulder in thanks. I notice he's got a bottle of the dark stuff in his hand. Fuck. Whatever is going down is big.

He turns to face us. Eyes red rimmed. "Today, Bolt made a discovery, and it's the reason the Mendez are declaring war."

"What is it that they think we got?" I ask, but Rags shakes his head.

"It's not what, it's a who."

All the air leaves my body as something else starts to take over. "Who?" I know he hears me because he turns, snapping to look in my direction.

"Arya Mendez."

"The daughter of Gino Mendez." Cas spits the name. We all knew she existed. The Mendez's little fucking princess. The recon we had on her was she's this perfect little princess that fell into line. Covered in pearls and poised words. Also, one of the heirs to The Mendez family and fortune.

"Didn't she get butchered with her parents?" Rev asks. A deep growl comes from Rags, but it's what we were all led to believe that she died with her parents.

"Watch what you're saying." My father warns. What is fucking happening? Rags turns back to the table.

"Her mother and Gino were killed because Carlo wanted her. Arya was fifteen at the time."

I might not give a shit for the little Mendez princess, but that was fucked up and twisted, even for Carlo, his own niece. Bile rises in my throat as my stomach twists. Rev slams a knife into the table.

"At fifteen? Sick prick." His voice is as lethal as the look in his eyes.

Rags nods as a low growl escape. "She escaped and has been running ever since. She's managed to evade Carlo and us for the last four years."

This chick is impressive enough to be able to dodge not only our Club, but also the Mendez family; that's some great fucking skills.

Cage frowns. "Why is everyone after this Arya chick?"

Rags closes his eyes, letting out a shuddering breath. "For different reasons. Mendez wants her back because Carlo is obsessed with her like a degenerate asshole. She's just turned nineteen, so my guess is, now he can legally take her as his wife." He rubs his hand over his face, looking tired. "We set up our own tails on her, and we've had some leads. That's what Bolt was doing last time you were up. Like I said that girl is fucking smart, too smart for her own good." Rags and Bolt share a look with a small grin.

"Okay, I get it, this bitc-" Before I can finish the sentence, Rags has clocked me in the jaw, sending my head sideways.

"Watch your fucking mouth, boy."

I look at my old man, who nods. I grind my jaw, stopping only out of respect.

"I get this bit-chick has had a rough start, but what the fuck has it got to do with the Mendez knocking on our door? They think we are hiding their little princess. Jailbait, that's not our style, and everybody knows it, including Mendez. What the fuck would we want with a little mafia princess?" We weren't into sex trafficking and underage girls like those cunts.

He grunts. "I guess he found out her connection to us. I'm positive she is not even aware. Arya is my daughter, not Gino's. She's Bolt's sister."

We all look at each other, none of us were expecting that. There have been no whispers over the years of Rags having a daughter, no permanent bitch in his life, apart from the one… shit, twenty years ago.

"It happened when you were sent away?" I ask, but already know the answer from the darkness in his eyes a mixture of hurt and remorse.

"You're all too young to remember her. She came here a few times. Rose gave birth before I left. Nothing I regret more than getting on that plane. We found her again when she was five, but things were too dangerous for us to keep in contact. I struck a deal with Gino, but bikers and Mendez are like oil and water. I could never turn up every Saturday for a visit. Instead, I watched my baby girl grow up through photos until she ran, and we've not had a sighting--until today."

Fuck, and he came back to his Ol' Lady married, moved away with his daughter and Bolt missing.

"Ain't your fault, Pop, we had eyes on her." That doesn't surprise me, it now all makes sense why he moved and started a new chapter. I bet my cut it's because his daughter is up that way.

"They hurt her," he chokes out. "They fucking hurt her bad enough that she ran and never fucking stopped. We don't know what happened in that house."

The emotion in his voice hits all of us. Searching for her the last four years, knowing she's in danger, we all understand their meltdown. My old man and I would be fucking screwed if anything happened to Layla, and even worse if she were running for her life but kept slipping through our fingers. I slap his back, squeezing his shoulder in understanding. Telling him we are behind him.

Sketch and Cage walk in, Storm starts filling them in when Sketch stands, his face looking pale.

"Arya?" Rags nods. Sketch's eyes widen, looking straight at me. I know whatever he says is going to change everything. It's as if he's holding the match and I'm the fucking fuse. "Arya, fuck! She told me her name when she first got here, but I didn't think about it again. Fuck, brothers, it's Rae. They are after Rae."

Cas jumps up. "Rae is twenty-two, not nineteen. And she sure as shit ain't no princess. Are you sure?"

Sketch shakes his head. "She must have a fake ID. Fuck. If she is running, then it makes sense."

An eerie silence fills the room, and the tension grows like a storm cloud. I look at Bolt and Rags for confirmation. They both nod their heads as it all clicks why Bolt reacted to me the way he did. Rae is his fucking sister. She fitted so well because she belongs here.

I stand slowly, and for once it's not ice that fills my veins, but red-hot lava.

Every one of the emotions that I have buried for years clashes together, flying to the surface and making a brand new one I can't even put a name to. The locked-up anger releases, burning through me like hell's flames ready to explode.

"They are not fucking touching her. Do you hear me!" I roar, eyeing every brother, all who seem to watch me as if they never saw me before. Rev's eyes flick to the other brothers, even he's unsure of the man in front of now. Maybe now they completely understand what I'm capable of.

"I'm laying claim to her right fucking now. She is mine." My voice comes out low, a deathly whisper. I turn to Rags, feeling the smirk crawl across my face as my eyes fill with fury, and my body vibrates with anger. "They even breathe the same air as her, and they will regret it. Carlo wants a message, then he can have one; Rae is fuckin' mine." I thump my chest, right above my heart. Each word is drenched in threat and laced with a promise.

The doors to the church fly open, as Red runs in, she's deathly pale and shaking as tears run down her face.

"Rae. She's gone," is ripped from her as she breaks.

My vision doesn't turn black, it turns bright fucking red. Any semblance of my sanity is now destroyed.

They made a grave mistake taking her. They chose conflict. They stole the last of my humanity, the only person who grounded me, made me real.

I stand there letting everything take over me, all the heightened emotions to destroy the man I am. Ice is gone.

I am the thing of myths and legend, forged in conflict. I am death.

The prophecy says The Red Horsemen, representing war and bloodshed, rose out from the second seal. It is a time of murder, assassination, bloodshed, revolution, and war.

The Horsemen have risen. We are bringing it all and coming straight for Carlo......

CLAIMED

Coming March 12th, 2021

Buckle up – I promise this wild ride isn't finished yet!
Can Ice save Rae in time?
What is Rae hiding?

Pre-Order Now: Amazon-
https://books2read.com/u/bw7QKO

Add to TBR: https://bit.ly/CLAIMEDGR

ACKNOWLEDGMENTS

Thank you so much for reading Captured!
I hope you enjoyed reading part one as much as I enjoyed writing it.
If you did, please consider taking a few seconds to leave a review –
they mean so much to authors.

A massive thank you to the wizard master and best friend who is my
editor **Imogen Wells**—You can find her hanging out at Final Polish
Proofreading.

Thanks to **Krissy** at Word Bunnies (www.authorbunnies.com) for
proofreading Captured.
To my **beta readers and ARC readers** who all took time out of their
busy schedules to read Captured, thank you!
Mog and Gen, who put up with me messaging and calling all the
way through writing this book. You kept me from deleting it all and
made me push that damn button. Lol Thank you for being the best
sound boards and friends a girl could want. Love your faces!
Sophie and Clayr, thanks for waving those pom-poms and cheering
me on every step of the way. (They are so not the pom -pom type
Lol)

To my tribe: Where do I even begin with all of you? Lol Thank you
for being the sassy, dirty- minded women that I love. For getting my
sick sense of humor, and coming along on this crazy journey with
me. For your naughty meme's and hilarious banter. I would not be
here without you.
**So, thank you, Gen, Imogen, Sophie, Andrea, Brenda, Clayr,
Marnie, Julie, Megan, Rhiannon and Robyn. Love your faces.**

My Husband: Thank you so much for believing in me and holding my hand through it all. For bringing me cups of tea when I locked myself away. For the endless questions you let me run past you. Most of all, thank you for helping my dreams come true—I love you always.

My Babies: I love you all so much. Don't forget, never give up. You can achieve anything you put your mind to. You have already got your number one cheerleader.

Thank you all!!!

ABOUT RAVEN

"Hey!", (waves like a crazy woman).
So, this book has been in the process for years. I left it, come back to it, scraped it and re-wrote it.
I knew I needed to get Ice and Rae's story told though, and they left me crying, swooning and wanting to chuck my laptop. Lol.
I love dark romance. The forbidden. I enjoy finding the beauty in the pain and Love in tragedy.
Love isn't always a fairy-tale- sometimes it hurts like a bitch and can tear you apart, before putting you back together again.

Want to know more about me? If you are fluent in smartass sarcasm, don't mind adult language and, have questionable morals. I have a Facebook group called Raven Rebels. (https://www.facebook.com/groups/2195670413843598/). Where I hang around and post all my latest news.

Facebook page:
https://bit.ly/FBPAGERAVEN
Facebook group:
https://bit.ly/FBGROUPRAVEN
Goodreads:
https://bit.ly/GRRAVEN
Bookbub:
https://bit.ly/BBRAVEN
Instagram:
https://bit.ly/INSTARAVEN

ALSO BY RAVEN AMOR

Available Now
http://mybook.to/Ownedbyhim
https://books2read.com/Nera

Coming February 12th, 2021
https://books2read.com/capturedRedHorseman

Coming February 16th, 2021

Amazon US: https://bit.ly/StalkersUS
Amazon UK: https://bit.ly/StalkersUK
Amazon CA: https://bit.ly/StalkersCA
Amazon AU: https://bit.ly/StalkersAU

Coming March 12th, 2021
Pre-Order Now: https://books2read.com/u/bw7QKO

TBR: https://www.goodreads.com/book/show/56285184-claimed

Printed in Great Britain
by Amazon